Echoes & Embers

by Melody K. Smith

ISBN: 979-8-9990074-5-2

This series exists because I did not do it alone.

It was written in borrowed hours, stubborn hope, and more cups of coffee than anyone should admit to. It was finished because of the people who showed up when I faltered, who reminded me to rest when I forgot, and who believed in Emerdeen even when the story was still arguing with me.

Emerdeen is more than a setting. It is my belief that care is power, attention is love, and control is not the same thing as strength. Writing these three books changed me. It taught me to trust community, to stay curious, and to choose meaning over certainty.

To everyone who supported this work, fed me, grounded me, challenged me, and let me wander long enough to return with a story—thank you. You are woven into every thread.

And to the readers who found themselves here: welcome. The lantern is lit.

-   *melody*

"Look carefully around you and recognize the luminosity of souls. Sit beside those who draw you to that.".

- Rumi

Chapter One: Static in the Thread

Cassie's coffee tasted like doubt.

Not burnt or bitter or bland. That would've been easy. She could fix a burnt cup. But this? This was something subtler. A gentle hesitancy at the edges of her usual morning ritual. A pause before the pour. A barely-there fuzz between the intention and the outcome.

She held the mug close to her face, letting the steam ghost her cheeks. Stirred & Spellbound was still quiet, the front windows hazy with the condensation of a too-humid spring. The greenhouse plants were stretching toward the sunrise in lazy curls. Her favorite monstera had nudged one of the rune stones off the sill again, and the scent of moss and lemon balm hung in the air like a lullaby.

Everything looked right. Everything felt off.

Cassie narrowed her eyes at the mug. "You're supposed to taste like conviction. Or maybe determination with a cinnamon finish. Not existential crisis with a hint of bergamot."

The mug, traitorous thing, said nothing.

Baz had already gone out for a walk. He'd left a note on the counter scribbled in his slanted, sleepy handwriting: *Needed air. You were making that noise in your sleep again. Back before lunch.*

That noise.

She didn't remember dreaming, but she'd woken with her heart pounding and her fingers clenched tight around the throw blanket. It had taken her several minutes to realize she wasn't still inside one of the vignettes.

And even then, she wasn't entirely sure.

Cassie exhaled slowly and stepped over a rogue basket of dyed raffia. The Spellbound part of their sanctuary had become increasingly cluttered with charm ingredients, half-built spellbooks, and the ever-multiplying glass jars that seemed to breed when left alone too long. She really needed to clean. Or organize. Or burn it all down and start fresh.

Instead, she sipped the not-quite-right coffee and wandered to the back door.

The door creaked like it was trying to tell her a secret.

She stepped into the morning mist and let it settle into her curls. The Hollow shimmered in the distance, threads of golden light twisting like lazy smoke above the tree line. Everything was exactly as it should be.

And yet. There it was again. That sensation. The static at the edges. A low-level hum that made her shoulder blades itch.

Magic had always been a little wild here, but lately it felt dissonant. Like a string pulled too tight on an old fiddle. Some days, her vignettes wouldn't anchor properly. Other days, her minor spells overcorrected. Like the time her gentle rain charm turned into a full-on thunderstorm over her front porch. Baz had come home soaked and laughing.

"It's the Hollow adapting," Morgan had said last week, fingers weaving invisible threads in the air during their new workshop series. "It's becoming what you all need. What you are."

Cassie hadn't argued, but the unease had nestled behind her ribs and refused to leave.

She leaned against the railing, letting her eyes travel down the stone path to the community garden Bram had coaxed back to life. Tiny bursts of green were peeking through the soil, though Bram swore he hadn't planted anything there. Not yet. The land was doing its own remembering.

6

That wasn't always comforting.

Cassie turned her head at the sound of a rusted engine coughing up the road. A car, late-model and full of dents, crept past the property and kept going. Not a local. She knew every car that rattled through Emerdeen, and this one didn't belong.

Probably just passing through. Probably.

She tapped her mug three times with her index finger, a habit that started as spellwork and had morphed into something more like superstition.

Three taps. Anchor me here.

Three taps. Let me see clearly.

Three taps. Keep the weird on a leash today.

The coffee still tasted like doubt, but she drank it anyway.

Cassie stood on the porch longer than she meant to, letting the mist curl around her ankles. The porch steps still creaked on the second board, something Baz promised to fix and never quite got around to. Just like the corner gutter that leaned too far and the half-buried wind chime that kept trying to sing even though it had lost two notes.

She liked the broken things. The not-quite-rightness of it all.

Except when it came to her magic.

The Hollow pulsed in the distance, quiet and golden and steady. It wasn't doing anything unusual. And yet something in her belly coiled like a wind-up clock. The kind that ticks even when you don't want it to.

She thought of the dream, or whatever it had been.

She remembered fog. And hands not her own, threading something together and then pulling it apart strand by strand. Each thread glowed, and each one sang in a language her waking mind couldn't hold on to.

It hadn't been frightening. Just hollowing. Like being scraped out with a silver spoon and left half-lit.

She reached into her cardigan pocket and pulled out a crumpled note card. She hadn't meant to keep it, but she hadn't meant to throw it away either. Morgan had slipped it to her after last month's full moon gathering.

When your thread hums strange, it read in Morgan's looping script, *don't pull it tight. Let it speak first. Then follow.*

Cassie snorted softly. "Easy for you to say, Oracle Barbie."

She tucked it back in her pocket and turned to go inside but paused.

A blue thread had appeared overnight, looped gently around the railing. Not woven. Not tied. Just resting. Almost like it had placed itself there. It wasn't one of hers. Wasn't part of a spell, at least not one she'd cast.

The wind didn't move it. She didn't touch it.

Instead, she just watched it, strangely still in the moving air, like a held breath.

Back inside, she stepped barefoot across the creaky wood floors and through the arch into her craft room. Or maybe portal staging ground was more accurate now.

Half-finished vignettes lined the wall, each one in various states of creation. A moonlit cemetery, a coffee shop with glowing runes scrawled on the menu, a riverbank lined with tiny thread trees and paper boats. All hers. All paused.

The one she couldn't look at lately sat on the far shelf.

She had started it after they came back from the Hollow the last time, when the magic felt rich and certain and unshakable. The vignette was meant to be her offering to Baz, a miniature of the greenhouse porch at dusk, with the ivy just starting to curl and a small rocking chair in the corner.

She had enchanted it to hum like his laugh when touched.

But somewhere along the way, the thread wouldn't hold. The glue repelled the magic. The spell slipped off the structure like water on wax. She had tried again and again. And then finally, she stopped trying.

Cassie closed the door to the room without entering and leaned her forehead against the frame.

Something was unraveling. Not fast. Not loudly.

But definitely.

Baz returned mid-morning with dew on his boots and a bag of fresh scones tucked under his arm. Cassie heard the door creak and his soft "Morning, wild thing," before she saw him.

He kissed her temple as he passed into the kitchen. She leaned into it for half a second longer than usual, like anchoring herself to a familiar song.

"I got the orange cranberry ones. You're welcome," he called, rifling for plates.

"Bless you and your bakery diplomacy," she murmured, following him in.

He raised an eyebrow. "Rough morning?"

She hesitated and he noticed.

"Magic go weird again?" he asked gently, sliding her a plate and sitting across the table.

"Define 'weird.'"

"That thing where your coffee tastes like an existential crisis again?"

"Exactly that."

Baz smiled, slow and crooked. "Maybe your magic is just picking up on your mood."

She looked up. "You think I'm an existential crisis?"

He took a long sip of tea. "I think you're overdue for rest. And maybe a break from everyone else's problems for, like, five minutes."

Cassie didn't answer. She picked at the edge of her scone.

"Cass." Baz leaned forward. "I know this place keeps us busy. But you haven't made anything for yourself in weeks. Not even a miniature rock garden."

"I've been... busy."

"You've been carrying too much."

That was probably true. She wanted to argue, but there was no heat behind it. Instead, she tucked a leg under her and leaned forward, chin in her hand.

"Did you see the blue thread outside?" she asked.

Baz nodded. "Didn't touch it. Didn't feel like mine to move."

She exhaled, both grateful and unsettled.

Something was stirring.

And she had a feeling they were going to need all their threads for what came next.

Chapter Two: The Skeptics Arrive

Fi hated dirt roads. She hated them even more when they were damp and pretending not to be mud. The car fishtailed just enough to make her curse out loud, and the GPS on her phone blinked out for the fourth time in half an hour.

"Do we even know where we're going anymore?" she snapped.

From the passenger seat, Fox tilted his head without looking up from his book. "We're going where the dead aunt's will told us to go. Don't hit a tree."

"That's very helpful, thank you." Fi jerked the wheel slightly to avoid a pothole the size of a baptismal font. "Maybe next time, you can drive the haunted inheritance mobile."

"It's a perfectly normal car," Fox said mildly. "The cassette player just screams a little when it's humid."

"You scream a little when it's humid."

Fox turned a page. "I accept that."

The car rounded a bend and dipped into a hollow so dense with green it looked like something out of a painting. Moss coated every surface that didn't move, and even a few that probably did. Fi slowed down, both out of caution and some half-felt instinct not to anger the landscape.

She didn't like it.

Too quiet. Too soft. Too eager to be believed.

They passed a wooden sign carved with careful letters. *Emerdeen. Founded 1849.* Someone had painted ivy leaves along the edges. Beneath that, in smaller, newer letters: *Magic Rooted Here.*

Fi made a noise halfway between a snort and a sigh.

"Magic," she muttered. "Of course."

Fox finally looked up. "Let it go. We're here for legal reasons, not spiritual ones."

"I know that. But I swear if someone hands me a crystal and tells me it aligns my water chakra, I'm going to align it into their forehead."

"You're thinking of the sacral chakra," Fox said absently. "Water's the element, not the location."

Fi glared at him.

He shrugged. "What? I read things."

They crested the last hill, and the town came into view. Quaint didn't quite cover it. Emerdeen looked like someone had commissioned a folk artist and then let a hedge witch do the finishing touches. Painted porches, twinkling lanterns strung between trees, herbs growing out of mailboxes. A cat wearing a knit hat watched them from atop a fence post with blatant judgment.

Fi pulled up in front of a cottage that matched the photo from the lawyer's email. It had stone steps, a front door the color of blackberries, and a wind chime made of silver spoons. One spoon shimmered with a faint gold thread that definitely wasn't part of the design.

Fox leaned forward, peering out the window. "Well. This looks extremely cursed."

Fi killed the engine. "Let's get this over with."

Inside, the cottage smelled like lavender, cedar, and something else she couldn't name. The windows were clean; the furniture draped in sheets that looked like they hadn't been disturbed in years. Still, it didn't feel abandoned.

It felt... expectant.

Fox opened a cabinet in the kitchen and whistled low. "This woman had a tincture collection like an apothecary."

"She also had an antler nailed above the back door." Fi poked it with a broom handle. "Is that a blessing or a warning?"

"Could be both."

They found the deed in a folder tucked inside an old recipe box. Fi scanned it quickly and rolled her eyes.

"Well, we own it. For better or weirder."

Fox turned in a slow circle, his eyes landing on a shelf of tiny glass bottles labeled in cramped handwriting: *Clarity. Courage. Reversal. Moonwater, aged seven days.* He smiled, not mockingly but with a kind of gentle amusement.

"Want to bet the local library also sells spells?"

"I want to bet that if we stay more than a week, one of these people tries to read our aura."

Fox plucked a bottle labeled *Luck, mild* off the shelf. "You could use some."

Fi flicked the cap at him and wandered back toward the front door. She paused when she saw someone across the street, standing beneath a wooden sign carved with leaves and moons. A woman, maybe forty-something, with wild dark curls, wearing an oversized cardigan and holding a mug like it was the last warm thing on earth.

The woman tilted her head slightly, as if she could sense the exact moment Fi saw her. Then, calmly, she raised her hand in a small, deliberate wave.

Fi didn't wave back. Instead, she turned and let the door shut behind her.

"Locals," she muttered.

Fox appeared at her side, reading the label on a mason jar filled with dried blue petals. "She looked nice."

"She looked like she knows what my dreams mean."

"Do they mean something?"

"They mean I need a nap and a sandwich."

Fox looked over his shoulder. "You're going to like it here."

"No," Fi said firmly, "I am going to catalog this place, clean out the cobwebs, flip the deed, and be gone before the next full moon."

Fox smiled, as if he knew something she didn't.

She hated that smile.

Chapter Three: The Thread Across the Street

Cassie didn't wave back.

She had, quite clearly, waved first. It was a polite neighborly gesture, the kind of small act that said, I see you, I know you're new, I'm the kind of person who waves instead of stares.

And yet the woman across the street had stared anyway. Stared like she was cataloging Cassie's soul and finding it entirely too much trouble.

Cassie stood at her front window for another minute, mug warm in her hands, watching the strange siblings disappear into the blackberry-doored cottage.

She hadn't known anyone was moving into Marlene Carrow's place. Then again, that house had a way of staying empty until it didn't. Marlene had died two years ago, no funeral, no official goodbyes. Just gone. The house had been quiet ever since, although Cassie had sometimes seen candlelight in the upstairs window.

Now someone was finally in it.

She took another sip of coffee and frowned. The taste had shifted again. Less doubt now. More… curiosity, with a soft undernote of caution.

Cassie's magic, like most things in Emerdeen, didn't always announce itself with trumpets and sparks. Sometimes it whispered through coffee beans and left strange threads on your porch.

She set the mug down and reached for her cardigan. The blue thread from earlier was still outside, still untouched, still perfectly still in the breeze. She didn't remove it. Not yet.

Instead, she pulled a different thread from her pocket. This one was silver, braided with green silk, meant to be used for quiet observation. A kind of magical periscope.

Cassie tied it loosely around the porch railing and let the charm settle. It didn't allow her to spy. That wasn't how the magic worked. But it did let her feel when someone nearby tugged at the edges of the town's energy, whether knowingly or not.

The thread twitched.

She raised an eyebrow.

Across the street, the cottage window flickered. Not light exactly, but presence. Something watching back.

Cassie's skin prickled.

She had expected tourists this season. Curious travelers. People wanting to peek into the place that had started appearing in obscure travel blogs and niche TikToks. Emerdeen was beginning to get a reputation, especially since Morgan's workshops had started drawing the spiritual crowd.

But these two weren't tourists.

The woman had the look of someone trying very hard not to belong. The man seemed more curious than cautious, though she'd sensed the same resistance in him, dulled by patience.

Skeptics.

Skeptics always made the magic restless.

Cassie stepped down from the porch and walked a slow circle around her greenhouse, pretending to inspect the ivy trellises. She reached out to the oldest vine near the door, ran her fingers along the leaves, and whispered, "Watch gently."

The vine tilted.

Cassie went back inside.

She didn't need to make contact with the newcomers just yet. But she did need to prepare. Skeptics had a way of knocking things loose—intentionally or not.

She passed by the vignette room again, still closed. Still not ready.

Instead, she wandered into the workshop nook. A few dried bundles of rosemary and lemon balm hung over the sink. A charm jar labeled *Soften stubborn hearts* sat crooked on the shelf, next to another that simply read *Patience*.

She didn't need a spell today. She needed information.

She opened the drawer beside the bookshelf and pulled out her old scrying map. It was hand-painted, bordered with protective sigils and tangled roots. At its center sat a tiny replica of Emerdeen, the buildings etched in careful miniature detail. Each resident's home had a different rune beneath it. Each place, a thread.

She pressed her finger to Marlene Carrow's cottage.

The rune blinked once. Then changed.

Cassie sat back.

The rune now glowing beneath the house wasn't for shielding or sleeping.

It was the rune for disruption.

Not danger. Not harm.

Just change. Reluctant, rumbling change.

Cassie stared at it for a long time, then traced the surrounding paths. The Hollow glowed dimly in the distance. The threads that connected her to Baz and to Morgan and to Bram were stable, woven, familiar.

This new one was loose. Wiggling. Testing the weave.

She folded the map carefully and tucked it back in the drawer. No need to sound alarms. Not yet.

Still, as she turned to go, she whispered one word to the house.

"Watch."

The spoon chime outside rang once, gently, in response.

Chapter Four: Nothing Moves Unless You Name It

Fi had a rule. Several, actually, but this one was written in metaphorical stone at the top of the list. *Don't name things.*

Naming gave shape. Naming gave weight. Naming made things real.

So, she didn't name the twitch in her stomach when she passed the old stained-glass lantern hanging from the neighbor's porch. Or the flicker in her peripheral vision when she looked too long at the ivy crawling across the mailbox.

She absolutely didn't name the pressure in her chest when she glanced across the street and saw the woman standing still as a statue, watching her with what looked far too much like knowing.

Fi slammed the front door behind her and tossed the keys onto the nearest flat surface. The cottage echoed with quiet in the way old houses always did. Not abandoned, just... reserved.

She kicked off her boots and stalked into the kitchen, suddenly determined to unpack something. Anything. She opened a cupboard, found a box labeled *Cinnamon: Past Life Blend*, and promptly closed it again.

Fox wandered in with his usual slow-motion serenity. "Did the house offend you, or are you just warming up to yell at the wallpaper?"

Fi ignored him and ripped the tape off a box labeled *KITCHEN STUFF* with a little too much enthusiasm. Inside, she found three mismatched mugs, a broken tea strainer, and a crumpled receipt from a gas station in Missouri.

Fox plucked one of the mugs and ran a finger around the rim. "We should get groceries."

"We should get the place exorcised," Fi muttered.

Fox opened the fridge. "Half a lemon and something that might once have been yogurt."

Fi exhaled through her nose and sat on the floor, legs crossed. She stared at the cottage around them. The walls were painted a soft, mossy green. The floor was old oak, the kind that creaked when you so much as looked at it funny. And the window above the sink framed the Hollow in the distance like a painting someone had enchanted to move only when you weren't watching.

"This place is ridiculous," she said aloud. "It's curated whimsy. We're living inside a Pinterest board that got possessed by Stevie Nicks."

Fox leaned on the counter, biting back a smile. "And yet here we are."

"Only because the will said so. Only because flipping the property is the fastest way to get back to real life."

He tilted his head. "Define real."

Fi narrowed her eyes. "We've already been through this. Real is observable. Repeatable. Explainable. Magic is... none of those things."

"Maybe not to you."

Fi bristled.

Fox walked over and handed her a jar. Inside were small pieces of ribbon, folded paper, dried rose petals, and what looked suspiciously like glitter.

"This was in the bedroom closet," he said. "I think it's a charm jar."

Fi stared at it. "It's a mason jar full of craft scraps."

"Same thing, depending on the story you want to tell."

She didn't respond.

Fox lowered himself to the floor beside her. "Why do you hate it so much?"

"I don't hate it."

"You do."

"I don't believe in it," she said finally. "And it bothers me that everyone else does. That they just... lean into it. As if wishing hard enough turns coincidence into design. As if you can chant over a candle and get clarity instead of smoke."

Fox nodded slowly. "You know the funny thing about disbelief?"

"What?"

"It's still a kind of faith. You just don't like calling it that."

Fi glared at him. "Do you want me to throw this glitter jar at your head?"

He held up his hands in mock surrender. "Just saying. You might want to leave a little room in your worldview for surprises."

"I like surprises I can measure."

They sat in silence for a moment. The floor creaked, even though neither of them moved.

Fi looked at the window again.

The neighbor's porch was empty now, but something about the air across the street felt charged. She didn't like it. Not in the way she didn't like mushrooms or folding laundry, but in the way she didn't like when someone looked at her and saw too much.

"I don't trust this town," she said.

"You don't trust most towns."

"This one feels like it's watching."

Fox looked down at the jar in her hand. "Then maybe name it."

Fi blinked.

"Name the feeling," he said. "Name the weird. Name the thread. Nothing moves unless you name it."

She set the jar down, harder than she meant to.

"You're starting to sound like them."

"I'm starting to listen."

Fi stood. "Well, I'm starting to need a sandwich. Grocery run?"

Fox grinned. "Only if we stop by that shop with the dangling herbs in the window."

"I swear, if you join a coven before I get Wi-Fi—"

"Too late," he said, heading for the door.

Fi followed, muttering under her breath, the jar of ribbon and rose petals still quietly glowing behind her on the floor.

Chapter Five: What the Wind Forgets

Morgan woke before dawn, as they often did these days, with the distinct sense that something had shifted.

Not in the dramatic, sky-rending way people imagined when they thought of magic. No lightning bolts. No prophecies. Just a quiet rearranging. A nudge to the ribs from the universe that whispered, Look again.

They sat up slowly, letting the covers fall away, and pressed a palm to their chest.

Still there. Still them. But humming with something new.

The window above the bed was cracked open just enough to let in the breeze. It carried the scent of earth and clover, sweet and low like a lullaby. The Hollow was breathing deep today. And breath always meant something was about to begin.

Morgan dressed without rushing. A soft black tank top, loose linen pants, the turquoise wrap they'd dyed last month under the waxing moon. Clothes that moved when they moved. Clothes that let their body speak before their mouth caught up.

They tied back their hair and paused by the mirror, meeting their own gaze with a small nod.

"I see you," they said quietly. "Still here."

The walk to the studio was peaceful, the air soaked in the kind of damp that promised wildflowers by noon. The studio itself, tucked near the edge of the clearing, still held traces of last night's class. Threads of ribbon hung from the rafters. Chalk runes dusted the corners of the wide wood floor. A circle of tea lights sat unlit on the altar near the window.

Morgan inhaled deeply, then let their fingers move through the air as if plucking invisible threads. The room responded.

A soft flicker in the candles. A vibration in the floorboards. Nothing sharp or demanding. Just presence. Recognition.

But underneath it, something else.

A knot.

They paused. It wasn't dangerous. Not yet. Just unfamiliar. Like a new guest sitting too close to the salt bowl.

Morgan moved to the window and looked toward the far side of town.

They couldn't see the Carrow house from here, but they didn't need to. Their body knew where the thread had landed. Not the way a map knew. The way a web did. A single tremble, felt across the whole weave.

New people.

Not seekers. Not practitioners. Something more complicated.

They stepped outside and grounded both feet in the grass, letting their toes curl into the damp moss.

"Show me," they whispered.

The breeze shifted.

Not a vision. Not a name. But a pressure against their skin, like the first drop of rain before a storm gets brave enough to speak.

Morgan tilted their face to the sky.

"Alright," they said. "Let's meet the uninvited."

By late morning, a few of the regulars had wandered into the studio. Rowan was setting out yoga blocks. Mina was arranging candles by color again, claiming the full spectrum helped her think straighter. Morgan let them chatter, only half-listening.

They could still feel the thread humming beneath it all.

It wasn't malevolent. But it was resistant. And resistance had a way of either softening or shattering. Morgan hoped for the first.

They moved toward the altar and reached for the tea lights, pausing before lighting them. Instead, they rearranged them into a new shape.

Not a circle. A hinge.

Something about that felt right.

Morgan stood back and crossed their arms, studying the quiet, rearranged flame-space.

Someone new had arrived. Someone who didn't believe in what they couldn't name.

But Morgan knew belief was optional.

Magic didn't require permission. It only asked that you listen.

And Morgan, above all else, listened well.

Chapter Six: The Shape of Skepticism

Cassie brought muffins. Not because she felt particularly generous that morning, but because it gave her something to hold, and holding things helped her think. That, and Morgan always forgot to eat on days when the wind was too talkative.

Morgan raised an eyebrow as she stepped through the studio door. "Bribery?"

"Peace offering," Cassie replied, setting the basket on the windowsill. "And also, maybe a pre-apology, in case I decide to yell about someone new."

"I already ate my emotional muffin for the day but thank you." Morgan pulled a stool closer and gestured for her to sit.

Cassie didn't, not right away. She moved slowly around the space, letting her fingers trail the edge of a bench, the surface of a folded mat, the rim of a half-finished charm bowl. The studio always felt different from the greenhouse. Calmer. Spacious, but charged. Like it was always on the edge of becoming something else.

"You felt it too," she said finally.

Morgan didn't have to ask what she meant. "I felt the knot form around three in the morning."

Cassie nodded. "It tugged again around eight."

They sat in the stillness for a moment, each watching the other with a familiarity earned over dozens of moons and moments shared. Cassie sighed and finally lowered herself onto the stool.

"Siblings," she said. "Marlene Carrow's niece and nephew. They moved in across the street."

Morgan smiled slightly. "The ones with the iron aura and the 'prove me wrong' posture."

"That's them."

"She doesn't believe in anything."

"No. And he believes in too much to say so out loud."

Morgan nodded again, more thoughtfully this time. "Balance and friction. Curious pairing."

"She gave me the kind of look that could split wood." Cassie rubbed her temples. "And I waved. Like a complete Midwestern idiot."

"You are a Midwestern idiot," Morgan said, reaching for a muffin.

Cassie allowed herself a small smile.

Morgan broke the muffin in half and studied the crumb. "So. Why does it bother you?"

Cassie tilted her head. "Which part?"

"That they're skeptical. That they're here. Or that they're here now."

Cassie didn't answer right away. Her gaze drifted to the charm bowls again, then to the wide window where the light filtered in soft and strange.

"I don't know," she said. "It's not like I expect everyone to bow to the moon and burn herbs on schedule. But something about them feels... off pattern."

"Because they didn't choose this place," Morgan offered.

Cassie looked at her.

"Everyone else who's come to Emerdeen recently came looking for something. Healing. Magic. Belonging. Even if they didn't say it that way." Morgan leaned forward, hands loose on their knees. "These two? They inherited a house. That's not a calling. That's logistics."

Cassie nodded slowly. "Maybe that's what's scraping me raw. They're not here with wonder. They're here with a clipboard and a countdown clock."

"And yet," Morgan said, picking up the other half of the muffin, "they're here."

Cassie pressed her fingers to her coffee mug. "I don't think she likes me."

"That could be good for you."

She gave Morgan a look.

"Dislike sharpens the edge. You've been dulled lately."

"I've been exhausted lately."

Morgan shrugged. "Same thing."

They sat in silence for a few more breaths. The candles on the altar flickered without breeze.

Cassie finally said, "What do you think they'll do?"

Morgan folded the muffin paper into a triangle. "I think they'll try to resist. I think the town will push back. I think one of them will see more than they want to. And the other will say it was a trick of the light."

Cassie hummed. "You're not worried?"

"I'm always worried. I just don't let it drive the cart."

Cassie rose and walked to the window. The Hollow shimmered faintly in the distance, the trees exhaling soft green energy. She placed a palm against the glass.

"I just wish I knew why they were really here."

Morgan joined her at the window. "The same reason we all end up here."

Cassie arched a brow. "Which is?"

"To remember something we forgot. Or to forget something that never served us."

Cassie didn't reply. She just kept her hand on the window, staring out toward the town that always seemed to be waiting for the next story to unfold.

Chapter Seven: The Weight of Her Quiet

Baz wasn't sure when Cassie's silence had started carrying weight, but lately it felt heavier than anything he could lift.

Not the kind of silence that followed deep sleep or focused crafting or even her habitual brooding with a cup of too-strong tea. This was different. This silence had shape. It hovered around her like fog that wouldn't quite lift, clinging to the hem of her cardigan and the corners of her mouth.

She was quiet in the mornings. Cassie was never quiet in the mornings.

He watched her now from the back porch, pretending to be fixing the hinge on the greenhouse door. She stood across the garden, staring at nothing and everything, her hands wrapped around a mug he was pretty sure had gone cold twenty minutes ago.

She hadn't moved in ten.

Baz tightened the screw on the hinge and wiped his hands on the rag in his back pocket. He thought about walking over to her. Thought about pulling her into a hug, tucking her under his chin the way she let him when the world was too loud.

But Cassie didn't always do well with comfort when she hadn't asked for it.

He settled for speaking softly. "You're going to get root rot if you keep standing still like that."

Cassie blinked and turned slowly, like she was returning from a place he couldn't see.

"Sorry," she said, offering a smile that didn't quite reach her eyes. "Lost in thought."

"That thought owe you money or something? You looked ready to fight it."

She snorted, and for a moment the air between them eased.

Baz crossed the grass and joined her. He didn't touch her. Just stood close enough that she could reach for him if she wanted. Sometimes that was what love looked like. Proximity without pressure.

"You want to talk about it?" he asked.

She shook her head. "Not yet. It's not loud enough to name."

Baz nodded. He knew that feeling. The way a worry could be present without form, like a shadow with no body to cast it. He'd lived with enough ghosts of his own to recognize the signs.

"New folks moved into the Carrow place," she said after a pause. "Marlene's niece and nephew."

"I saw them drive in. Red hatchback that's seen better decades."

Cassie nodded. "They don't believe."

"In magic?"

"In any of it."

Baz squinted toward the road. "Well. That'll be fun."

"They're skeptics," she added. "The sharp kind. The ones who don't just disbelieve but need everyone around them to agree that nothing's real unless it can be dissected."

"Sounds exhausting."

She turned toward him. "It is. And they've only been here twelve hours."

Baz tilted his head. "So, why's it hitting you this hard?"

Cassie opened her mouth, then closed it again. She looked down at her mug, frowned, and handed it to him. He took it without question.

"I don't know yet," she admitted. "I just feel like they're tugging on threads I didn't know were loose."

Baz nodded and drank from her mug. Cold. Definitely tea. Definitely not enough sugar. He didn't flinch.

He studied her for a long moment. The wind played in her curls. The vines near the porch reached toward her like they always did. The land loved her. The Hollow hummed in her bones. But still, there was something about the way her shoulders stayed slightly lifted, like she hadn't taken a full breath all morning.

"You've been quiet lately," he said.

Cassie looked up, startled by the honesty.

"Not angry quiet. Not even sad quiet," Baz went on. "Just… distant. Like you're half-here. Like you're already inside the next thing, and I don't know if I'm invited."

She stared at him.

He didn't backpedal. "You don't have to fix it. I just need to know if I'm still holding the same thread you are."

Cassie stepped closer and laid her forehead against his chest. She didn't say anything for a long time. Baz stood still, heart steady, arms loose at his sides.

Eventually, she said, "I think I'm afraid that I've already woven the ending, and I'm just now catching up to it."

Baz gently touched the back of her head. "Then maybe we unravel a little. And start fresh."

She didn't answer, but she didn't pull away either.

The wind shifted again. And somewhere down the road, the first thread of something new began to shimmer.

Chapter Eight: The Spark That Watches

The bell above the shop door didn't chime the usual way when she entered.

Cassie was arranging bundles of dried lemon balm near the register when the sound cut through the room, sharp enough to make her fingers still. It was the same bell it had always been, the one she'd enchanted years ago to ring softly, like a breath drawn in welcome. Normally it sounded warm. Familiar. A promise that whoever crossed the threshold had done so with at least a scrap of sincerity.

Today, it sang too bright.

Clear and ringing, like sunlight glancing off glass at the wrong angle. Like being noticed.

Cassie looked up.

The woman standing in the doorway did not belong to this place.

Not yet at least.

She filled the frame of the door with practiced ease, as if she'd already imagined herself there before ever arriving. Her velvet coat was the color of overripe cherries, lush and deliberate, the fabric catching the light as she shifted her weight. Silver embroidery climbed her cuffs in curling vines, intricate enough to suggest both wealth and patience. Her boots were spotless. Expensive. Not made for mud or uneven paths.

Her hair spilled over her shoulders in waves of gold and honey, artfully undone in a way that took time to perfect. Even her luggage felt intentional. A single vintage suitcase, leather softened by care rather than use, the kind of object meant to be noticed.

Cassie blinked once.

The woman smiled.

"Hello," she said, voice smooth and warm, like cream poured slowly into coffee. "Am I too early to be enchanted?"

Cassie's brows knit together. "Sorry?"

The woman stepped fully into the shop, and the air shifted with her. Her perfume followed, peonies layered over something darker and warmer beneath, like woodsmoke clinging to silk. She extended her hand with unhurried confidence.

"Avalon," she said. "Just Avalon. Though I do get called a few other things in certain circles."

Cassie hesitated only a fraction of a second before taking her hand.

It was warm. Too warm.

Not unpleasant, exactly, but unmistakable. There was something beneath the surface of her skin, something taut and humming, like a live wire wrapped carefully in velvet. Cassie felt it brush her awareness before she could pull back.

"Cassie," she said evenly. "Welcome to Stirred & Spellbound."

Avalon's eyes moved then, cataloging the shop with open fascination. They were green. Not the soft kind. Emerald sharpened to a point, bright and assessing. Her gaze lingered on the charm bundles hanging from hooks, the apothecary jars lined with handwritten labels, the tray of custom rune tokens resting on the counter as if they belonged there.

"You've made it lovely," Avalon said, almost absently. "I was told this town might be… interesting. Magical, even."

Cassie folded her arms loosely. "Told by who?"

Avalon laughed softly. "Oh, you know how whispers work. One leads to another." She tilted her head, studying Cassie now. "And I've always had a good ear for the interesting ones."

There it was again. That low hum beneath the words. Not quite sound. Not quite sensation. The unmistakable feeling of something coiled and waiting.

Cassie stepped out from behind the counter, grounding herself through motion. She reached for a bundle of rosemary, its scent sharp and familiar, and pressed it into Avalon's hands.

"Protection," she said lightly. "Never a bad place to start."

Avalon's lips curved. "Are you suggesting I'll need it?"

Cassie shrugged. "Depends on how long you're planning to stay."

Avalon slipped the rosemary into her suitcase with careful precision. "Long enough to find what I'm looking for."

"And what's that?"

Avalon glanced toward the door as if listening for something only she could hear. "I'm not entirely sure yet. But I always know when I'm getting close."

She turned then, her attention snagging on the framed photograph above the fireplace.

Baz. Laughing in the garden, dirt streaked across his hands, a riot of orange calendula blooming behind him. The image radiated ease. Belonging.

Something flickered across Avalon's face. Interest sharpened into focus.

Cassie felt the shift like a breeze suddenly cut short.

"I should go check in," Avalon said, stepping back toward the door. "But I wanted to introduce myself first. Make a good impression."

"You've made one," Cassie replied. She wasn't sure what kind.

Avalon smiled wide and radiant. "I'll be seeing you."

The bell rang again as she left. This time, it sounded too sweet.

Cassie stood very still in the center of her shop, listening to the echo fade. She pressed her fingers to her temples, then to the steady beat of her pulse.

The ward woven into the threshold, the one that glowed gently in the presence of true intention, was still there.

Still shimmering.

But it flickered at the edges now.

As if it didn't quite know what to make of the intention that had just walked in.

Chapter Nine: Patterns in Threes

Morgan didn't flinch when Cassie walked into the studio unannounced.

They were sitting on the floor, surrounded by half-finished spellwork and scraps of dyed gauze, cross-legged like a child in the middle of story time. The circle around them was marked with river stones and loose lavender buds. Candlelight flickered against the rune-carved walls, soft but steady.

Cassie didn't speak right away. She toed off her boots and stepped into the circle without asking, lowering herself across from Morgan with a huff that carried more weight than breath.

Morgan looked up, brows arched.

"That bad?"

Cassie rested her elbows on her knees and stared at the candle between them.

"She smiled at the photo of Baz."

Morgan made a low noise in their throat, not quite amusement, not quite concern. "Define smiled."

"The way someone smiles when they find the prize in a scavenger hunt."

Morgan leaned back on their palms. "So, she's shiny and dangerous."

"She's too shiny. Like someone turned up the saturation on her whole being."

"Name?"

"Avalon."

Morgan blinked. "Well. That's subtle."

Cassie snorted. "Right? Who names themselves after a mythical island known for illusions and seduction?"

"Someone who's either extremely self-aware or dangerously not."

"She bought rosemary," Cassie said. "I gave it to her. She looked me straight in the eye and said, 'Are you suggesting I'll need it?'"

Morgan let out a soft whistle.

"She set off the bell," Cassie continued. "Not in the usual way. It rang too bright. Like it was announcing royalty. Or warning me."

Morgan sat up straighter, gathering the scattered threads near their knees. "So. That makes three."

Cassie looked at them.

"Three new people in three days," Morgan said. "Siblings who don't believe. A woman who believes too much."

Cassie leaned back, crossing her arms. "The town's never had this many outsiders at once. Not since the first binding."

"And even then, they trickled in. One by one. This is... condensed."

"Like the Hollow is pulling threads tighter. Or drawing them in fast before we know what they're for."

Morgan tapped a finger against the floor. "Did she feel familiar?"

Cassie hesitated. "No. That's what's bothering me. Most people who come here have a little bit of familiar on them. A thread that hums, even if it's buried. She felt... off-frequency. Like someone singing in the right key but the wrong song."

Morgan stood and stretched, brushing herb dust from their clothes. "We'll watch her."

"I'm already watching her."

"Good. But we'll do it quietly. No jumping to conclusions. She might be lost, not malicious."

Cassie rose too, but slower. "You didn't see the way she looked at Baz."

Morgan raised a brow. "What does he think?"

"Haven't told him yet."

Morgan tilted their head. "Avoiding it?"

"Waiting for the right moment."

"Cass."

Cassie sighed. "Fine. Avoiding it a little."

Morgan walked to the altar and adjusted one of the stones. "Don't wait too long. Magic thrives in the unspoken, but so does miscommunication."

Cassie wandered to the window. The light had shifted again, casting everything in gold that didn't quite feel like warmth.

"Three new people," she said. "One who doesn't believe. One who doesn't want to. And one who believes in something she's already decided she's meant to have."

Morgan joined her, hands in their pockets.

"Three's a sacred number," they said softly. "Beginnings, middles, ends. Past, present, future. Maiden, mother, crone. It always circles back."

Cassie nodded. "What if this isn't a beginning?"

"Then it's a middle," Morgan said. "And middles are where all the choices live."

They stood together, shoulder to shoulder, watching the road where everything new seemed to come from lately.

And somewhere, beyond the trees, the Hollow listened.

Chapter Ten: Field Notes and False Starts

Fi had officially entered what she referred to as data-gathering mode, which mostly meant walking through town with her phone, a small notebook, and a deeply principled refusal to make eye contact with anyone carrying a crystal larger than a quarter.

Fox called it "light stalking."

She called it "research."

The distinction mattered to her.

Emerdeen was the kind of place that invited conclusions, and Fi did not trust anything that eager to be understood. She kept her shoulders squared, her steps measured, and her attention deliberately fractured between storefronts, signage, and the expressions of people passing by. Observation without absorption. That was the goal.

They were halfway down Main Street when the smell hit her first. Nutmeg. Butter. Something warm and nostalgic enough to feel manipulative.

Fi stopped short in front of a bakery window stacked with hand-painted loaves and chalkboard signs promising comfort like it was a contractual obligation. Just beyond it hung a small iron sign shaped like a crescent moon, gently swinging despite the lack of wind.

"'The Hollow & Hearth,'" Fi read aloud. "Apothecary, tarot, herbal blends." She snorted. "Oh look. A bingo square."

Fox tilted his head, taking it in with less hostility and more curiosity. "You're being awfully snide for someone who has willingly entered three metaphysical shops in two days."

"Willingly is doing a lot of work in that sentence," Fi replied.

"You bought a moonstone bracelet yesterday."

"I bought a bracelet," Fi said, already pulling out her notebook. "The moonstone part was optional."

Fox leaned over her shoulder as she began to write, amused.

Day 2, Emerdeen.
• Magic-to-practicality ratio: 3 to 1
• General tone: aggressive whimsy
• Locals: suspiciously kind
• Energy: ...weirdly soft?
• Fox is falling for it
• Must remain grounded

She paused, pen hovering, then added one more line.

• Possible atmospheric manipulation via suggestion? Investigate further.

Fox chuckled. "You know, if you keep writing about the energy like it's a science experiment, it's going to start experimenting back."

Fi snapped the notebook shut. "Let it try. I've got skepticism and sarcasm. They're both excellent insulators."

They kept walking.

The town's central square opened ahead of them, framed by tall trees whose branches were draped with ribbons, paper charms, and small bells that chimed softly when the air moved. The sound was pleasant enough to be suspicious. At the center of the square sat a wide stone fountain, its water smooth and undisturbed.

Too smooth.

Fi slowed without realizing it.

The breeze stirred the ribbons overhead. Leaves shifted. Bells rang.

The fountain did nothing.

Fox noticed at the same time she did. "No ripples."

"No wind response," Fi agreed.

They approached cautiously, circling the fountain like it might suddenly confess something. A small sign was bolted to the stone base, its lettering neat and deliberate.

Make a wish.
Tell no one.
Wait three days.

Fi scoffed. "Vague instructions. Classic misdirection."

Fox leaned in closer, squinting at the water's surface. "It's not reflecting anything."

Fi frowned. "What do you mean?"

He pointed. "Look. No trees. No sky. No us. It's just... water. Flat. Blank."

She stared.

At first, she told herself it was a trick of light. Or stone. Or maintenance. But then she saw it, just beneath the surface. Not a reflection. Not movement.

A shimmer.

Like a thread pulled tight enough to catch light but not break.

Her chest tightened before she could stop it.

Fi stepped back abruptly. "Okay. That's enough field work for today."

Fox turned toward her, his expression easy but attentive. "You alright?"

"Perfectly fine," she said, already pivoting away. "Still grounded. Still immune to suggestive surfaces and community-theater sorcery."

Fox followed, grinning. "You sure? You looked a little like you saw—"

"Don't."

He lifted his hands in surrender. "Not saying it. Just noting that you're walking faster."

"I'm walking purposefully."

"To where?"

Fi stopped, exhaled once, and recalibrated. "Lunch?"

Fox considered this. "Sure. But you're buying. For calling my recording equipment 'podcast paraphernalia.'"

"It is podcast paraphernalia."

They turned the corner toward a small café painted with stars and trailing ivy, their argument slipping easily back into familiar rhythm.

Behind them, unnoticed, a single thread of gold curled up from the surface of the fountain, stretching briefly in their direction before dissolving into the afternoon light.

Emerdeen, patient as ever, waited.

Chapter Eleven: Salt in the Honey

Avalon hated the word "delicate."

People used it when they meant something was fragile or unfinished. She had been called delicate once, by a man who liked the way her voice broke when she cried. That man had found himself hexed with three years of unfortunate romantic coincidences. Nothing dangerous. Just inconvenient.

Avalon didn't believe in breaking hearts. But she absolutely believed in redirecting energy.

And hers was currently fixed on Emerdeen.

She sat beneath a copper wind sculpture outside the café, its spirals spinning lazily in the warm afternoon air. A cup of rosehip tea rested untouched beside her journal, its pages inked with neat, looping handwriting.

Day One:

- *Initial spell pinged strong resonance near greenhouse. Male signature. Grounded. Unaware of potential.*
- *Town saturated with latent magic. Wards subtle but old. Could be co-opted with care.*
- *Most concerning presence: woman at shop. Owns the space. Protective. Intuitive. Possible romantic entanglement with target.*
- *Her name is Cassie.*

Avalon closed the notebook and smoothed her hand over the cover like a secret.

She wasn't here to hurt anyone. She simply believed that the heart could be persuaded. Baz—if that was the name he still went by—had a light inside him she recognized. A tether. A pull.

Some people met by chance. Others met by design. And Avalon knew the difference.

He belonged with her.

Not in the way of fairytales or fated love stories. In the way a spell finds its source. A match to a spark. A river to its stone.

She had loved before. But not like this. Not with the certainty that came before the feelings.

The Hollow itself had whispered to her in her dreams weeks before she arrived. She had seen golden threads pulling her forward. A garden flooded with lanternlight. And a man whose voice she hadn't heard, but who somehow knew hers.

It wasn't obsession. It was intuition. And now that she was here, all she had to do was wait for the right moment.

She stood to leave just as someone passed close enough to bump her shoulder.

"Oh—sorry," Avalon said automatically, stepping aside.

But the woman didn't return the smile. She was older than most of the townsfolk Avalon had seen so far. Broad-shouldered, with silver-shot hair and hands that looked like they had never stopped doing useful things.

"No worries," the woman said curtly. "Just didn't see you there."

Avalon paused, letting her charm rise like breath. "I don't think we've met. I'm Avalon."

The woman gave a short nod. "I know."

Avalon tilted her head. "Do you?"

"Small town," she replied. "Name like yours doesn't go unnoticed."

Avalon's smile didn't falter. "And you are?"

"Bram sends me when someone new forgets their grounding salt," the woman said. "You're the one who bought moonroot and fever balm yesterday without a stabilizer."

Avalon blinked. "I don't need a stabilizer."

The woman shrugged. "Everyone does. Even people who think they glow brighter than they do."

Avalon's posture sharpened. "Are you always this welcoming?"

"Only to the ones who already think they own the place."

There it was. The unmistakable scrape of resistance.

Avalon laughed softly. "I'm not here to own anything. Just to explore."

"And if you find something that doesn't want to be found?" the woman asked.

Avalon smiled wider. "Then I ask it nicely."

The woman leaned closer, her voice low. "Be careful what you ask. This place has a way of answering in ways you don't expect."

Avalon's smile didn't falter, but her fingers curled slightly at her side.

The woman turned and walked back toward the apothecary, braid swinging with each confident step.

Avalon watched her disappear around the corner, then opened her notebook again.

- *Addendum: elder female presence. Protective. Tied to local lore. Watch closely.*
- *Increase protection charms before next interaction with Cassie.*

She tucked the notebook away and turned her gaze back to the road.

Baz hadn't seen her yet. Not properly. But he would. And when he did, he would remember what she already knew.

They were meant to spark something together.

Cassie just hadn't figured that out yet.

Chapter Twelve: The Fray Beneath the Fabric

Cassie woke with her heart racing and the unmistakable taste of burnt sugar on her tongue.

Not literal sugar. Magic sugar. The kind that stuck to your bones when someone tried to sweeten what should have been left alone.

She swung her legs out of bed and pressed her feet to the floor, grounding herself. One deep breath, then another. Her body wasn't in danger. Not physically. But something had curled too tightly in the threads last night, and it had snagged her in her sleep.

She looked toward the window.

No wind. No birdsong. Just stillness. Like the town had hit pause.

Cassie wrapped herself in her cardigan and padded down the hall to the back room—the one she used for quiet sensing, for deeper listening. The space was simple: a low bench, her woven altar cloth, a bowl of salt, and a shelf of tiny vials filled with local river stones and foraged bones.

She didn't light a candle. She didn't need to. The tension in the room lit itself.

Cassie closed her eyes and whispered the grounding phrase.

Thread to soil, soil to breath, breath to heart.

Her pulse steadied. She reached outward, not with her hands, but with her intention. Into the weave of the house. Into the garden. Into the gentle, shimmering stretch of magic that bound the Hollow to the rest of Emerdeen.

And there it was. A snag.

No. A fray.

Someone had tugged at the threads with the wrong kind of hunger.

Cassie opened her eyes and moved to the altar, pulling down a small silver spool of thread. She let it unwind into her palm and whispered a request: Show me where the spell slid sideways.

The thread moved. It arched gently in the air, then twisted left, pointing not toward the Hollow, not toward Bram or Morgan, but outward.

Toward town. Cassie followed.

By the time she reached the path behind Stirred & Spellbound, the thread had gone slack. The energy was still humming, but more like a wire pressed too close to static. The wards she'd woven around the shop hadn't broken, but they were itchy now. Mismatched.

She knelt by the garden gate and pressed her fingers to the soil. The rosemary didn't lean toward her like it usually did. The ivy near the porch had curled inward, as if bracing against something it couldn't name.

Cassie stood slowly.

Someone had cast something last night. Not a large spell. Not an obvious one. But a charm, perhaps. Something sticky. A drawing-in. A focus.

It wasn't malicious.

But it wasn't careful, either.

Cassie returned inside, her feet moving by memory, and opened the drawer beneath the main counter. She pulled out her charm ledger - a book bound in thread and sealed with a sigil only she and Morgan could break.

She opened to a fresh page and wrote:

- *Subtle charm interference detected*
- *No rupture, but fraying present in greenlines and garden weave*
- *Root pattern suggests intent of attraction, not healing*
- *Likely target: Baz*

Her pen hovered.

She added, quietly:

- *I knew she looked too shiny.*

She closed the book and set it on the shelf. She didn't want to tell Baz yet.

Not because she didn't trust him, but because something about this spell, this attempt, felt like it needed to be witnessed first, before it was named aloud. Magic had a way of listening in.

She needed to see how deep it was willing to dig before she started pulling threads.

Outside, the wind finally moved. The ivy relaxed. The rosemary tilted.

But somewhere beneath the soil, the fray still hummed.

Chapter Thirteen: Charms and Coincidences

Baz didn't consider himself the suspicious type. He liked people. He liked conversations that ran long and strange. He believed in the good in people, even when they were a little odd around the edges.

So, when he saw her with that red velvet coat, wide smile, suitcase perched too perfectly beside her at the bakery counter, his first instinct wasn't alarm.

It was curiosity.

"Hi there," she said, turning to him with the ease of someone who expected to be noticed. "You look like you know which pastries are safest."

Baz smiled. "Depends on your definition of safe. Cinnamon braid will lull you into a sugar coma. Blueberry scones can be weaponized if day-old. The shortbread's diplomatic."

She laughed, light and clear. "Diplomatic sounds like a reasonable start."

He gestured to the barista, who already knew his order. "One diplomatic shortbread, coming up."

The woman extended her hand. "Avalon."

He shook it. "Baz."

Her eyes lit, just slightly. "Of course it is."

Baz blinked. "Of course?"

She gave a small shrug. "It suits you."

He didn't ask what that meant. Instead, he took the paper bag and leaned on the counter. "Just visiting?"

She picked up her tea and gave a soft, content sigh. "Something like that. This town called to me."

Baz raised an eyebrow. "Called to you how?"

"Oh, you know. The usual way." She twirled a strand of hair around her finger. "Dreams. Gut feelings. Irresistible impulse. That kind of thing."

He laughed. "Sounds like a sales pitch for moving to the Hollow."

"I'm very persuasive," she said.

Baz didn't doubt that. She had that polished kind of charisma, like someone who knew exactly how she looked under candlelight and intended to stay there.

He took a bite of his shortbread and studied her over the rim of his coffee cup. She wasn't fidgeting. She wasn't scanning the room like a lost tourist. She was placed. Positioned.

"You here on your own?" he asked.

"For now," she said. "But I tend to find company wherever I go."

Baz nodded slowly. "Well, Emerdeen's a small place. Folks tend to notice new energy."

"I'd hope so," she said, smiling again. "I didn't come here to go unnoticed."

Something about that rubbed the wrong way, but Baz couldn't name why. He didn't get the sharp flash of warning that Cassie sometimes talked about; no voice in the back of his mind, no sudden chill. Just a quiet unease. Like someone had moved his favorite tool an inch to the left.

Avalon sipped her tea and leaned in slightly. "You've been here a while, haven't you?"

"Few years now," he said. "Moved for the plants. Stayed for the people."

"And someone in particular?" she asked, voice light but not careless.

Baz's jaw ticked.

Cassie.

The question wasn't inappropriate, not on its face. But the way she said it felt too pointed. Like she already knew the answer and was weighing its significance.

"Yeah," he said simply. "Someone in particular."

Avalon's smile didn't falter, but it cooled.

"I'm glad to hear that," she said. "Connections are important in places like this."

Baz nodded. "They are."

They stood in silence for a moment, shortbread and tea between them.

"Well," she said, adjusting her coat. "I suppose I'll be seeing more of you."

He didn't say anything.

She left with a swirl of perfume and the sound of her heels clicking smartly across the wood floor.

Baz turned back to the counter.

"Was that the lady who bought all the heartseed oil?" the barista asked.

Baz frowned. "What?"

"She was in the shop next door yesterday," the barista said. "Cleared them out. Said she needed ingredients for something romantic."

Baz said nothing.

But the unease settled a little deeper now.

Not alarm. Not accusation.

Just friction.

And in his pocket, a grounding charm made of hematite and thread that Cassie had charmed for him months ago, was suddenly warm.

Chapter Fourteen: What She Buried

Fi hadn't meant to wander.

She'd meant to go for a brisk, no-nonsense walk to clear her head. Something with a set number of steps, maybe even a timer. But somehow, she ended up two blocks off the town square, past the little library with the hand-painted rocking chairs and the alley strung with mismatched lanterns.

The sky was the kind of pale gray that made the world look quieter than it was.

She stopped in front of a crooked little shop that didn't have a sign.

Just a small hand-painted stone by the step that said, *Leave what no longer fits. Take only what hums.*

Fi blinked at it.

A wind chime clinked overhead, soft and uncertain.

"Absolutely not," she muttered, and turned around.

She was halfway back to the street when she heard someone humming.

Not a recording. Not birdsong.

A person.

Soft and low and strangely familiar.

She paused. There was no one in sight.

The street was still. No movement, no voices.

Just the hum.

And it sounded like her mother.

Fi spun on her heel and walked faster.

Back at the cottage, she dropped her phone on the counter, kicked off her shoes, and went straight to the tin box under the sink. The one she hadn't opened in two years. The one she'd told herself she only kept because shredding paperwork was annoying.

She sat cross-legged on the floor and opened the lid.

Inside: a tarot card. The Two of Swords. A photo of her and her mother at a Renaissance fair, arms looped, grinning like fools. A receipt for rose quartz. A letter, unsigned, but she knew the handwriting. Loose and messy, full of certainty.

You've always had the gift, Fi. You just stopped looking.

She stared at the card.

It had been a joke at first. Her mother, all scarves and stardust, had claimed the "gift" ran in their bloodline. Said her grandmother used to read tea leaves and set bones to guide the lost. Fi had indulged it in the way you do when someone you love wants to believe something.

Until it got serious.

Until it became prophecy, not possibility.

Until the day her mother told her she was destined to lose someone and then did.

That was the last reading. The last time Fi picked up a deck. The last time she let magic near her without armor.

Grief had a way of solidifying into logic. Skepticism had been easier than rage.

She shoved the box closed.

Fox found her in the kitchen later, staring into a cup of tea she didn't remember making.

"You alright?" he asked.

"Define alright."

He sat across from her and waited.

Fi looked up. "Do you remember what she said?"

He didn't ask who.

She continued. "Mom. About how the town would find me someday. That it would whisper."

He nodded.

"I heard humming today," Fi said. "Out loud. From nowhere. And for a second, I thought it was her."

Fox studied her. "Do you want it to be?"

"I don't want it to be anything," she said. "Because if it is something, that means she wasn't wrong. And if she wasn't wrong, that means I've spent two years fighting something real."

"And if it's not real?"

"Then I've built my whole life around refusing a ghost."

Fox leaned forward, elbows on the table. "You don't have to believe anything. But you do have to be honest about what you're feeling."

Fi looked down at her hands. They were shaking, just a little.

"I don't know what I'm feeling."

"That's a start," Fox said.

She nodded.

And outside, on the edge of the garden, a single hummingbird hovered in the air. It didn't move toward the flowers. Just lingered.

Then vanished.

Chapter Fifteen: The Language of Thread

Cassie didn't mean to find her.

She had only meant to take the long way home from Bram's, arms full of lemon verbena and a stubborn strand of ivy that had refused to stay rooted. The kind that crept where it pleased, no matter how carefully Bram had tried to train it. Cassie liked plants like that. They reminded her that obedience was rarely a virtue in the natural world.

She wasn't even supposed to pass the Carrow cottage.

Her feet simply turned when her thoughts grew crowded. They had a habit of doing that, choosing quieter paths when her mind needed room to stretch.

That was how she saw Fi.

She was sitting on the porch steps, legs folded beneath her, elbows braced on her knees. She wasn't holding her phone. No book. No coffee cup or notebook to signal occupation or defense. She was just sitting there, staring toward the trees at the edge of the property like they were saying something just beyond her grasp.

Not pleading. Not threatening.

Inviting.

Cassie stopped at the gate and waited, the way you did when you weren't sure if your presence would be welcome. She considered moving on. Respecting the solitude. Silence could be a kind of care too.

Then Fi spoke, without turning her head.

"Are the plants in this town always that expressive?"

Cassie smiled before she meant to.

"Only when they're listening," she said.

Fi shifted slightly, just enough to acknowledge that she'd been joined. Her eyes were red-rimmed, though whether from lack of sleep or a stubborn moment she hadn't yet named, Cassie couldn't tell. Her voice, when she spoke again, was steady. Controlled.

Cassie stepped closer to the porch. "Mind if I sit?"

Fi shrugged faintly. "It's a free country."

Cassie lowered herself to the edge of the step, careful not to crowd her. Close enough to offer company. Far enough to leave room for refusal.

They sat in the kind of silence that didn't demand explanation.

Cassie adjusted the bundle of herbs at her feet, then reached into the pocket of her sweater and drew out a small spool of thread. Nothing special at a glance. Soft gray cotton, slightly frayed at the edges. Not enchanted. Not marked. The kind of thing you could find in any sewing kit, forgotten in a drawer.

She rolled it slowly between her fingers.

Fi noticed.

"Some people use cards," Cassie said quietly. "Or bones. Or tea leaves." She glanced down at the thread. "I use this."

Fi finally turned toward her. "To see?" she asked.

"To feel," Cassie replied. "Sometimes a thread shows me where tension lives. Sometimes it tells me where a story pulled too tight and never loosened again."

Fi watched the movement of Cassie's hands. "That seems… open to interpretation."

Cassie smiled. "So is everything that matters."

They fell quiet again. A breeze moved through the trees, rustling leaves in a way that sounded almost conversational. Somewhere farther off, something creaked and settled, wood adjusting to the day.

Cassie held out the spool.

No flourish. No explanation. Just the thread resting open in her palm.

Fi stared at it like it might suddenly grow teeth.

"I'm not doing magic," she said.

Cassie didn't withdraw her hand. "Good. Neither am I. Just holding it."

Fi hesitated. Her fingers hovered, then closed around the loose end. The thread felt ordinary. Light. Harmless.

They sat there, each holding one end, the line stretched gently between them.

Cassie gazed toward the Hollow, where the trees thickened and the air seemed to fold in on itself just slightly. "I don't need you to believe in all of it," she said softly. "But the land listens better when you stop yelling at it."

Fi scoffed. "I don't yell."

Cassie gave her a sideways glance.

Fi exhaled, the tension easing just enough to be honest. "Fine. I debate loudly."

"That's fair," Cassie said.

They didn't smile, exactly. But something in the space between them softened. The thread warmed faintly where their fingers touched, or maybe that was just skin adjusting to contact.

Cassie gave the thread a small tug.

Not a test. Not a challenge.

Fi responded instinctively, tugging back.

Just a flicker. Just enough.

Cassie stood slowly, gathering her herbs. "If you ever want to see how the thread works," she said, "the real kind, not the metaphor, come by the shop."

Fi looked up at her. "Will I be charmed into believing something I don't?"

"No," Cassie replied easily. "But you might remember something you didn't know you forgot."

Fi didn't answer.

But when Cassie walked away, she noticed the thread still looped loosely around Fi's fingers, trailing across her palm like a question she wasn't ready to ask out loud.

And that, Cassie thought, was how it usually began.

Chapter Sixteen: The Thread She Didn't Drop

Fi sat on the porch steps long after Cassie disappeared from view.

The late afternoon light shifted slowly, turning the dust in the air golden, then dulling it again. Somewhere down the road, a car door closed. A bird argued with another bird. Life continued with irritating normalcy.

The thread in her hand did nothing.

It didn't glow. It didn't hum. It didn't pulse with latent power or reveal hidden symbols when she squinted at it sideways. It was soft gray cotton, slightly frayed where it had been wound and unwound too many times. The kind of thing that came free with sewing kits and got lost under couch cushions.

And still, she couldn't bring herself to drop it.

Not because it was magic.

Because it might be.

Because it had passed from one hand to another without coercion. Because it had been offered, not pressed. Because Cassie had not asked for belief or participation or gratitude. Just attention.

Fi hated that.

Not the thread itself, but what it stirred. The subtle shift in her internal footing. The way certainty, her long-standing companion, suddenly felt less like armor and more like habit.

Doubt crept in quietly, not as a challenge but as a question.

Are you sure?

It sounded inconveniently like her own voice.

Fi curled her fingers around the thread and pushed herself to her feet. The porch boards creaked beneath her weight, grounding her in the ordinary physics of the moment. Wood. Gravity. Balance. Things she trusted.

Inside the cottage, the air was warm and faintly herbal. Fox had left a mug half-full of something steeped and forgotten on the counter, the scent unfamiliar but not unpleasant. The radio played low in the corner, an old jazz tune crackling softly, like it was reaching for something it had almost remembered.

She closed the door behind her and leaned against it, eyes shut, breathing out slowly.

Get a grip, she told herself. It's a piece of thread.

But that wasn't entirely true anymore.

She crossed the room to the small worktable by the window, the one she had cleared for practical things. Groceries. Receipts. The growing paper trail of relocation and responsibility. Without meaning to, she had turned it into something else.

A place where questions landed.

Fi set the thread in the center of the table. It lay there innocently, unremarkable against the wood grain. No shimmer. No pull. No demand.

And yet.

It wasn't nothing.

Because for the first time in longer than she wanted to admit, Fi didn't feel angry about not knowing something.

Anger had always been her first response. Anger at being misled. Anger at false authority. Anger at systems that pretended mystery when they meant control.

This was different.

This was curiosity.

Unsettling. Suspicious. Deeply inconvenient.

She reached for her notebook, the one she'd been using to catalogue Emerdeen with the precision of someone determined not to be impressed. She flipped past pages filled with bullet points and barbed commentary.

Aggressively quaint.
Moon appears to be emotionally manipulative.
Locals suspiciously unbothered by ambiguity.

She stopped at a blank page.

Her pen hovered.

Then she wrote:

• *Cassie handed me a thread today.*
• *No spell. No instruction. Just a choice to hold it.*
• *Felt like someone handing me the end of a sentence I forgot I was supposed to finish.*

Fi leaned back in her chair, surprised by the honesty of it.

After a moment, she added one more line.

• *Didn't drop it.*

She closed the notebook carefully, as if not to startle the thought into retreat. She reached out and picked up the thread again, rubbing it gently between her fingers.

There was no voice in her head. No revelation. No ancestors lining up to explain themselves.

Just the quiet, unfamiliar weight of possibility.

And that, Fi realized with a mixture of irritation and awe, might be the most dangerous thing of all.

Chapter Seventeen: Honey in the Hemlock

Avalon lit three candles before dusk, all in shades of pink and gold. The kind that softened the air, the kind that bent the light just enough to make the edges of truth blur.

She'd gathered the ingredients carefully. Not from the town's usual shops; she didn't need Cassie's fingerprints on her work. She brought most of it with her, tucked in compartments and charm-lined pouches. Dried rose petals. A sliver of honeycomb. A piece of a poem, torn from a page and folded like a secret. She added a pinch of heartseed oil and whispered the name.

"Baz."

Just the name. Not the rest of the spell yet.

She wasn't foolish enough to bind. Not yet.

Binding was messy. Noticeable. It made magic twitchy, and men even worse.

No, she was crafting an invitation. A door gently opening. A shift in the wind that might make him glance over his shoulder. She'd always believed you could catch more affection with suggestion than force. Let the spell do the winking. Let the charm hum quietly beneath his feet.

Avalon sat cross-legged on the floor, eyes closed, voice low.

"Not to take, only to draw. Not to cage, only to call. Let his heart lean toward mine. Let his gaze return more than once. Let the warmth find its source."

The candles flickered. The honey warmed.

And the thread began to unwind.

She smiled.

The next morning, she dressed with care. Something soft, but not too soft. Intentional. She let her hair fall just enough over one eye and wore a sprig of rosemary tucked behind her ear, just enough protection to keep herself centered, but not enough to dull the signal she was sending out.

She wandered toward the greenhouse with a basket of fresh apples and no real excuse.

Baz was outside, sleeves rolled, dirt on his forearms, coaxing a stubborn vine into cooperation.

He looked up as she approached.

"Morning," he said easily, the same way he would greet anyone.

She smiled as if it mattered. "I thought you might enjoy these."

He wiped his hands on a cloth and eyed the apples. "Didn't take you for a fruit-bearing wanderer."

"I contain multitudes," she said, setting the basket down.

Baz nodded once. "Appreciated."

Avalon waited for him to say more.

He didn't.

Instead, he turned back to the vine and gave it a small encouraging tap. "You're going to need a little more shade if you want this to root well. Late sun's been burning the edge."

Avalon crouched beside him, brushing a stray leaf from her knee. "You speak to them like they answer."

He smiled faintly. "They do."

"In words?"

"In results."

She studied him. "You're not like the others."

Baz shrugged. "I just listen better than most."

Avalon reached into her pocket and pulled out a charm - small, round, wrapped in rose thread. She held it out, casual but deliberate.

"I made this," she said. "Just a little something for clarity and confidence. Nothing binding."

Baz didn't take it.

Instead, he glanced at it. Then at her.

"Clarity and confidence," he repeated.

"It helps people see what they want," she said, her voice softening. "What they need."

Baz dusted his hands on his pants and stood.

"That's the thing about clarity," he said. "Sometimes it shows you something you didn't want to see."

Avalon blinked.

"I appreciate the gesture," he added. "But I'm already pretty clear on where I stand."

He turned and walked back toward the greenhouse.

Avalon stayed crouched beside the vine, charm still in hand.

It hadn't failed. Not completely.

But it hadn't worked the way it should have.

The air around her shifted. Slightly colder. Slightly stiller.

The charm string snapped in her fingers.

In the Hollow, the old threads stirred.

And far away, in a drawer beneath Cassie's altar, a silver thread curled tighter on its spool.

Chapter Eighteen: The Weight of Unspoken Things

Baz didn't tell Cassie.

Not yet.

He told himself it was because there wasn't anything concrete to report. A stranger had come bearing apples and pleasant conversation. No raised voices. No overt spellwork. Nothing that warranted alarm bells or a town meeting or one of Cassie's quiet, careful circles.

Still, his hands itched after she left.

It was the kind of sensation he trusted more than logic. A residual awareness, like static clinging to skin long after you'd stepped away from faulty wiring. The rosemary along the garden path, which usually leaned toward him when he passed, stayed stubbornly upright. The leaves did not turn. The stems did not sway.

He washed his hands once at the sink. Then again.

The water ran clear, cool, grounding. It helped, but not enough.

Baz stood in the doorway of the greenhouse and scanned the rows, trying to convince himself he was imagining the shift. The lavender looked slightly dulled at the tips, its color muted like fabric left too long in sunlight. Not dying. Not sick. Just… withdrawn.

The charm she had offered him still flickered behind his eyes.

Small. Round. Wrapped in rose-colored thread. Pretty in the way objects designed to be persuasive always were. Polished enough to imply care. Purposeful enough to suggest inevitability.

He hadn't touched it.

He hadn't needed to.

Some things announced themselves without contact.

Baz stepped outside and began his usual perimeter walk, tracing the edge of the garden in a slow, deliberate loop. It was a habit he had developed long before Emerdeen, back when he trusted systems more than instincts. When he needed to think, he moved. When he needed to listen, he let his body do the work.

The plants were quiet, but not empty.

The soil didn't hum the way it usually did beneath his feet. There was no resonance, no gentle feedback loop of care and response. Instead, the ground felt hesitant. Like something had paused mid-sentence.

He crouched near the calendula beds and pressed his palm into the earth.

Warm.

But not welcoming.

Baz frowned.

This wasn't a breach. No ward had been crossed. Nothing aggressive had entered the space. But it felt as though someone had whispered into the garden without asking first. A suggestion had been planted, subtle and careful, curling into the air like an idea you couldn't quite trace back to its origin.

He stood and brushed the dirt from his jeans.

He knew that texture.

He had lived most of his life under it.

Expectations. Assumptions. The unspoken weight of what people wanted him to be. What they thought he should build, how he should behave, who he should become if he just applied himself correctly.

There was a tone to it. A pressure. When someone wanted something from you badly enough, the space between grew dense.

Avalon had left that density behind.

Baz made tea he didn't drink. Lit a candle he didn't need. He adjusted a tool that was already aligned, anything to keep his hands busy while his mind circled the same conclusion.

This wasn't about magic.

It was about entitlement.

When Cassie arrived later with her familiar knot of lemongrass and thyme tucked under her arm, she stopped short in the doorway. She didn't speak right away. She just looked at him, taking in the set of his shoulders, the way his breath didn't quite reach his chest.

"You okay?" she asked.

"Sure," Baz said automatically.

Cassie's eyes narrowed, not with suspicion, but with recognition. "You're too quiet."

"I'm always quiet."

"You're quiet with volume," she replied. "This is different."

He didn't argue.

She stepped inside, set the herbs on the counter, and crossed the space between them without urgency. She placed her palm lightly against his chest, just over his sternum. Not a spell. Not a reading. Just contact.

"You feel like static," she murmured.

Baz swallowed. "She offered me something."

Cassie's hand stilled.

"A charm," he added quickly. "For clarity. Confidence."

Cassie's mouth tightened, the humor draining from her expression.

"I didn't take it," he said. "I wouldn't."

"I know," Cassie replied. "The charm didn't land. But it brushed the threads. That's what I felt this morning."

He exhaled, the breath leaving him in a rush. "She wants something."

Cassie nodded once.

"She thinks she's owed it," he continued, the words settling heavily between them.

This time Cassie's fingers curled slightly into his shirt. Not fear. Not anger.

Protection.

"I'll handle it," she said.

Baz covered her hand with his. "I don't want this to turn into a war."

"It isn't a war," Cassie said softly. "It's a boundary."

He met her eyes. "I didn't invite her in."

"I know," she whispered.

They stood together in the quiet, both holding the weight of something newly named. Outside, the rosemary finally bent toward the doorway, responding not to resolution, but to attention.

The balance hadn't returned.

But it was listening again.

And for now, that was enough.

Chapter Nineteen: Unravel, Return

Cassie didn't slam drawers. She didn't pace the shop or mutter half-formed threats into the corners of the room. There was no rush of air, no crack of heat or light, no dramatic punctuation to announce that something had gone wrong.

She moved slowly instead.

The kettle went on the burner. Water measured. Tea steeped just long enough to be strong without bitterness. She wiped down the counter, not because it needed it, but because it gave her hands something steady to do while her thoughts aligned.

Only then did she light a candle. Only then did she gather the thread.

Not the silver thread she used when she needed to listen to the weave itself. Not the enchanted strands reserved for vignettes or thresholds. This was the plain gray cotton she offered freely to guests. The kind she kept wound loosely in a shallow bowl by the register. The kind that accumulated meaning not through power, but through repetition.

The thread of ordinary choice.

She carried it into the back room and cut three lengths with careful precision.

One for Baz.

One for the space between them.

One for whatever had attempted to intrude without consent.

Cassie sat at the small table by the window and let the thread run through her fingers. She felt its softness. Its slight resistance. Its honesty. Thread like this didn't pretend to be unbreakable. It trusted you to handle it with care.

She didn't curse.

She didn't bind or restrain or push back against what had brushed too close. Force invited force. Control invited escalation.

Instead, she whispered what she already knew to be true.

"Return what does not belong.
Restore what was not broken.
Reinforce what is freely given."

The words were not demands. They were reminders.

She knotted the first length carefully, fingers steady.

"Baz," she said softly, "as you are. As you choose."

The second knot followed, looser, breathing space into its shape.

"Our bond," she murmured, "as it lives. Not as it's claimed."

The third knot was small and deliberate.

"Let borrowed magic fray before it roots."

The candle flame wavered once, then settled. Not in response. In agreement.

Cassie braided the three threads together slowly, not rushing the rhythm. When she finished, she wrapped the braid around a smooth river stone, cool and patient in her palm. She stepped outside and tucked it gently into the soil beneath the rosemary bush, pressing the earth closed again with her hands.

A quiet spell.

A grounding point.

Something Avalon would never see but might feel later. Like the subtle discomfort of realizing your words don't land the way you expected. Like the way your name sounds slightly wrong when spoken by someone who doesn't know you.

Cassie rose slowly and brushed the dirt from her palms, breathing in the scent of rosemary and damp soil.

This wasn't fear.

This was clarity.

Avalon had arrived wrapped in velvet and suggestion, in sparkle and entitlement, in magic designed to impress and persuade. Cassie didn't need any of that. She had a greenhouse that responded to her presence. A shop that shimmered when she laughed. A relationship built not on inevitability, but on choices made with clear eyes and dirty hands.

Let Avalon try.

Let her craft and coax and cast.

Cassie wasn't interested in stopping her.

She was only interested in making sure nothing stuck.

Chapter Twenty: The Stitch Beneath the Silence

Morgan felt it in the soles of their feet.

Not a jolt. Not a tremor that rattled the bones or sent warnings skittering up the spine. It was subtler than that. A settling. Like a rug that had been nudged off-center over time and finally eased back into alignment without anyone making a show of it.

They were in the studio, sweeping chalk dust into a shallow copper bowl, when the shift moved through them. The broom slowed in their hand. The air seemed to exhale.

Stillness.

Not the brittle quiet that gathers before a storm, tight and anticipatory.

The quiet that follows a decision.

Morgan paused mid-sweep, one palm resting against the wall, grounding themselves in the familiar texture of plaster and paint. They closed their eyes and tipped their head slightly, the way you did when listening for something just beyond sound.

There.

A subtle change in the weave.

Cassie's magic always had a recognizable texture. Earthy and practical, threaded through with care rather than spectacle. It didn't announce itself. It settled into places. Strength that came from mending rather than force. The kind of magic that knew how to hold without gripping.

This working was no different.

But it had teeth.

Not sharp. Not aggressive. Defined.

Morgan smiled, a small, knowing curve of the mouth. Not unkindly. Not surprised at all.

They straightened, set the broom aside, and crossed to the altar shelf. Their fingers brushed over familiar objects as they passed. Smooth stones worn pale by years of handling. Small jars layered with wax drips and handwritten labels. Nothing dramatic. Nothing rare.

They selected a slip of plain muslin and a fresh sprig of lemon balm, its scent bright and reassuring. With careful hands, they wrapped the herb into the cloth and tied it closed with a simple knot.

Just enough to hold space.

Not because Cassie needed protection.

But because Morgan understood how magic rippled. How one choice, once made, tugged on nearby threads whether anyone intended it or not. Support wasn't about interference. It was about resonance.

They stepped outside and turned toward the Hollow.

The trees acknowledged them as they passed, leaves shifting with a sound that felt like greeting rather than wind. Morgan moved without hurry. Not hiding. Just listening. Their steps found the softer ground instinctively, avoiding stones and roots without conscious thought.

Every place had a heartbeat. Emerdeen had many.

The shop pulsed steady and warm. The greenhouse hummed with quiet diligence. The studio held its breath in anticipation of the next gathering. The Hollow breathed deep and old.

And threaded between them all now was the pulse of connection between Baz and Cassie, once soft and private, now wrapped deliberately. Chosen.

Morgan knelt beside a twisted birch near the path, its roots gripping moss and soil with patient insistence. They pressed the sachet gently into the earth, tucking it among the roots as if returning something borrowed.

No chant.

No blessing.

Just a whisper meant for listening ears.

"For clarity to stay clear," Morgan said softly.
"For connection to stay chosen."
"For want to stay out of the way of what already is."

The birch shifted slightly, bark creaking in quiet acknowledgement.

Morgan rose and drew in a slow breath, letting it settle low in their body.

Avalon had begun to pull. That much was evident. Not violently. Not yet. But sleekly. Persistently. The kind of wanting that slid between boundaries and pretended not to see them.

Wanting alone didn't make someone dangerous.

Entitlement did.

Morgan turned back toward the studio; footsteps light but sure. Cassie had done what needed doing. Cleanly. Without spectacle.

The weave had felt it.

And threads, once reminded of their purpose, had a long memory.

Chapter Twenty-One: Names That Remember

The second time Fi came into the shop, she didn't knock.

Cassie had left the door open. On purpose, maybe.

The air was cool and pine-scented, the windows propped wide with smooth stones. A string of wind chimes whispered gently overhead with thread spools, tiny scissors, and ceramic moons clinking in a language no one really taught, but everyone felt.

Cassie looked up from the counter. "Back so soon?"

Fi gave a half-smile. "Thought I'd return the thread."

Cassie glanced at her hands. "You're not holding it."

"I mean the idea of it," Fi said. "The metaphor."

Cassie smiled. "Ah. The dangerous kind."

Fi wandered a little, eyes skimming the shelves. "You label everything like it's an invitation."

"Maybe it is."

"To what?"

Cassie leaned against the counter. "Choice. Curiosity. Something you forgot you wanted."

Fi picked up a jar labeled *For unraveling with grace* and snorted softly. "Charming."

"Literally," Cassie said.

They lapsed into quiet.

Then Fi asked, almost casually, "Is Cassie short for something?"

Cassie arched a brow. "Fishing?"

Fi shrugged. "Curious."

Cassie hesitated. "It's short for Cassia."

Fi's eyes widened slightly. "That's actually... beautiful."

"It was my grandmother's name. My mother named me after her, but I didn't grow into it for a long time."

"So why the short version?"

Cassie gave a soft, self-deprecating laugh. "Because 'Cassia' felt like a prophecy, and I wasn't ready to be that girl yet. 'Cassie' could hide behind coffee and snark. Cassia had to listen when the wind talked."

Fi nodded slowly. "Makes sense."

She set the jar down and turned. "Mine's short, too."

Cassie looked at her.

"Persephone."

Cassie let the name settle in the space between them.

"That's not one you hear every day."

Fi's mouth twisted. "Try growing up with it and see how many pomegranate jokes you get before high school."

Cassie smiled. "So, you became Fi."

"It sounded sharper," she said. "Harder to romanticize. Less floral, more 'don't try me.'"

"Fits," Cassie said.

Fi crossed her arms. "You think names matter?"

Cassie nodded. "Names carry intention. Even the ones we run from."

Fi looked away, toward the open door.

"It was my mother's favorite myth," she said quietly. "Persephone. The girl who ate the seeds and split her life. Queen of the Underworld, whether she asked for it or not."

Cassie said nothing.

"And I guess," Fi added, "when she died, the name felt heavier. Like I had to carry both halves."

Cassie's voice was soft. "But Fi lets you breathe."

Fi looked back at her. "For now."

They stood in silence for a moment. Not awkward. Just aware.

Cassie broke it gently. "Want to help me label some new tinctures? I promise not to enchant anything while you're watching."

Fi smiled. "No promises about sarcasm."

"I wouldn't dare ask."

Chapter Twenty-Two: Cracks in the Exit Plan

Fox was sitting on the back porch with a sketchpad balanced on his knee and a cat he absolutely insisted he did not feed draped across his shins like royalty granted temporary clemency.

The cat's tail flicked once, slow and imperious, as if daring either of them to dispute ownership.

The sun had just slipped past the trees, leaving the sky streaked with soft oranges and bruised purples. It was the kind of light that made Fi want to catalog wavelengths and atmospheric conditions so she wouldn't accidentally fall into reverence.

She pushed the screen door open with her elbow and dropped a folded tea towel onto the railing. "We own too many mugs."

Fox glanced up, pencil still moving. "We inherited too many mugs."

"Well, half of them say things like *Blessed be the brew*," Fi said. "I refuse to drink out of anything that feels like it came with a complimentary incantation."

Fox smirked. "Didn't stop you from stealing the cinnamon one."

"It was clean and had a decent handle," Fi replied, settling beside him and curling one leg beneath her. "That's not witchcraft. That's ergonomics."

The cat opened one eye and regarded her with profound disinterest.

Fox let a few beats pass, then said, "You're quieter than usual."

Fi tilted her head toward the trees. "I had a conversation today."

"That does sound terrible."

"With Cassie."

Fox's pencil stopped mid-line.

"Ah," he said carefully.

"She asked about my name," Fi continued. "The real one."

He finally looked up, studying her face the way he always did when something mattered. "And you told her?"

"I didn't plan to," Fi said. "It just… came out."

Fox waited. He was good at that.

"And you're still breathing," he said after a moment. "So, I assume she didn't try to bind you to the moon or make you wear a flower crown."

Fi snorted despite herself. "She was gentle."

He raised an eyebrow.

"Annoyingly so," Fi added.

Fox closed the sketchbook and set it aside. "You sound like someone who didn't hate it."

"I didn't like it," Fi said quickly. "But I didn't hate it."

They sat with that, the porch boards cooling beneath them as the day slipped fully into evening.

"She makes you feel," Fi said slowly, "like maybe magic isn't about power or control. Maybe it's just… paying attention really hard."

Fox smiled, soft and unguarded. "That's kind of beautiful."

"I know," Fi said, scowling at the horizon. "Which is deeply inconvenient."

Fox leaned back against the railing; hands folded loosely over his stomach. "So, what now?"

Fi rubbed her thumb along the seam of her jeans. "I don't know. It's not like one conversation changes anything."

"No," Fox agreed. "But sometimes it opens a door you didn't realize was there."

Fi didn't respond.

The cat stretched luxuriously, claws flexing against Fox's leg, entirely unconcerned with existential thresholds.

"I found the property assessment," Fox said gently. "The land alone could sell well. Some developer's already left a flyer in the mailbox."

Fi rolled her eyes. "Of course they have."

He hesitated. "Do you still want to sell it?"

Fi exhaled slowly. "That was the plan."

Fox met her gaze. "That's not an answer."

She swallowed. "I don't know," she admitted. "This place... it's weird. It breathes. And I keep feeling like if I leave too fast, it might follow me."

Fox nodded, unsurprised.

Fi stared out into the darkening woods. "And the worst part?"

"What?"

"She remembered my name," Fi said quietly. "Like it meant something."

Fox placed his hand lightly on her knee, grounding, steady. "It does."

Fi didn't pull away.

She didn't speak again.

Above them, the first star blinked into the sky, quiet and certain, like a truth that didn't need permission to exist.

Chapter Twenty-Three: The Thread That Would Not Hold

Avalon woke with the uneasy certainty that something had slipped through her fingers.

She lit her usual candle. Stirred honey into her tea. Reached for her charmwork journal with fingers that still moved in perfect grace. But when she opened the page where Baz's name had been inked into the binding spell, the thread sewn into the margin was slack.

Not broken.

But limp.

The energy that once shimmered faintly across the page now felt dull. Tired. Like it had been undone gently, not forcefully. As if someone had not fought her magic but simply returned it.

She frowned. Avalon did not believe in failure.

Only recalibration.

She re-read the charm three times. Checked her ingredients. Whispered a new intention over the rose-threaded spool she had used the day before.

Nothing shifted.

The air in the cottage felt wrong too. Stiller than it should have been. Not heavy, just unwilling.

The rosemary by the windowsill had turned toward the corner instead of the light.

Avalon stood abruptly and moved to the center of the room. She spread her arms and closed her eyes, calling the magic up from her ribs and out through her hands.

She whispered. She summoned. She asked.

Nothing came.

The threads were not listening.

No. Worse. They were listening to someone else.

Later that morning, she returned to the garden path near the greenhouse, the one she had walked before with carefully rehearsed ease. She waited until she saw him. Baz, bent over a row of snapdragons, laughing softly at something Cassie said from the porch.

He was not wearing her charm.

He had never accepted it.

But he looked even further from her reach now than he had when they first met.

Cassie turned, eyes flicking up, and caught Avalon standing there.

She did not smile.

She did not scowl either.

She simply looked.

And Avalon felt it.

The full weight of something ancient and precise. Not power in the dramatic sense, but power in the knowing. Cassie's gaze was not aggressive. It was calm. Balanced. Like someone who had already bound the edges of a spell long before anyone thought to test it.

Avalon turned before they could speak.

She walked slowly back to the road, fury blooming quietly behind her ribs. It was not rage. Not yet. But the sharp edge of being denied something she had already counted on.

She whispered to the wind.

"You do not know what I have given up for this."

The wind did not answer.

The rosemary still faced the corner.

And in the folds of her velvet coat, the thread she had enchanted began to fray.

Chapter Twenty-Four: The Places That Remember Us

Cassie waited until dusk.

Not because of the light, or the tradition, or any dramatic impulse. She simply knew the garden listened best in the hours between. When the air hung softer. When the plants exhaled. When even the stones were willing to shift a little.

She walked the boundary of the shop in slow steps, fingers brushing low rosemary and high ivy, murmuring words that didn't need to be loud to be heard.

"Hold what is whole. Invite what is honest. Redirect what is not ours to carry."

Each word settled into the soil. Each breath wove a little tighter into the rootwork already in place. The wards here had grown up with her. They were part of the walls, the windows, the beams that held the roof up when storms came. But even the strongest weavings needed tending.

Something had tested the edges.

And though it had not broken through, it had left scuff marks.

Cassie reached the back porch and knelt beside the old lantern that marked the westernmost corner of the property. She lit a new wick, dipped her fingers in saltwater, and whispered her mother's phrase for steadiness.

Baz's footsteps sounded on the porch behind her.

"You're stitching again," he said gently.

She didn't turn. "She tried to thread something into you. I felt it yesterday."

"I know," he said.

Cassie looked up then, surprised by the lack of hesitation in his voice.

"She gave me a charm," he continued. "I didn't take it, but I felt the spell slide past anyway. It didn't land. Not fully. But it touched something."

Cassie rose slowly, brushing dirt from her hands. "I've reinforced the shop. The garden too. She won't get in again. Not through the magic."

Baz stepped forward, brushing a strand of hair from her face. "You always move like this. Quiet. Steady. No big gestures."

"That's how real things last," she said.

He took her hand and pressed his palm to hers. "I want you to know... I didn't hesitate. Not even for a second."

Cassie's throat tightened. "I know."

"I've had people try to choose for me before," he said. "I don't want that again."

"You won't get that here."

He smiled, small and soft. "I know that too."

They stood under the porch lantern, fingers still twined. The salt in the air had a sweetness to it now, like something had been released from tension.

Cassie reached into her pocket and pulled out a charm. Just thread, lavender, and hematite. The simplest kind.

"For protection," she said. "But more than that, for remembering."

Baz held it carefully. "I already remember."

Cassie smiled. "Good. Then let it help the garden remember too."

They stood together for a while longer, until the last light dipped beneath the trees.

And inside the shop, the wards pulsed once. A quiet affirmation. The thread was holding.

Chapter Twenty-Five: The Ritual Between the Lines

Cassie found Morgan on the porch with two mugs of tea already steeped and waiting, steam rising in lazy ribbons. The air had that early morning stillness that seemed to belong only to Emerdeen, where even silence had texture.

"You always know when I need to sit down," Cassie said as she joined them.

Morgan handed her the mug. "It's one of my quieter spells."

Cassie smiled, but she could already feel it. The magic in the air wasn't loud, but it was present. Watching. Listening.

"The Hollow pulsed last night," Morgan said. "It wasn't alarming. Just awake."

Cassie nodded. "I felt it too. Like something was stretching out its limbs after a long sleep."

Morgan took a sip of their tea, then added, "It passed through the old Carrow property."

Cassie glanced up. "Fi and Fox's place?"

Morgan nodded. "There's movement in the house. Not just them. The house itself."

Cassie let out a breath, slow and thoughtful. "Makes sense. It's been quiet for so long. Like it closed itself up after their aunt passed."

Morgan hummed in agreement. "She kept to herself, but she respected the land. That house was kept in balance. It wasn't flashy magic, but it was steady."

"She never talked much about her family," Cassie said. "I didn't even know she had a niece and nephew until the letter was read."

"They inherited it cleanly?"

"Completely. Deed and all," Cassie replied. "Fi told me they were planning to sell it, but she's hesitating now."

"Because of the house?" Morgan asked.

"Because of something the house remembers," Cassie said. "It's like the land's reaching for her."

Morgan tilted their head. "It would. Blood remembers blood. Even if the people forget."

Cassie looked toward the north road where the Carrow house sat just out of view. "I used to walk past it as a girl and swear I could hear someone humming inside even when the lights were out."

"That sounds about right," Morgan said. "There are notes that only certain houses hold."

"She's beginning to hear them," Cassie added. "Fi. She doesn't know what it is yet, but she's not running either."

"Not yet."

Cassie smiled faintly. "She told me her full name yesterday."

Morgan blinked. "That's a big step for someone so determined not to believe in magic."

"Persephone," Cassie said softly.

Morgan gave a low whistle. "That is not a casual name."

"It carries something. Her mother loved the story, apparently. I wonder if the aunt did too. That house doesn't feel neutral. It feels expectant."

Morgan leaned back against the porch rail. "You think it held the magic quiet while it waited?"

"I think it folded itself small so it wouldn't scare them off," Cassie said. "But now it's unfolding again."

Morgan nodded slowly. "We should check in. Not to intervene. Just to witness."

"I'm not sure they're ready for us to step inside just yet," Cassie said.

"Then we wait."

They both turned toward the hill, sipping their tea as the light shifted gently over the treetops.

"She's not leaving," Cassie said.

Morgan didn't answer with words. They just smiled.

Chapter Twenty-Six: Where the Hollow Bends

Morgan did not sleep when the Hollow shifted. It was not that the ground moved or the trees cracked. The change was more like a breath held too long. Something in the weave had tightened. A new thread pulled. They felt it in the soles of their feet. In the tips of their fingers. In the part of their chest that always hummed when the Hollow was speaking.

They stood barefoot in the center of the studio, eyes closed, pulse steady. The energy curled around them like mist. No words. No direction. Just that soft pressure. An invitation with no explanation.

They wrapped a shawl around their shoulders and stepped out into the night. The path to the Hollow was familiar by now. Worn by footsteps, softened by moss. They did not need a lantern. The moon gave enough. And the Hollow preferred its visitors arrive gently, not blinding the way with artificial light.

Branches rustled above them. A soft sound. Not warning. Not quite welcome either. Just awareness.

Morgan moved slowly, letting the rhythm of the place guide their pace. The farther they walked, the quieter the world became. Even their breath seemed to shift into something measured. The kind of silence that feels watched but not judged.

When they reached the clearing, the air felt different. Not heavy. Not light.

But bent. As if something had pressed into the weave and left a shape behind.

Morgan stepped into the center of the space and turned once in a slow circle. The trees stood tall around them. Lanterns hung from a few low branches, unlit but gently swaying. The ground beneath their feet pulsed faintly.

They knelt and placed one hand flat on the earth. The Hollow always remembered what had been asked of it. And something had just been asked.

Not by them. Not by Cassie. Not by anyone they could name.

But the request had echoed. Soft, but deep. The kind of request made with the whole body. The kind that did not ask for power. The kind that asked to be ready.

Morgan closed their eyes and leaned into the hum of it.

It was not Avalon's voice. It was not Fi's, or even Fox's.

It was older than the newcomers. Familiar. Rooted.

Cassie.

She had asked something. Not out loud. Not in ritualized words. But in intention. The Hollow had felt it. And now, so had Morgan.

They did not need to know the question. They only needed to make space for the answer.

Morgan stood and walked to the edge of the clearing. From the pouch at their side, they pulled three stones that were worn smooth by water and time. They placed them in a triangle at the center of the space and whispered a soft word of holding.

Not to bind. Not to shield.

To remember.

Then they sat, wrapped the shawl tighter, and waited.

They did not know what would come. But they trusted the path.

Chapter Twenty-Seven: What Houses Remember

Cassie found Morgan on the porch with two mugs of tea already steeped and waiting, steam rising in lazy ribbons. The air had that early morning stillness that seemed to belong only to Emerdeen, where even silence had texture.

"You always know when I need to sit down," Cassie said as she joined them.

Morgan handed her the mug. "It's one of my quieter spells."

Cassie smiled, but she could already feel it. The magic in the air wasn't loud, but it was present. Watching. Listening.

"The Hollow pulsed last night," Morgan said. "It wasn't alarming. Just awake."

Cassie nodded. "I felt it too. Like something was stretching out its limbs after a long sleep."

Morgan took a sip of their tea, then added, "It passed through the old Carrow property."

Cassie glanced up. "Fi and Fox's place?"

Morgan nodded. "There's movement in the house. Not just them. The house itself."

Cassie let out a breath, slow and thoughtful. "Makes sense. It's been quiet for so long. Like it closed itself up after their aunt passed."

Morgan hummed in agreement. "She kept to herself, but she respected the land. That house was kept in balance. It wasn't flashy magic, but it was steady."

"She never talked much about her family," Cassie said. "I didn't even know she had a niece and nephew until the letter was read."

"They inherited it cleanly?"

"Completely. Deed and all," Cassie replied. "Fi told me they were planning to sell it, but she's hesitating now."

"Because of the house?" Morgan asked.

"Because of something the house remembers," Cassie said. "It's like the land's reaching for her."

Morgan tilted their head. "It would. Blood remembers blood. Even if the people forget."

Cassie looked toward the north road where the Carrow house sat just out of view. "I used to walk past it as a girl and swear I could hear someone humming inside even when the lights were out."

"That sounds about right," Morgan said. "There are notes that only certain houses hold."

"She's beginning to hear them," Cassie added. "Fi. She doesn't know what it is yet, but she's not running either."

"Not yet."

Cassie smiled faintly. "She told me her full name yesterday."

Morgan blinked. "That's a big step for someone so determined not to believe in magic."

"Persephone," Cassie said softly.

Morgan gave a low whistle. "That is not a casual name."

"It carries something. Her mother loved the story, apparently. I wonder if the aunt did too. That house doesn't feel neutral. It feels expectant."

Morgan leaned back against the porch rail. "You think it held the magic quiet while it waited?"

"I think it folded itself small so it wouldn't scare them off," Cassie said. "But now it's unfolding again."

Morgan nodded slowly. "We should check in. Not to intervene. Just to witness."

"I'm not sure they're ready for us to step inside just yet," Cassie said.

"Then we wait."

They both turned toward the hill, sipping their tea as the light shifted gently over the treetops.

"She's not leaving," Cassie said.

Morgan didn't answer with words. They just smiled.

Chapter Twenty-Eight: The Shift in the Stillness

Fi woke before her alarm, which was rude in itself.

She lay in bed for a moment, blinking up at the ceiling and trying to figure out what had pulled her out of sleep. There hadn't been a sound, no nightmare, no storm. Just a subtle wrongness in the air.

Or maybe not wrong.

Just… altered.

The light filtering through the curtain was softer than usual. The kind of soft that felt watched. Not in a predatory way. In a patient one.

Fi sat up slowly and looked around the room.

Nothing was out of place.

The worn dresser still stood stubbornly by the far wall. The curtain still billowed a little in the breeze from the cracked window. Her mug from last night's tea sat on the bedside table, half full and completely cold.

But something had changed.

She swung her legs over the side of the bed and padded barefoot to the door, stepping carefully. The hallway creaked, same as it always did, but the floorboards felt warmer than they had yesterday. Less sullen. Less tired.

She paused halfway down the stairs.

The smell hit her first. Not coffee. Not Fox's overzealous toast experiments.

Lavender.

Not sharp, not perfumed.

Real.

Crushed lavender, earthy and fresh, like someone had walked through the garden and left the scent behind them.

Fi moved slowly into the kitchen.

It was empty.

Fox had left a note near the breadbox: *Gone into town. Back with snacks or a story.*

She frowned. Nothing in the room looked different. But it felt different. The air was charged, like a room where someone had just been laughing or crying and you walked in a second too late.

She reached for her favorite mug without looking.

And paused.

It wasn't on the hook where she always left it.

Instead, it was already sitting on the counter.

Clean. Warm.

Like it had just been washed and set out for her.

Fi stared at it for a long moment.

She picked it up slowly and held it in both hands. No inscription. No trick. Just warm ceramic and faint heat.

"I did not do this," she muttered.

The silence answered with nothing at all.

She placed the mug down and moved toward the back window, the one that overlooked the small patch of garden their aunt had once tended. Most of it had gone wild by now. But this morning, one of the rosebushes was blooming.

It hadn't been yesterday.

Fi narrowed her eyes. "Oh no you don't."

The bush didn't answer, obviously.

But the bloom tilted slightly toward the window.

Fi stared back at it.

She folded her arms.

"I'm not enchanted."

The bloom held its ground.

"I don't care what the porch smells like, or who warmed the mug, or what this house thinks it remembers. I'm not staying."

The bush did not retreat. Nor did it bloom any further.

It just… was.

Stubborn.

Like her.

Fi sighed and turned away.

She made tea. Sat down. Opened her notebook.

And before she could stop herself, she wrote:

- The house is paying attention.
- Lavender without source. Mug moved.
- Rosebush blooming out of cycle.
- I don't like being watched.
- I also don't hate it.

She stared at the last line and sighed again.

It was going to be a long morning.

Chapter Twenty-Nine: What Fox Found

Fox didn't have a destination in mind when he left the house that morning.

He'd scribbled a note for Fi in case she woke up before he returned. He figured she'd roll her eyes. He hoped she'd read it twice anyway.

The air was already warm, laced with something that felt like the edge of citrus and the beginning of summer. He followed his feet more than the road. The path curved past the bakery, where something with cardamom called to him, and through the square, where a couple of vendors were already setting up cloth tents and baskets of herbs.

Fox paused near a booth filled with bottles and loose paper. The woman behind it didn't look up, just hummed softly as she arranged her jars. He almost moved on, but a slip of paper pinned to a small wooden board caught his eye. It read:

"If you find what doesn't belong, hold it gently. It might be waiting for someone else."

Fox blinked. He stepped closer. The paper fluttered as if exhaling.

The vendor looked up at last. Her eyes were the soft kind that knew too much. "Looking for something?"

"Nope," he said. "Just wandering."

She smiled. "That's when the town usually speaks."

"I thought that was the Hollow's job."

She tilted her head. "The Hollow speaks with trees. The town prefers misplaced objects and awkward timing."

Fox laughed. "That tracks."

She handed him a folded map.

He raised an eyebrow. "You give maps to everyone?"

"Only the ones who look like they're about to find something they didn't lose."

He took it without opening it, thanked her, and moved on.

It wasn't until he passed the old chapel, which is now more moss than wood, that he realized he'd left the main road. He hadn't even noticed the turn.

The path narrowed and led to a small grove behind a fence that had given up being a barrier years ago. There, nestled between two trees, sat what looked like a mailbox.

Not just a regular one, but a tall, cast-iron box with vines curling up its base and initials carved carefully into the side: *J.M.C.*

Fox stood in front of it for a moment, unsure why he had stopped.

There was a sound. A faint clink.

He looked around.

No one.

Then he noticed the slot. It was open just a crack. Inside, barely visible, was a folded piece of parchment. Not damp. Not dusty. Fresh.

He hesitated.

Then he reached in and pulled it out.

The writing was delicate but sharp:

"Not all inheritances are paper and deeds. Some are memories that wait in the roots."

Fox stared at the words.

There was no signature.

He turned the paper over. Nothing on the back. No date. No explanation.

He folded it carefully and tucked it into his pocket.

The map felt heavier now.

He took it out, unfolded it slowly.

The town looked familiar. Mostly.

But in the top right corner, where the Carrow property should have been marked with a simple nameplate, there was a circle drawn in red thread. Not ink. Actual thread, stitched into the page.

And written next to it, in small looping script:

"The house remembers more than you."

Fox folded the map slowly, holding it between his fingers like it might say something else if he gave it time.

He didn't know who J.M.C. was.

He didn't know why a message had been waiting for him.

But he knew one thing now for certain.

They were not just here to sell a house.

Chapter Thirty: What She Is Willing to Risk

Avalon had stopped pretending this was still subtle.

Her room smelled of burnt sugar and crushed petals. Candles guttered in uneven lines across every flat surface. The velvet coat lay abandoned on the floor like a shed skin. Her hair hung loose and tangled around her shoulders, no longer artfully arranged, but pulled and twisted through restless hands.

She stood barefoot in the center of the cottage, breathing too fast.

It should have worked.

The honey charm.
The invitation spell.
The rosemary thread.

All of it should have woven into him by now.

But instead, the magic had begun to recoil.

Not violently. Not dramatically.

Quietly.

Which was worse.

Because quiet resistance meant someone had already answered her before she could.

Avalon slammed her palm onto the table.

"You are supposed to notice," she whispered.

She dragged open her trunk and began to pull things out in frantic handfuls. Crystals clattered across the floor. Bottles rolled. Bundles of dried herbs scattered like bones.

From the bottom of the trunk, she withdrew a small wooden box bound with tarnished brass hinges.

She hesitated only once before opening it.

Inside lay a charm she had sworn she would never use again.

Black thread.
A folded scrap of mirror.
A vial of something that shimmered faintly, like crushed stars.

This was not a drawing charm.

This was a convergence.

A spell that bent coincidence. That thinned resistance. That made paths cross whether they wanted to or not.

It did not bind.

But it cornered.

Avalon swallowed hard.

"I am not asking for control," she whispered to the empty room. "I am asking for a chance."

She lit one final candle and set the charm at its base.

Then she spoke his name.

Not softly this time.

"Baz."

The flame shuddered.

Outside, the wind surged through the trees like a held breath finally released.

The next afternoon, the greenhouse door jammed.

Not badly. Not broken.

Just enough to stick.

Baz tried the handle once. Then again.

He frowned and leaned into it.

At that exact moment, Avalon rounded the corner of the path, breathless and wide-eyed, clutching a basket of flowers.

"Oh," she said, as if surprised. "It's stuck?"

She hurried forward, dropping the basket and grabbing the door with him.

Their hands brushed.

The static cracked.

Baz flinched.

Avalon inhaled sharply.

For one brief moment, the air between them pulled tight.

Then the door swung open.

Baz stepped back immediately.

"I have to go," he said, too quickly.

He did not look at her.

Avalon stood frozen, heart racing, fingers trembling.

Something had answered her spell.

But not in the way she had meant.

And somewhere beneath the garden soil, the threads groaned under the strain.

Chapter Thirty-One: When the Thread Bites Back

Avalon didn't sleep.

She lay on top of the covers, fully dressed, eyes open and fixed on the ceiling as if it might eventually confess something useful. Her fingers rested flat against her chest, splayed just slightly, as though she were afraid her heart might slip loose if she didn't keep track of it.

The room was immaculate. Too immaculate. Every surface curated, every object placed with intention. Normally that kind of order soothed her. Tonight, it only amplified the silence.

The silence pressed back.

It was heavy in a way she hadn't encountered in years. Not the absence of sound, but the presence of attention. The kind of quiet that waits to see what you'll do next.

Avalon exhaled slowly through her nose and replayed the ritual in her mind, step by careful step.

She had done everything correctly.

The convergence charm was old, elegant, precise. It didn't force outcomes. It didn't bind. It merely leaned. A gentle nudge at the edge of possibility. A way to invite two threads closer together and see what sparked.

No shortcuts. No distortions. No improvisation.

It was meant to create opportunity.

But something had slipped.

She had felt it the moment Baz stepped away from her outside the greenhouse. The reaction hadn't been curiosity or hesitation. It had been instinctive withdrawal. The kind of recoil a body makes before the mind can catch up. The same way animals move away from tainted water before they ever taste it.

That wasn't what she had asked for.

Avalon sat up and swung her legs over the side of the bed. Her bare feet touched the floor, and for just a second the boards felt warmer than they should have been.

She stood and moved to the window, lighting a candle and setting it carefully on the sill. An anchor. A habit. She poured tea she didn't intend to drink, the steam curling thin and sour in the air.

"These things settle," she murmured to herself. "Energy rebalances."

But the tea tasted bitter the moment it touched her tongue, sharp and metallic. She set the cup aside with a frown. The candle flame bent sharply to the left, guttering as if caught in a draft that didn't exist.

Avalon's jaw tightened.

Then came the knock. Not at the door.

From beneath the floorboards.

A single knock. Deep. Resonant. Not sound so much as pressure.

She froze.

Another knock followed, slower this time. Measured. Patient.

Her hands began to shake, and that frightened her more than the sound itself. She whispered a grounding spell she hadn't needed in years, the words stiff in her mouth, the cadence off.

The knock came again.

Avalon crossed the room quickly and knelt beside her suitcase, fingers fumbling slightly as she unlatched it and pulled free her travel altar. The black cloth felt heavier than usual as she unwrapped it, the brass clasps cold against her skin.

The white stone at its center was split clean in two.

Not cracked. Not fractured.

Corrected.

Avalon stared at it, her breath shallow.

The convergence had answered.

But so had the land.

And the land had not negotiated.

This was not a warning. Warnings invited adjustment. This was something else entirely. A response. A refusal. A quiet, unmistakable no.

By the time dawn crept into the edges of the room, the rosemary on the windowsill had collapsed in on itself, its leaves gray and brittle as if winter had passed through overnight. The candle refused to relight, the wick blackened and inert no matter how many matches she struck.

Avalon moved to the mirror, needing to see something solid.

Her reflection blinked a half-second after she did.

She staggered back, heart hammering.

"This is not how it was supposed to go," she whispered.

Outside, birds skirted her rooftop, their calls shifting course as if redirected by an unseen current.

Inside, the rose-thread she had used for the convergence began to unravel where it lay coiled on the table, loosening stitch by stitch. The fibers curled inward as they came apart, soft and gray and soundless.

Like ash settling where fire had been denied.

Avalon sank onto the edge of the bed, staring at the floor.

For the first time since she'd arrived in Emerdeen, she understood something essential.

She had not entered a place that could be charmed into compliance. She had stepped into a system that corrected imbalance without malice.

And it had noticed her.

Chapter Thirty-Two: Familiar Shadows

Fi was not one for browsing.

She made lists. She followed maps. She preferred places with straight aisles, clear labels, and someone behind the counter who didn't ask questions. But Emerdeen had no respect for straight lines or predictable errands, so she found herself weaving through the market stalls with no real direction.

Fox was off somewhere with a story in his pocket and another snack likely half-eaten. The house had felt too full of questions that morning, so Fi had grabbed her jacket and gone outside without deciding where she was going.

Now she was walking past a row of book crates in the square when the hair on the back of her neck lifted.

She turned her head instinctively.

There, across the fountain, stood a woman in a black coat with her face turned just slightly away. The light caught on a dark braid and a shimmer of fabric that looked more ceremonial than seasonal. She wasn't moving. Just standing still among the movement, as if the town were passing around her instead of through her.

Fi narrowed her eyes.

The woman turned.

And Fi froze.

It was the eyes.

Not their color, though they were strange and sharp, like ice melting inward, but the way they locked on to her.

Not recognition.

Assessment.

The look you give someone when you're trying to decide whether to speak a name aloud or keep it buried.

Fi's stomach twisted.

She didn't know this woman. She was sure of that.

Except she wasn't.

The woman's gaze didn't break.

Fi took a step forward.

Avalon blinked once and turned away, disappearing behind a row of herb barrels without a word.

Fi remained rooted to the spot.

The moment had lasted maybe five seconds.

But her heart was racing like she'd just outrun something.

She moved toward where the woman had vanished, rounding the stall with deliberate steps.

Nothing. She was gone.

Fi turned in a slow circle, scanning the crowd.

Still nothing.

She shook her head. Tried to laugh it off. Failed.

There was something about that woman. Not just the clothes or the stare or the way she disappeared like smoke.

Something deeper.

She knew that feeling.

She had met people before who carried magic like a scent, something you couldn't name but could always detect just before the storm.

And worse—

She felt like she had seen her once, years ago. Somewhere colder. Somewhere with snow.

A memory flickered: a market in a northern town, a woman brushing past her shoulder, leaving a whisper of warmth and something else… not quite kindness.

Fi reached into her coat pocket and pulled out her notebook. Her fingers trembled slightly as she wrote:

- Saw her.
- Same woman? From Geneva?
- Still don't know her name.
- Still feels like she knows mine.

She looked up once more, eyes scanning the square.

The market continued around her, untouched.

But the air tasted different now.

Like a match had been struck but not yet blown out.

Chapter Thirty-Three: The Snag in the Weave

Cassie was sorting dried elderflower in the back room when the pulse hit her.

It wasn't a knock. Not a spark. Just a tug.

Like one thread in a tapestry had caught on something sharp.

She stilled immediately, hands hovering over the ceramic jar.

The shop was quiet, lanterns flickering gently. Nothing broken. Nothing loud.

But the magic had twitched.

Cassie set the jar down and closed her eyes.

The air was wrong. Off-balance. Like the silence after a storm that hadn't reached the ground but still made the trees bow.

She reached beneath the table for the satchel she only used when things began to unravel. Inside, she found her sensing thread - the one she spun herself during the last equinox, dyed in rosemary and rose ash.

She moved through the shop slowly, letting the thread trail behind her fingers.

The weave responded, reluctantly.

It wasn't frightened. It was irritated.

Tense. Tired.

The feeling was strongest at the doorway, where the boundary wards met the path. Something had pushed against the threshold recently.

Not to break in, but to brush past. Like a guest who wanted to be remembered without ever introducing themselves.

Cassie stepped outside.

The wind lifted her hair gently, curling it toward the northern part of town. Toward Avalon's cottage.

Cassie didn't need confirmation.

The thread in her hand trembled faintly.

Avalon had done something. Not just clumsy charmwork or shallow intention. She had tried to bend the weave itself. Force a crossing. Pull a moment out of alignment.

And now the land was pushing back.

Cassie knelt by the rosemary bush near the porch. It was her marker plant, her early warning system. A little wild. A little chatty. But honest.

The leaves were curling at the edges. Not burned. Not broken.

Just stressed.

"Too tight?" Cassie whispered.

The bush gave no answer, but the soil felt dry beneath the surface.

She touched it lightly with one palm.

"I know," she said. "I'll fix it."

Inside, she lit a single candle and laid out her cards. Not for divination.

For anchoring.

The Weaver. The Mirror. The Threshold.

And a fourth she hadn't drawn in months: The Snarl.

Cassie stared at it.

The Snarl was a warning. Not of evil, but of knots made without care. Of magic tangled in ego. Of spells cast with a clenched fist instead of an open hand.

She placed her fingers lightly on the card.

"Show me what she's done."

The candle flared.

For a heartbeat, Cassie saw Baz's face - not in pain but recoiling. As if from heat.

Then Avalon's eyes, wide and sharp and glassy, blinking in a mirror that blinked a half-second too late.

Then a thread, black and slick, pulled too tight and starting to snap.

Cassie sat back and exhaled.

She didn't have the full picture yet. But she had enough to start the unweaving.

She would not strike Avalon.

But she would not let her sink her hands into the soil again either.

This place had learned to trust her.

And she would protect what trusted her.

Chapter Thirty-Four: Circuits and Roots

Baz was in the greenhouse sorting seedlings when he heard the crunch of footsteps on gravel behind him. The sound carried differently here, softened by glass and growing things, as if the space itself absorbed sharp edges before they could do harm.

"Hope I'm not interrupting a sacred ritual," Fox called, voice easy but respectful in the way people get when they realize they're standing somewhere that matters.

Baz smiled without turning. He lifted a small tray of basil, checking roots that had just begun to curl white and confident against the soil. "Only if you consider transplanting basil sacred."

Fox stepped into the warmth of the glasshouse and stopped short, the door swinging shut behind him with a quiet click. Sunlight filtered through the panes above, catching on condensation and turning it into something like suspended breath.

"Honestly," Fox said, lowering his voice, "I kind of do. This place feels like it could talk back if I asked it nicely."

"It might," Baz said, finally turning. He brushed soil from his palms and wiped them on his jeans. "But tone matters."

Fox huffed a laugh and wandered slowly between the tables, eyes scanning the neat rows of seedlings. Everything was labeled. Everything had room to grow. Nothing was crowded or wasted.

"Everything here has a place," Fox said.

"That's the idea," Baz replied. "Plants don't like guessing games."

Fox stopped near the rosemary, running his fingers just above the leaves without touching. "I don't get it," he admitted. "Magic. Or I didn't. I still don't, fully. But it doesn't feel random. It feels… structured."

Baz raised an eyebrow. "You were expecting chaos?"

"I was expecting smoke and mirrors," Fox said. "A lot of dramatic nonsense meant to distract people from the fact that nothing was actually happening." He gestured around them. "But this feels like a system. Like design. Clean. Intentional."

Baz tilted his head, considering that. "I've never thought of it that way."

"When I was in school," Fox continued, warming to the idea, "I studied systems. Feedback loops. Energy transfer. You tweak one variable and the whole thing adapts. Or collapses, if you're careless." He glanced at Baz. "This feels like that. Like responsive architecture."

Baz nodded slowly. "Magic works the same way. It isn't about forcing outcomes. It's about relationship. How you speak. How you listen. How you adjust when the answer isn't what you expected."

Fox leaned against a worktable. "So... responsive code."

Baz laughed softly. "If that metaphor keeps you honest, I'll allow it."

Fox smiled, then sobered. "I'm not trying to mock it. I'm trying to understand what it means when a place seems to remember you. When it reacts to who you are, not just what you do."

Baz met his gaze. "Emerdeen remembers everything. Not just big rituals or dramatic moments. It remembers care. Neglect. Patience. What you choose when no one is watching."

Fox swallowed. "Fi doesn't want to believe any of it."

"She doesn't have to," Baz said gently. "Belief isn't the entry fee."

Fox frowned. "Then what is?"

"Honesty," Baz said without hesitation. "With yourself. The town can tell the difference between disbelief and denial."

Fox looked down at his hands. "She's starting to feel it," he admitted. "The house. The land. She won't say it, but it's… tuning itself around her."

Baz's expression softened. "That means it's listening."

Fox straightened, tension flickering through him. "And if you ignore that?"

Baz didn't hesitate. "Eventually, something answers for you."

They stood together in the low hum of the greenhouse, surrounded by green life doing exactly what it had been asked to do. Sunlight shifted. A leaf unfurled somewhere nearby.

Fox reached out and gently touched the basil seedling at last, careful not to bruise it.

"I don't think I want to leave," he said quietly.

Baz smiled, warmth spreading through his chest. "Good," he said. "The basil was getting attached."

Chapter Thirty-Five: What the Walls Remember

The house had been discreet all morning.

Not silent.

Fi was learning there was a difference.

Silence was something you imposed. Something you chose or were forced into. The quiet here was different. It had texture. Breath. Intention.

And today, it was watching her.

She stood in the hallway with a cup of coffee, staring at the crooked frame on the wall that had refused to stay straight since they moved in. She had fixed it four times already. It tilted again every night.

Now it was perfectly level.

Fi narrowed her eyes.

"Don't start being helpful," she muttered.

The wall did not reply. But she felt it.

The air had weight to it. Not oppressive. More like someone had just been standing in the room a moment before she entered.

She turned toward the staircase.

There, resting on the third step up, was one of Fox's sketchbooks. Closed. Balanced. Set down with care.

Fi picked it up. It was warm.

She opened it without meaning to, flipping past rough outlines of trees and garden walls until she reached a newer page.

He had drawn the greenhouse. In full detail. Line for line. And not from memory. From presence. From intimacy. Like someone who had stood in the middle of it and been changed.

Fi closed the sketchbook and held it against her chest.

Fox had gone soft on this place. She could feel it.

And the house had felt it too.

She stepped back into the kitchen, where sunlight had begun to stretch across the floor in a pattern she didn't recognize.

The old tiles, always scuffed and uneven, now shimmered slightly where the light touched them.

She crouched, ran her fingers along the line where two tiles met.

Warm. Not from sun.

From within.

The house was responding to him. Not to her.

And she hated how that made her feel.

Unchosen.

Or worse, out of sync with something that had once been hers to refuse.

She stood too quickly, knocking her mug off the counter. It shattered across the floor.

"Damn it," she hissed.

She dropped to her knees and began picking up the pieces, breath short and sharp.

Behind her, the hallway light flickered once.

Just once.

A flicker like acknowledgement.

Like apology. Or warning.

Fi sat back on her heels with a piece of the handle still clutched in her hand.

Fox was changing.

And the house had already welcomed him.

Chapter Thirty-Six: The Quiet Undoing

Cassie had never believed in ripping magic out by the roots.

It damaged too much in the process. The threads that held things together were delicate. Tense them too hard, and you snapped what had taken years to grow. Undoing a charm required more than power. It required listening. Precision. Consent from the land itself.

She stood in the greenhouse just before dusk, sleeves rolled to her elbows, hands covered in the soft dust of crushed lavender and ground nettle. She had cleared a circle in the center—nothing drawn or carved, just space made clean and open.

On the table beside her sat three objects.

A spool of deep gray thread.
A copper thimble.
And a single rosemary cutting tied with black ribbon.

Cassie took a long breath and closed her eyes.

She did not speak Avalon's name. To do so would give the charm a tether. Instead, she whispered the name of the place the charm had landed.

"Baz."

The threads stirred.

Not painfully. Just aware.

She stepped into the circle and laid the rosemary at its center.

"This is not yours," she whispered. "Return it."

She felt the pushback.

Not from Baz. From the charm itself.

It wanted to stay.

Cassie opened the thread and began to unspool it slowly, walking the circle's edge in a wide arc.

With every step, she said one word.

"Truth."
"Choice."
"Home."
"Refusal."
"Release."

The wind picked up slightly. The lantern above the table swung.

When she reached the thimble, she stopped.

It was the anchor. The vessel that would catch what was being removed. She set it gently on the soil.

Then, without speaking, she pulled the thread tight between her fingers and closed her eyes again.

This was the hard part. Feeling where the charm still clung.

It wasn't in Baz. Not anymore.

But it hovered.

In the places where he had walked. In the spaces Avalon had crossed. It had drifted like smoke, trying to hold.

Cassie followed it. She reached gently through the weave, not with force, but with invitation.

You don't belong here.

The charm pulsed once in reply.

I was invited.

Cassie whispered back, "Not by him."

She closed her hand, and the thread looped into itself.

The energy tightened. Resisted.

Then, released.

A small shiver ran through the greenhouse floor.

The rosemary blackened at the edges. The thimble spun once, then stilled.

Cassie opened her eyes.

It was done. Not erased.

But unhooked.

She picked up the thimble and dropped it into a salt bowl. The charm inside would dissolve by morning.

She stepped out of the circle, careful not to scuff the edges.

Then she sat on the porch, face tilted toward the fading sun, and whispered,

"Let that be enough."

The threads settled. The weave exhaled.

And from the soil, a new sprout pushed upward.

Chapter Thirty-Seven: The Shattering

Avalon woke with the crushing sensation that something had been taken from her.

It wasn't a noise that startled her awake, nor a dream she could name. It was absence. A hollowing. As if a cord that once ran through her chest had been severed in the night, leaving behind the echo of something she could no longer reach.

She reached instinctively toward the charm she had placed at her bedside - the convergence thread bound in ritual and intention.

But her fingers touched only ash.

The fine powder clung to her skin, silvery and soft, and for a moment, she did not move. She stared down at the remains, heart pounding, mouth dry.

The spell was gone.

Not dormant. Not resisted.

It had been undone.

Undone with a precision she did not expect, and a softness that made it worse. There had been no backlash, no magical blow to warn her. The charm had been unraveled as one might unlace a boot - gently, deliberately, with no intention of returning it to place.

Her breath caught in her throat. The edges of the room sharpened around her as panic bloomed under her ribs.

She rose too quickly from the bed, dizziness washing over her. The room tilted slightly, though nothing moved. She grabbed the edge of the windowsill to steady herself and scanned the space as if the magic might be hiding in a corner, waiting to return.

But it wasn't.

She reached for the convergence mirror across the room. It stood tall and cold in its frame, ringed in brass and runes of her own carving. She had used it many times before, always careful, always powerful. She stared into its surface.

The glass did not show her reflection.

It shimmered once—flat, blank, impersonal—and then held nothing.

Her stomach turned.

"No," she whispered. "No, you don't get to erase me."

She crossed the room in two quick strides, pressing her hands against the frame.

"I was seen," she said aloud. "I was seen."

But the mirror would not answer.

Behind her, the candles on the altar shelf had gone dark. Not extinguished, not blown out. Just inert. The wicks refused to catch even when she struck match after match. The flame would rise for a breath and then die midair, flickering like a sigh of refusal.

Avalon's fingers shook as she tried again. And again.

The silence in the room grew thicker, not with darkness, but with indifference. It wasn't that the cottage hated her. It had simply decided she no longer belonged.

The realization sent something sharp and hot through her.

Grief. But beneath it, fury.

All that she had poured into this place, all the ways she had tried to entwine herself with its magic—with his magic—had been returned to her empty. Not broken. Not scattered. Just quietly placed back into her hands as if to say, "No."

Her voice cracked as she let out a single, low sound. It wasn't quite a scream. It was the sound before one. The inhale of someone who has just realized she lost something that was never hers to keep.

With a stiff breath, she turned toward her trunk and began gathering her belongings with rigid efficiency. The velvet coat, now wrinkled and stained with old rosewater. The polished stones. The remaining vials of tincture and salt. The scraps of thread and intention that had once made her feel sovereign.

She didn't stop to fold anything. She simply packed.

Her basket toppled once, and she left it.

By the time the sun crested the horizon, Avalon was already at the edge of town.

She did not say goodbye. She did not glance back.

She left the door to the cottage open, the curtain at the window swaying gently in the morning light. There was no note, no spell of closure. Only a single rose left upright in the soil by the front gate, its stem cleanly cut, its bloom sharp and full.

It was not a gesture of gratitude.

It was a final word.

A mark of presence. Proof that she had been here.

And that she had not been welcomed to stay.

Chapter Thirty-Eight: A Calm Between

Baz found Cassie in the garden, barefoot, her hands in the earth like it was a conversation.

She didn't turn when he approached. She didn't need to. He stepped softly enough that the plants barely noticed, settling beside her on the low stone wall that edged the lavender beds.

For a long moment, they said nothing.

The sun had already crested the ridge and was casting long gold lines across the garden. The rosemary looked brighter than it had in days. The bees had returned to their usual lazy rhythm. Even the wind felt less tangled.

Cassie wiped her hands on her apron and finally looked up.

"You feel it too," she said.

Baz nodded. "It's quieter. Not just the air. The threads."

Cassie tilted her head. "The soil's breathing again."

"I didn't know it had stopped."

"It didn't stop," she said. "It held its breath."

Baz glanced around. The trees looked softer. The house behind them felt less watchful.

"She's gone," he said.

Cassie didn't ask how he knew. She had felt it too. The sudden release. The charm she had undone had left more than magical residue, it had left an opening. A letting go.

"Do you think she'll try to come back?" Baz asked.

Cassie pressed her palm flat to the earth and waited a beat before answering.

"No," she said. "Not here. Not now."

Baz leaned back on his hands and looked up at the sky, pale and cloudless. "Feels like the first time I've been able to breathe since she arrived."

Cassie smiled, small and private. "You were never caught. But she tried to sew herself into something that didn't belong to her."

"She wanted a shortcut," Baz said. "To something that only grows slowly."

They let that truth hang between them for a while.

"She didn't understand how this place works," Cassie added. "It doesn't reward hunger. It responds to care."

Baz looked at her, his voice softer. "You always did take the slow path."

"Because I know where it leads," she replied.

They shared a look—uncomplicated, unguarded. A thread between them humming low and steady.

"I think things are shifting again," Cassie said after a moment. "But this time in a good way."

"You mean Fi and Fox?"

"I mean everything," she said. "The shop. The Hollow. The garden. The way the town is listening again."

Baz reached down and plucked a leaf from the thyme growing by his feet. He rolled it between his fingers. "So, what now?"

"We rest," she said. "We breathe. We make soup. We let things grow."

Baz laughed. "You always make it sound so simple."

Cassie stood and stretched, brushing dirt from her palms. "It is. Until it's not."

She offered him her hand.

He took it.

And for a while, they simply walked the edge of the garden, side by side. Not solving anything. Not bracing for anything. Just moving together through the quiet that had returned.

Neither of them noticed the shadow that passed beneath the roots of the oldest tree, far at the edge of the property. It did not carry malice.

But it carried memory.

And memory, when left unspoken, has a way of blooming.

Chapter Thirty-Nine: What Was Left Behind

The house had been unusually quiet all morning.

Not watchful. Not heavy.

More like it was waiting to see if Fi would notice.

She hadn't intended to go rummaging through the attic. She'd gone looking for extra blankets, maybe an old trunk she could repurpose as a coffee table. But when she pulled down the ladder and climbed into the low-beamed space above the second floor, something shifted under her skin.

It smelled like cedar and old books. The kind of attic that wasn't haunted but remembered everything. She swept the beam of her flashlight in a slow arc. Dust swirled in the air like snow.

Boxes, mostly. Labeled in her aunt's tight script. *Winter linens. Holiday. Kitchen overflow.*

Then, behind a wardrobe draped in a yellowed sheet, she spotted a wooden chest.

It was low to the ground, with no markings. No latch. Just a slight shine to the corners where it had been handled over time. She reached out and ran her fingers along the edge.

Warm.

Of course it was warm.

Fi sat cross-legged in front of it and hesitated.

She told herself it was just a box. But the stillness around it said otherwise.

She lifted the lid.

Inside were layers of folded cloth, faded but clean. Beneath them, a stack of notebooks wrapped in ribbon. Not journals. Spellbooks.

Fi stared at them for a long time.

The top one had a small, pressed flower tucked into its corner. Marigold.

Aunt Thea had never talked about magic.

Not directly. Not openly. She had kept herbs in the pantry and bundles over the windows. She had insisted on fresh rosemary at the door and left bowls of water out on full moons.

But she had never called it what it was.

Fi pulled out one of the notebooks and opened it.

The handwriting was neat, but informal. Observational. Notes and recipes, yes, but also thoughts. Reflections. The margins were full of questions.

The rosemary boundary held again. Why does the light shift just before it fails?

Is there a difference between memory magic and place magic?

Fox is too young to feel it, but maybe Fi could, if I showed her where to look...

Fi froze.

The words blurred slightly.

She turned the page.

More notes. More recipes. More quiet longing.

Her aunt had wanted to share this. Not in a loud, pushy way.

But in a waiting-for-the-right-time kind of way.

Fi closed the notebook and sat back, blinking hard.

This wasn't just a hidden stash of supplies. It was a conversation that had never started.

A door that had been left open just enough for her to see through, but only if she chose to walk closer.

Behind her, something creaked softly. A board shifting. The house settling.

Or perhaps, acknowledging.

Fi stood and looked around the attic once more.

There were no secrets left in this space. Only truths that had waited.

She packed the notebooks gently into a basket and made her way down the ladder.

As her feet hit the hallway floor, the light above her flickered, not sharply. Just once. A breath. A nod.

And far below, in the roots of the house, something old stirred and settled again.

Not disturbed.

Relieved.

Chapter Forty: Things We Thought We Knew

Fox found Fi on the back porch, barefoot and wrapped in the oversized cardigan she only wore when she was sorting through something too big for words.

She didn't look up when he approached, but she slid the basket closer to the edge of the step like she wanted him to see it. That was her way. She didn't call people in. She let them decide whether to step closer.

Fox sat beside her and peered inside.

Notebooks. Old, worn, ribbon-tied. The edges were curled slightly, the way pages do when they've been touched often.

He picked up the top one.

The pressed marigold fell into his lap.

"I found them in the attic," Fi said quietly. "Aunt Thea wrote them."

Fox didn't answer right away. He flipped gently through the pages, stopping at a line written sideways in the margin.

Everything listens, if you're willing to speak gently enough.

"She never said anything," he murmured. "Not once."

Fi nodded. "She said a lot. Just not in the way we expected."

He looked at her. "You think this is why she left the house to us?"

"I think she knew we'd need it more than we wanted it."

He returned the notebook to the basket and rested his arms on his knees. The yard stretched out in front of them, overgrown but not unwelcoming. The light had changed somehow since he came back from the greenhouse. Softer. More honest.

"Did you know?" he asked. "That she was one of them?"

Fi shook her head. "Not really. But now that I think about it, there were signs. All those things she did that felt like quirks."

"Like making us bury copper under the porch."

"Or the way she always whispered to the windows during storms."

Fox exhaled. "I thought she was just weird."

"She was," Fi said with a faint smile. "But not in the way we thought."

They sat with that for a moment.

The kind of silence that meant the world was rearranging itself, just slightly, and neither of them wanted to look directly at the shift.

"Do you think this changes what we're doing here?" Fox asked eventually.

Fi looked out across the yard. "It doesn't change why we came. But maybe it changes whether we leave."

Fox was quiet.

Then, "I don't think I want to go."

She didn't answer right away.

Instead, she pulled one of the books from the basket and held it out to him. "There's a page marked near the back. Something about threadwork and boundary spells."

Fox took it, hands steady.

"I think she wanted us to find this," Fi said softly.

He turned the pages until he found the ribbon.

There, scrawled across the top of the page in their aunt's looping handwriting, were the words:

Some homes are built to protect. Others to remember. But a few rare ones… they do both.

Fox read it twice.

Then he closed the book and said, "Let's see what this house still remembers."

Chapter Forty-One: The One Who Stayed

Cassie was pruning calendula along the west side of the greenhouse when she heard the hesitant steps behind her.

Not Fi's.

Lighter. Quicker.

She didn't turn.

"Lost something?" she called.

Fox cleared his throat. "Maybe. Or maybe I just figured you'd know what I didn't know I needed."

Cassie smiled and snipped one last bloom before turning to face him.

He was holding a small notebook in both hands. The ribbon had come loose and fluttered in the breeze.

"I figured if anyone could tell me more about Aunt Thea, it'd be you," he said, offering it to her. "Fi found these in the attic."

Cassie took the notebook gently, her eyes scanning the cover, the frayed edges, the careful folds.

"She used to buy these at the old stationery shop before it closed. Always picked the ones with the rough paper, even though they bled ink. Said it kept her honest."

"So, you knew her well?" Fox asked.

Cassie motioned for him to follow and led him to the shaded bench near the rosemary beds.

"She wasn't one for crowds or gatherings. Never joined the coven, never attended rituals. But she helped more people in this town than most realize."

Fox sat down beside her. "How?"

"Quietly," Cassie said. "That was her magic. She called it living in the layers. She'd charm a jar of jam to keep the peace in a household. Leave a sprig of basil under a neighbor's porch when someone was about to fall sick. She never wanted attention. Just to make things steadier."

Fox looked down at his hands. "We had no idea."

"She kept it that way on purpose," Cassie said. "Not because she was ashamed. She just believed that if magic was real, it didn't need to be announced. It needed to be used."

Fox smiled faintly. "Fi's going to love that."

Cassie gave him a long look. "And how do you feel about it?"

He paused, then said, "Like something just clicked into place. Not loudly. More like when you walk into a room and it smells like home and you didn't know you missed it until just then."

Cassie nodded. "That sounds like Thea's kind of magic."

"She left us the house," Fox said. "But I think she also left us an invitation."

Cassie leaned back on the bench. "She trusted you'd decide what to do with it."

Fox hesitated, then looked out toward the woods beyond the property line. "You think it's the kind of house that remembers?"

Cassie didn't answer right away. She opened the notebook and flipped through a few pages, stopping at one in the middle.

"It's the kind of house that waits." She handed it back to him. "And I think it's been waiting for the two of you for a long time."

Fox traced his finger along the ink that curled across the page. His aunt's handwriting was clear and steady. A line near the bottom read:

I don't need to be seen to be known. I just need to leave the door open long enough for someone to walk through.

He looked up at Cassie. "Do you think Fi will stay?"

"I think she's already started," Cassie said. "She just hasn't told herself yet."

Fox grinned. "That sounds about right."

They sat for a few minutes more, not speaking, just letting the garden breathe around them.

When Fox stood to leave, he paused and added, "Thank you."

Cassie smiled. "Any time. And Fox?"

He turned.

"Tell the house thank you too. It's been waiting a long time to be heard again."

Chapter Forty-Two: What Grows Back

Morgan had learned to pay attention to the kind of magic that didn't announce itself.

Most people watched for sparks. They listened for bells, chased wind through open windows. But Morgan knew that real magic shifted beneath your skin first—just a subtle tightening along the ribs, or a thread of breath that didn't quite reach the bottom.

This morning, they felt it the moment they stepped barefoot into the garden.

It came not as a warning, but as a hum. A change in the way light touched the trees. A pause in the rhythm of the bees.

Something had stirred.

Not dangerously.

But deeply.

Morgan closed their eyes and followed the feeling northward, toward the old Carrow house.

The land there had been quiet for so long, holding its breath through the years of solitude. But now it was stretching. Exhaling. And not just because of who had arrived, but because of what was waking up in them.

They smiled.

The house wasn't just remembering.

It was preparing.

Morgan turned toward the path that wound behind the greenhouse and made their way toward Bram's cottage. If anyone would know what the land needed next, it would be him.

Bram was already in the garden when Morgan arrived, crouched low near the feverfew, muttering to himself as he moved a sprig from one pot to another.

"You talk to them more than you talk to people," Morgan said, stepping through the gate.

"That's because they argue less," Bram replied without looking up.

Morgan crouched beside him, picking a bit of mint and rolling it between their fingers. "The Carrow house is waking up."

"I know," Bram said. "The lemon balm told me."

Morgan raised an eyebrow. "She does love to gossip."

Bram finally looked up, his eyes sharper than usual. "It's not just the house. The land around it is loosening. Threads that have been knotted for decades are starting to move."

"I figured," Morgan said. "That's why I'm here."

Bram stood and brushed the dirt from his knees. "You want something to help them settle in."

"Something gentle," Morgan said. "But grounding. Especially for Fi. She's resisting it with everything she's got."

"She'll come around," Bram muttered, leading them to the back shed where his drying racks hung in low, fragrant lines. "The ones who resist it hardest usually fall the deepest."

Morgan smiled. "That sounds like personal experience."

"It is," Bram said, then added, "More than once."

He pulled down a bundle of dried agrimony, tied in faded blue twine. "For honesty. Helps you speak truths you didn't know were waiting."

"Good," Morgan said. "And something for memory?"

Bram handed over a pouch of crushed mugwort. "For dreaming. For finding the shape of what came before."

"And for Fox?"

Bram considered. "He's already half-rooted. Give him yarrow. He'll stay calm even when everything else begins to shake."

Morgan took the bundles with care, tucking them into the cloth satchel across their chest.

"Thank you," they said, then paused. "Do you think this ends well?"

Bram looked toward the ridge where the house stood, still mostly hidden behind trees.

"I think endings are just quieter beginnings," he said. "And I think that house has been waiting long enough."

Morgan nodded once.

As they walked back toward town, the satchel against their side warmed slightly.

The plants were ready.

The house was ready.

And soon, the siblings would have to decide whether they were too.

Chapter Forty-Three: Offerings at the Threshold

Fi nearly tripped over the bundle.

It was resting against the front step when she opened the door that morning, wrapped in soft gray cloth and tied with a sprig of fresh rosemary. No note. No instructions.

Just presence.

She frowned, crouching down to study it. The scent hit her first—earthy, crisp, with something wilder layered underneath.

"Morgan," she muttered.

Fox emerged behind her, stretching and still half-asleep. "What's Morgan?"

"This," she said, lifting the bundle.

He blinked. "They drop off mysterious plant bundles often?"

"Not yet," Fi said. "But it feels like them."

She carried it into the kitchen and set it gently on the table, unwrapping it with care.

Inside: four smaller bundles. Dried leaves, twisted stems, bits of root tucked neatly in parchment. It looked old and intentional, like something pulled from a personal apothecary.

Fox leaned in, curious. "That's agrimony, right? And yarrow?"

Fi raised an eyebrow. "Since when do you know herbs?"

"Since I spent an afternoon with Baz sorting seedlings. He labels everything."

Fi looked at the remaining bundles. Mugwort. Lemon balm. Subtle, supportive herbs. Not for casting. For grounding.

"For us," she said quietly.

Fox nodded. "Looks like."

She ran her fingers along the edge of one parchment slip and spotted a single line, written in graphite:

For memory. For softness. For standing still long enough to listen.

She didn't know if Morgan had written it or if it had always been there, waiting to be read. The house didn't offer answers.

It offered echoes.

"Do you think this means they want us to do something with them?" Fox asked.

Fi turned to the old stovetop kettle, already pulling down their aunt's chipped teapot. "We don't have to cast anything," she said. "Just steep it. Let it work through us."

Fox watched her. "You don't seem quite so annoyed anymore."

"I'm still annoyed," she said, tossing a glance over her shoulder. "But now I'm also curious. I think that's worse."

She steeped the mugwort first, letting it breathe in the ceramic.

Fox took the bundle of yarrow and turned it over in his hands. "Feels like the house is watching."

"It always is," Fi replied.

They sat in the stillness of the kitchen, the old teapot warming between them, herbs unfurling in the steam. No one told them what to say, what to feel, or what would come next.

But for the first time, Fi didn't feel like the house was pushing.

It was holding space.

Waiting, not for a decision, but for presence.

And as the scent of lemon balm drifted into the corners, Fi leaned back in her chair and exhaled.

The first dream would come tonight.

She didn't know how she knew.

She just did.

Chapter Forty-Four: The Quiet Rise

Cassie felt it before she saw it.

She had just finished tucking dried calendula into a jar behind the counter when the warmth curled through her fingertips like breath.

Not from her own threads.

From the land.

She stilled.

The Carrow house was stirring again.

Not in the erratic way Avalon's charm had rattled the boundaries, not with force or fracture. This was something deeper. A pulse. A low rhythm. Like the heartbeat of something that had been dormant for too long, beginning—just barely—to wake.

Cassie crossed the shop and opened the front door.

The late afternoon light had taken on a rich honeyed hue, thick and golden, casting long soft lines across the path. The wind was steady but not sharp. The rosemary by the steps vibrated faintly, its silvered leaves brushing toward the north.

Cassie followed its lean with her eyes.

The Carrow property sat just beyond the ridge, tucked into its own pocket of old soil and older story. She hadn't stepped foot near it since Fox and Fi had arrived—not out of avoidance, but respect. The land there would invite when it was ready.

Now, it was beginning.

She stepped onto the porch and stood still.

It was subtle.

A shift in pressure. A scent in the air that hadn't been there yesterday—mugwort, wild yarrow, a trace of lemon balm. It moved like steam off tea, slow and searching.

Cassie closed her eyes and reached out with her senses.

Not casting. Not weaving. Just noticing.

The house wasn't just holding them anymore.

It was answering them.

It heard their voices.

She felt it in the way the roots curled toward warmth again. In the threads that began weaving slowly, experimentally, like vines re-learning a trellis.

Magic was returning to the house, but not alone.

Memory was coming with it.

And somewhere in the space between those things, she caught a flicker of something else.

A presence.

Not malevolent. Not loud. But watchful.

Cassie opened her eyes.

It had not come from Avalon. It had not followed the siblings. It had always been there.

It had simply been waiting for the right ones to unlock it.

The land had long memories, and houses longer still.

Cassie stepped back inside and retrieved a small tin from the shelf labeled *Soil & Thread*.

Inside were woven charms, each stitched with a different purpose. She ran her hand over the row and stopped at one wrapped in green linen and knotted with three turns of copper wire.

It was a house-knot. A blessing. A soft ward meant not to protect from harm, but to remind the space it was loved.

Cassie slipped it into her pocket.

She didn't need to deliver it yet.

But soon.

The house was listening again.

And it would be good to say something kind while it still remembered how.

Chapter Forty-Five: The Dream Left Open

Fi didn't mean to fall asleep on the couch.

She'd left the mugwort steeping longer than she intended, and the brew had taken on a dusky sweetness, almost smoky. She drank it in sips, half-curious, half-daring it to do anything at all.

By the time the cup was empty, her limbs were heavy and her eyes would not stay open.

She meant to stretch. To move. To get up and write.

But sleep pulled at her.

Not with force. With invitation.

The dream opened slowly. Like a room she'd been in before but couldn't name.

The air was warm, full of dust motes suspended in amber light. She stood in the kitchen—her kitchen—but it wasn't now. The edges of the cupboards were sharper, the curtains floral instead of plain, and there was a faint hum in the walls.

Someone stood at the stove.

Fi took a step forward, and the floor creaked under her bare feet.

The figure turned. It was her aunt.

Younger. Brighter. Hair up in a loose knot. A smudge of flour on her cheek.

She was stirring something in a pot and humming low to herself, as if trying to keep herself from falling apart.

Fi tried to speak, but no sound came.

Thea looked up, as if she heard anyway.

Her expression shifted. Not surprise. Not recognition exactly.

But awareness.

"Are you here now?" she asked softly.

Fi nodded without meaning to.

Thea turned back to the pot. "I didn't think you'd ever come back. Not really."

She stirred again. The scent of rosemary and something bitter rose from the steam.

"I tried to keep it safe," she said. "But some things can't be held. They root too deep. They wait."

The kitchen lights flickered, and the edges of the room blurred.

Fi stepped forward. "What waited?"

Thea didn't answer.

She just reached over and opened the drawer beside the stove.

Inside was a bundle of keys. Twisted. Old. Some rusted, some polished. One was broken in half.

Thea touched the broken one.

"I didn't lock it," she whispered. "I just hoped no one would try the door again."

Fi looked down.

The keys were gone. The drawer was empty.

The room was darker now.

Behind her, a second door creaked open. One she didn't know existed in the waking world.

From within came the sound of wind, dry and distant, like it was blowing through something that hadn't breathed in a long time.

Thea's voice followed, quieter now.

"If it comes back… don't open it alone."

Fi turned toward the sound, but the dream was already shifting, the light thinning like mist at sunrise.

She woke with her hands curled tight into fists.

The teacup was still warm on the table.

The couch blanket was tucked around her shoulders, though she didn't remember reaching for it.

Somewhere in the walls, the old pipes groaned once, like an exhale.

Fi sat up slowly.

The house had spoken. Not in words.

In memory.

And beneath it all, in the quiet places between what was said and what was held back, she felt the warning.

Something was returning.

She just didn't know what. Not yet.

Chapter Forty-Six: Not All Shadows Cross Realms

Fi found Fox in the garden behind the house, kneeling beside the raised beds their aunt had built years ago from scavenged wood and stubborn persistence. The planks were uneven and weather-softened, corners darkened by years of rain and soil, but they held fast. Like Thea had intended. Like most things she left behind.

Fox was planting late-season greens, working methodically, hands deep in the earth. He moved with a careful patience that still surprised Fi sometimes, as if the garden had taught him a different rhythm than the one he used everywhere else. His face tilted toward the sun, eyes narrowed against the light, like someone trying to decide whether he belonged where he stood.

Fi lingered at the edge of the path longer than she meant to. The gravel pressed into the soles of her shoes, grounding her, reminding her that she was here and awake and not drifting through the echo of something else.

"I had a dream," she said at last.

Fox glanced over his shoulder, hands still sunk in soil. "A weird one," he said, "or a house one?"

"Both," she replied. "Definitely both."

He shifted his weight and sat back on his heels, brushing dirt from his palms onto his jeans without much concern for the stain. "Go on."

Fi crossed to the bench near the shed and sat, elbows braced against her knees, fingers laced together tightly enough to whiten her knuckles. She stared at the ground for a moment, gathering the pieces in the right order.

"It was the kitchen," she said. "Ours, but older. Before we repainted. Before the floorboard near the sink started squeaking." She

swallowed. "Thea was there. Younger. Not young-young, but…
lighter. Like she hadn't started carrying so much yet."

Fox's expression softened. "What was she doing?"

"Cooking," Fi said. "But she kept looking toward the hallway. Like
she was waiting." She paused. "For me, I think."

Fox tilted his head. "You think it was a memory?"

"I know it was," Fi said quietly. "But not just mine. Hers. The
house's, maybe. It felt… layered."

She rubbed her palms together as if trying to shake off the sensation.
"There was a door. One I didn't know existed. She touched the
frame and said she didn't lock it. She just hoped no one would try it
again."

Fox's brow furrowed. "Try what again?"

Fi hesitated. The dream clung to her like steam after a shower, hard
to see but impossible to ignore. "She told me not to open it alone.
That if it came back, we'd need to be ready."

He waited, letting the silence do its work.

"And I don't think she meant anything magical," Fi said finally.
"Not like what Morgan does. Not like the things this town carries."
She looked up at him. "This felt… heavier. More ordinary."

"You think it's from here," Fox said slowly. "Our world."

She nodded. "It felt grounded. Like something tied to our bloodline.
Not Emerdeen's threads. Ours."

Fox wiped his hands on his jeans and stood, gaze drifting toward the
far edge of the property where the grass gave way to trees and old
fence posts leaned at tired angles.

"You're saying Thea was protecting the house," he said, "not just from something strange... but from something familiar."

Fi followed his gaze. "Not everything dangerous comes with runes and mist," she said. "Some things wear normal skin. Some things knock like they belong there."

Fox was quiet for a long moment, the only sound the soft rustle of leaves and the faint hum of insects waking with the sun.

"You think it's a person," he said at last.

"I think it was," Fi replied. "Once."

They sat together in the garden's gentle hush, surrounded by things that grew because someone had tended them year after year. The raised beds. The soil. The choices that had kept the place alive.

After a while, Fox spoke again. "Then we don't open any doors without backup."

Fi let out a short, breathy laugh. "Deal."

She looked down at her hands, then at the porch boards worn smooth by decades of feet pacing, pausing, returning.

"We're not just here to inherit something," she said. "Are we?"

Fox shook his head. "No. We're here to finish it."

Behind them, in the shaded kitchen, the drawer beside the stove creaked open a fraction of an inch.

Waiting.

Chapter Forty-Seven: The Stranger Who Didn't Ask Twice

Morgan was elbow-deep in soil when the man arrived.

They didn't hear the gate open or the gravel shift under his steps. One moment they were humming softly to themselves, fingers weaving comfrey roots into the earth and the next, there was a shadow stretching long across the greenhouse floor.

Morgan didn't look up immediately. Most people around here announced themselves with footsteps, greetings, the gentle clatter of garden boots on old stone.

This man did not.

Morgan rose slowly and wiped their hands on a rag hanging near the potting shelf.

The man was tall and lean, his coat too dark for the weather, his expression pleasant in a way that felt rehearsed. His eyes didn't smile, even when his mouth did.

"Lovely place," he said, voice smooth as polished wood. "Smells like memory in here."

Morgan gave a neutral nod. "It usually does."

"Are you the gardener?" he asked, glancing around. "Or is this someone else's sanctuary?"

Morgan offered a half-smile. "Depends on who's asking."

The man chuckled, but the sound was shallow.

"No harm in being curious," he said. "I've been passing through, and I couldn't help but notice this town seems... different."

Morgan let the silence sit between them.

He didn't offer a name.

Didn't say what he was passing through from, or to.

Just that he'd noticed.

Different.

"Is it?" Morgan said at last.

The man tilted his head. "It breathes a little slower here. Like time takes its shoes off."

"Some people find that unsettling."

"Oh, not me," he said quickly. "I appreciate a place with secrets. Just curious how deep they go."

Morgan stepped aside and began gently watering a tray of seedlings. The air between them tightened, not with tension, but with precision. Like the man was tuning a string that had not yet been played.

"Do many people settle here?" he asked casually. "Or do they tend to move on?"

"Depends on what they're carrying."

"And what they leave behind?"

Morgan met his gaze. There was nothing obvious about him. No overt darkness. No looming threat.

But everything in Morgan's body told them the questions weren't for conversation.

They were for inventory.

"You looking to buy property?" they asked.

He smiled. "Maybe. Maybe just revisiting old paths."

Morgan arched a brow. "Funny. You don't seem the nostalgic type."

He shrugged. "I don't usually stop anywhere twice."

"And yet."

He didn't flinch.

Just looked past them, into the rows of growing things.

"Do the houses here remember?"

Morgan's heart tightened.

"What makes you ask that?"

The man finally turned to leave. "Just passing curiosity."

But as he stepped out into the light, he paused and added, "Some places remember the wrong things."

And then he was gone.

No name. No purchase. No trace of how he'd arrived.

Morgan stood in the greenhouse, staring at the door he'd walked through, the faint scent of ash lingering where no fire had burned.

Something had changed. Not loudly.

But completely.

Chapter Forty-Eight: Tea and Warnings

By the time Morgan reached Bram's cottage, the edge had returned to their voice.

Not sharp. Not panicked.

Alert.

They had taken the long way through the woods, skirting the edge of town where the path narrowed and the trees leaned closer together. It was a habit Morgan had learned young. When something unsettled the weave, you walked until your body remembered its own rhythm again. Heel to toe. Breath to step. Ground meeting ground.

It helped. Some.

But whatever the stranger had left behind clung anyway, thin and persistent, like the smell of smoke carried from a fire you could not yet see. Not dangerous yet. Not fully formed. But undeniable.

Bram opened the door before Morgan could lift their hand.

"You felt it," Morgan said, more statement than question.

"I felt you feeling it," Bram replied, already stepping aside to let them in.

The cottage wrapped around them like a held breath released. Warmth radiated from the hearth. Rosemary steam hung in the air, softening the sharpness at the edges of thought. Dried bundles of thyme, sage, and yarrow hung from the rafters like sleeping bats, their shadows swaying gently as the door closed behind them.

Bram moved with practiced ease, lifting the kettle from the hook as it began to whistle. "Sit," he said. "Then talk."

Morgan settled into the chair closest to the fire, palms resting on their knees, fingers still faintly streaked with soil. The heat sank into their bones slowly, the way it always did here.

"A man came to the greenhouse," Morgan said.

Bram poured water over the herbs already waiting in two mismatched cups. "Describe him."

"Tall," Morgan said. "Older. Or worn in a way that mimics age. He wore a coat too heavy for the weather, like he didn't trust the season." They paused. "He smiled without meaning it."

Bram slid one cup across the table. "Did he give a name?"

"No," Morgan said. "But he asked questions. Too many. About the land. About whether the houses remember what happens inside them."

Bram's hand stilled for a fraction of a second before he reached for the second cup. "He asked about memory."

Morgan nodded. "And when he left, he said something like an afterthought. 'Some places remember the wrong things.'"

Bram leaned back in his chair; eyes fixed on the fire. The flames reflected faintly in his pupils, not dancing so much as holding steady. When he spoke again, his voice was quiet.

"Not a man."

Morgan straightened.

"Not exactly," Bram continued. "Or not anymore. There are things that move through places like Emerdeen when the ground shifts. Old energies. Old griefs. Old beliefs that never learned how to rest." He met Morgan's eyes. "They wear skin. But they are not made of it."

"A revenant," Morgan offered.

"No," Bram said. "This is older than the dead rising. This is something that never left when it should have." He took a breath. "This is someone returned."

Morgan's fingers tapped once against the side of their cup. "Returned from where?"

Bram's gaze didn't waver. "From wherever they were told to stay quiet. From whatever threshold they were convinced they had the right to cross."

The fire popped softly.

Morgan swallowed. "Do you think he's tied to Fi's house?"

Bram nodded once. "Not to the house itself. To what the house witnessed. To what it refused to forget." His jaw tightened. "Places like that don't just hold love. They hold interference. They hold people who tried to overwrite something that wasn't theirs."

"He's looking for a crack," Morgan said.

"Yes," Bram replied. "And cracks appear when people start remembering out loud."

Morgan let out a slow breath through their nose. "He found me."

Bram reached for a small tin on the mantle and added two fresh leaves of vervain to Morgan's cup. "Then we make sure he doesn't find anyone else."

The steam curled upward, carrying the sharp, grounding scent. Morgan watched it rise and dissipate.

"The land's waking up," they said. "He felt it. And now he's circling."

Bram leaned forward, elbows resting on his knees, voice low but steady. "Then it's time to remind the land how to say no."

Morgan nodded slowly.

Outside, the wind shifted direction.

And the cottage, like the town beyond it, held its ground.

Chapter Forty-Nine: The Thing That Wasn't Buried

Fi was not planning to go outside.

She had just poured her coffee and settled into the narrow window seat beneath the stairs, the one that caught the late morning light just right. One of Aunt Thea's notebooks lay open in her lap, its pages crowded with slanted handwriting and margin notes that felt more conversational than instructional. Grocery lists shared space with half-formed thoughts. Observations about weather bled into reminders to rest.

Normal things. Comforting things.

Then the wind shifted.

It was not a gust. Nothing dramatic enough to rattle the windows or stir the chimes on the porch. It was precise. Directed. Like a breath exhaled through the keyhole of a locked room.

The back of Fi's neck prickled.

She sat very still for a moment, coffee warming her palms, listening to her own breath. The house had its usual sounds. The hum of the refrigerator. The faint creak of settling wood. Fox moving somewhere down the hall.

And beneath it all, something else.

Fi stood slowly and set the mug on the windowsill. She did not rush. Rushing felt like exactly the wrong response. She slipped on her boots and stepped out onto the porch, the screen door closing behind her with a soft click.

The garden looked unchanged.

Overgrown, yes. Familiar. The herbs still tangled together the way they always did when no one intervened. The curved path Fox had cleared near the mulberry bush remained visible, though already reclaiming itself at the edges. The low stone border they had joked about rebuilding sagged in places, stubborn but tired.

All of it felt like home.

And yet something tugged at her attention, persistent and sharp, pulling her gaze toward the far edge of the yard.

A shape.

Fi walked slowly across the grass, boots sinking slightly into the damp earth from last night's rain. She could feel her heartbeat in her wrists, steady but alert. At the fence line, half-hidden by ivy and a snarl of yellowing vines, stood an object that had not been there yesterday.

An iron stake.

Rusted. Pitted. Leaning slightly to one side, as if the ground itself had tried and failed to reject it.

She crouched beside it, careful not to touch.

There was no marker. No ribbon. No charm. No sign that it belonged to anyone who still cared for it.

Just a dull iron ring embedded at the top. The kind used to tie something down.

Or to keep something from slipping free.

Fi swallowed and reached out despite herself.

The moment her fingers brushed the metal, a flash tore through her skull, bright and merciless.

She saw a porch lit by oil lamp, shadows jumping across weathered boards. A man in a long coat stood near the back door, smiling too widely, his eyes not matching his mouth. A whispered argument hissed through the space between walls. Fear pressed low and urgent.

A child's voice, muffled. Hidden. Breathing shallow beneath floorboards.

And one word, forced out through clenched teeth, sharp as broken glass.

"Unbind."

Fi jerked her hand back, breath catching painfully in her throat.

The stake pulsed once beneath the ivy.

Then stilled.

Fox's voice called her name from inside the house, distant and unconcerned. She did not answer. She could not. The air around the stake felt wrong now, tight and compressed, as if the land itself had tried to grow over something poisonous and failed.

She rose slowly, backing away step by careful step.

The ground here felt bruised. Pinched. Like it remembered being violated.

Fi lifted her gaze toward the tree line.

For a moment, just a moment, she thought she saw movement beyond the fence. The edge of a coat. A figure standing where the light thinned and the woods deepened.

Watching.

Not approaching. Not yet.

Waiting.

Fi turned and walked back toward the house without looking over her shoulder again.

Some doors, she knew now, were never meant to be reopened casually.

And some things did not leave just because time passed.

Chapter Fifty: The Cleansing Fire

He did not think of it as stalking.

He thought of it as watching over.

The way a shepherd might keep to the hills while the wolves circle. The way a flame waits in the coals before it rises.

He had not used his real name in a long time.

Names tied you to the world in inconvenient ways.

He had shed his long ago, the day he burned the last of the journals his sister left behind.

She had been the first.

Or at least, the first he'd loved.

The first to fall into the lie of magic. The first to whisper to candles and claim that dreams were more than the echoes of a sleeping mind. The first to believe that herbs could protect, that intention could heal, that women who bled with the moon could claim the right to wield power without permission.

He had watched her change.

Had watched the fever take her.

Not of the body, but of the soul.

And when the charm she carried turned to ash in her palm; when the thing she had trusted betrayed her in the end, he took it as proof.

Magic was not salvation.

It was rot.

It was rebellion wrapped in beauty.

Deceit cloaked in ritual.

It was the snake that whispered, you can be as gods, and offered the apple in the language of roots and thread.

He had made a vow.

To find it.
Name it.
And cut it out.

Town by town.
Witch by witch.
Lie by lie.

Some resisted.

Some didn't see him coming until the final spark.

But Emerdeen was different.

It held the magic.

Not like a tool, but like a breath.

The ground itself remembered. The buildings hummed. The air tasted like spellwork and old promises.

It had taken him time to find the cracks.

But he had found them.

A shop that glowed too warmly.
A garden that grew in unnatural rhythm.
A girl with a line of old blood in her hands and the nerve to look him

in the eye.
A town that no longer feared its own darkness.

He had marked the boundaries.
Learned the names.
Listened for the weave.

They thought he didn't know what they were.

But he knew.

He'd seen towns like this before.
And he'd burned them clean.

This time, he would not wait for the rot to grow.
This time, he would strike first.

He opened his coat pocket and touched the charm wrapped in black cloth.

A relic from another place.
A talisman once stolen from the ashes of a fallen coven.

It would be enough to begin.

Let them sense him.
Let them prepare.

Faith did not require stealth.

Only conviction.

Chapter Fifty-One: The Line That Holds

The moment the outer ward shifted, Cassie dropped the spoon she was using to stir the honey.

It clattered against the counter, sending a soft drizzle of gold spiraling across the stove. But she didn't move to clean it. Her breath had gone shallow.

Not pain. Not magic. Not yet.

But pressure.

A tension just beyond the edges of town, brushing against the threads she'd buried years ago; quiet, protective ones, sewn into stones and hedgerows and the corners of porches. She hadn't felt them stir like this in years.

And when they did, it was never for anything good.

Cassie pressed her palm to the old oak counter and reached for the weave, her fingers brushing through layers of energy she usually let lie dormant.

There it was.

A disturbance. No malice, not in the loud sense. No wild magic. No cracking air.

But something far worse.

Intention.

A will with no invitation. A presence not seeking but judging.

Her jaw clenched.

It wasn't the first time.

She remembered the church steps.
Sixteen. Barely.

She had been lighting candles for her grandmother, murmuring words that were older than prayer and not printed in any bulletin.

The woman had grabbed her wrist as she passed—white lace gloves, hard eyes. "You think the Lord doesn't see what you're doing?"

Cassie had flinched but not pulled away.

The woman had leaned closer, breath like peppermint and scorn.

"Witchcraft in His house? He won't protect you when the fires come."

Cassie hadn't said anything then.

But the next week, all the candles in the sanctuary had refused to light.

And the woman never touched her again.

Now, as the threads at the edge of Emerdeen rippled, Cassie felt the same chill.

This wasn't wild magic or clumsy curiosity. This was something older, meaner.

Self-righteousness with a purpose.

She crossed to the corner cupboard and pulled out the salt jar, then the bundle of iron keys she hadn't touched since the last eclipse.

She didn't panic. But she did move with urgency.

Because people like that never arrived without plans. They didn't ask questions unless they already believed they had the answers.

And they didn't care what the truth was.

Cassie scattered salt at the threshold, whispering the soft, forgotten words that bound it to the land.

She pressed the iron key into the center of the floor and traced a circle around it with rosemary ash.

Then she closed her eyes.

She didn't call on the threads.

She reminded them.

You've held before.
You'll hold again.
We are not powerless here.
We never were.

The air thickened, just slightly.

The ward steadied.

But the pressure at the edge of town remained. Pacing.

Looking for an opening.

Cassie opened her eyes and reached for her coat.

If this was the beginning, she wasn't going to face it inside.

Not this time.

She was going to meet it where the line had been drawn.

Chapter Fifty-Two: Where the Threads Cross

Cassie didn't rush.

The path toward the edge of town was old and uneven, lined with the kind of hedgerows that had grown around stone markers no one wrote down anymore. She didn't need a map. She had walked it before after storms, after births, after other quiet reckonings.

She walked it now because something had crossed the boundary.

Not with blood or fire.

But with belief.

And belief, when shaped like a weapon, could do more damage than either.

The wind was still. Not absent. Just listening.

Cassie reached the split in the path where the sycamores leaned too far inward and paused beneath their shade. Her coat was unbuttoned. Her hands were bare. She didn't carry charms.

Only a single iron key strung on thread around her neck, and a satchel of salt and rosemary tucked beneath her arm.

The threads hummed beneath her feet.

Not warning. Waking.

The land knew what it meant when someone came with the intention to unmake.

Cassie stepped forward again, each footfall measured.

She passed the old Miller gate, long rusted shut. Passed the bend where Morgan had once buried a moonstone for safe passage. Passed the grove where Baz had etched runes into bark, half-drunk on honeywine, laughing and serious all at once.

The world changed slowly out here.

But it remembered fast.

At the last bend, she stopped.

The man was waiting at the far edge of the clearing.

Coat dark. Posture straight. Hands in his pockets like he wasn't trespassing, only observing.

Cassie didn't speak.

She didn't need to.

The threads gathered around her ankles, rising slightly, responding to her stillness.

He smiled.

It was a thin thing, more habit than warmth.

"You came alone," he said.

Cassie cocked her head. "Funny. I was thinking the same thing about you."

"I'm not a threat," he said. "Only a question."

"You're shaped like a threat," she replied. "And you're not a question. You're an answer you want everyone else to memorize."

He flinched—just barely.

Cassie stepped forward, onto the edge of the ward.

It rippled under her heel, then smoothed. She had reinforced it well.

"I know what you're here to do," she said. "And I'm telling you now, it won't take."

He tilted his head. "You believe you speak for this place?"

"I don't have to," she said. "It speaks for itself. I'm just one of the few who knows how to listen."

His gaze sharpened.

"Magic," he said quietly, "doesn't belong in the hands of the unrepentant."

Cassie's jaw set, but she didn't raise her voice.

"You mistake humility for guilt," she said. "And difference for danger. And that's not magic's failing. That's yours."

He didn't move.

But the weight in the air shifted.

She could feel him reaching—energetically, not physically. Testing. Probing the seams.

The ward held. But it wouldn't forever.

He would try again.

Cassie stepped back, deliberately, and let the silence stretch.

"Emerdeen doesn't need to be saved," she said. "It's already whole. You're the one trying to cut it open."

The man watched her.

Then, with no farewell, he turned and walked the treeline, disappearing back into the woods like mist moving backward through time.

Cassie didn't follow.

She stood at the boundary, breathing in the stillness he left behind.

And then, as gently as she could, she whispered to the threads below her feet:

Anchor here.

Hold fast.

We see him now.

Chapter Fifty-Three: What We Carry

The greenhouse was quieter than usual.

Morgan stood near the lavender row, weaving rosemary sprigs into a slow spiral, their fingers moving by memory. Baz leaned against the frame, one foot up on a low crate of drying calendula, arms folded but eyes sharp.

"He's not just watching," Morgan said. "He's measuring."

Baz nodded once. "Like someone looking for weak points in a wall."

Morgan adjusted the spiral. "Cassie went to meet him."

"She shouldn't have had to."

"She didn't ask."

Baz ran a hand through his hair, frustration barely contained. "It's not just him, though. It's what he brings with him. That look in his eyes—it's not new. It's old. It's the kind of certainty that never questions itself."

Morgan looked up. "It's the kind that burns things down and calls it grace."

They stood in silence, both of them watching the condensation bead across the glass. Outside, the afternoon light had thinned, the sky turning the color of early parchment. Something was waiting at the edge of that horizon.

Then the door opened.

Cassie stepped in, her coat still dusted with salt from the wards. Her face was unreadable, but her shoulders carried the kind of tension that meant she'd been holding something back for too long.

Baz straightened immediately. "You okay?"

She didn't answer at first.

Instead, she closed the door softly behind her and said, "I need to tell you both something."

Morgan gestured toward the wide bench near the herb-drying rack. Cassie sat. Baz joined her, close but not crowding, while Morgan remained standing, their arms crossed lightly over their chest.

"I've seen people like him before," Cassie said. "When I was younger. Before I came here."

Her voice was steady, but something flickered behind it.

"I was twenty. Living in a town that didn't have a name for what I did, only words for what it wasn't. I tried to stay small. Not out of fear, not exactly. Just out of survival."

Morgan moved closer.

"But even that wasn't enough," she continued. "There was a man. A minister's son. He'd show up at my shop and ask questions that weren't really questions. About candles. About herbs. About whether I believed."

Cassie took a breath. "One night, my windows were broken. The jars were smashed. Salt in the drains. Ash on the doorstep."

Baz's fists clenched on his knees.

"I moved two weeks later. Packed what I could. Left the rest. Told myself that silence was safer. That if I just didn't draw attention, I'd be fine."

She looked up at Morgan. "But that silence became a habit. Even after I got here. Even when the land whispered that I was safe."

Morgan's voice was soft. "And now he's stirred it back up."

Cassie nodded. "It's not just what he believes. It's what he's willing to destroy to prove he's right."

Baz spoke, low. "You think he'll hurt someone."

"I think," Cassie said slowly, "he doesn't care who he hurts, as long as he gets to be the one who defines what's real."

She reached into her coat and pulled out the charm key; the one she wore when she needed to remember who she used to be.

"I'm not afraid for myself," she said. "Not anymore."

Morgan and Baz waited.

"I'm afraid for what happens if we let him unmake this place. If we let someone like him tell the land it's wrong for remembering."

The silence in the greenhouse was thick and sacred.

Morgan stepped forward and knelt in front of her, hands on Cassie's knees.

"We're not going to let that happen."

Baz, still beside her, reached over and gently placed his hand over hers. "Not this time."

Cassie's voice was quieter now. "Then we need to be ready. Because he's not just looking for cracks in the wards."

She met their eyes, one at a time.

"He's looking for the cracks in us."

Chapter Fifty-Four: Something I Wasn't Supposed to Remember

Fi had barely slept.

The dream the night before had been vivid again—shadows in the doorway, whispers too close. But this time, something different had cracked through the murk. A face. A voice. A smell that made her stomach turn.

And this morning, when she stepped out to bring in the laundry she'd forgotten the night before, she saw him.

Across the street.

Not watching her. Not openly.

But present.

The man in the coat.

Polished. Still.

As if he belonged to a different weather pattern than the rest of them.

And when their eyes met just for a flicker, something ancient and cold lit up in her chest like frost on bone.

She knew him.

Not as the man he was now. But from before.

From long before.

The memory struck as she poured her coffee.

She was small. Maybe seven. Visiting her aunt's old house with her parents. Her mother had gone into the cellar to get jars. Her father was loading boxes in the truck.

Fi had wandered outside to where the trees began.

And he was there.

A man in a long coat, smiling too much.

Asking questions she hadn't understood.

"Does your aunt ever talk to the wind?"

"Has she given you anything to wear? A charm, maybe? A stone?"

He had crouched, hands on his knees. Friendly on the surface.

But his eyes—

They had looked past her. Not at her. Like she was only a hinge to something else.

Her mother had come running, then. Pulled her away. Angry. Terrified.

They never talked about it again.

Fi had forgotten.

Until now.

She left the house without finishing her coffee, clutching the journal she'd found in the attic.

The one with Thea's quiet warnings scrawled in the margins.

She needed to talk to Cassie.

Not just because Cassie would believe her.

But because she was afraid of what it would mean if Cassie didn't.

The bell above the shop door rang softly as Fi stepped inside. The scents wrapped around her immediately—sage, cedar, and the faintest hint of orange peel. The warmth of it eased her shoulders just a fraction.

Cassie looked up from the counter, brows knitting together as she took in Fi's expression.

"I need to talk to you," Fi said, voice tight. "Now."

Cassie motioned to the back room without hesitation. "Come on."

They sat across from each other, no tea this time, no ritual. Just presence.

Fi placed the journal on the table between them and said, "I know who he is."

Cassie didn't blink. "Tell me."

So, Fi did.

Every detail she remembered. The voice. The questions. The coat that looked too heavy for summer. The way her mother had gone pale and silent and never once explained what had happened.

When she finished, Cassie exhaled, slow and steady.

"I think he's been circling this place longer than we realized," Cassie said. "Maybe even before Thea anchored the house."

"I think he marks people," Fi said. "Marks children. Because he's looking for cracks early. Looking for weakness."

Cassie's mouth tightened.

Fi reached into her coat pocket and pulled out a small, pressed marigold from one of Thea's journals.

"She was trying to protect us," she said. "She knew. And I think she sealed something away because she couldn't stop him."

Cassie gently touched the flower.

"Then it's not just about keeping him out," she murmured. "It's about making sure no one invites him in."

Fi met her gaze. "Do you think he's the danger I dreamed about?"

Cassie didn't answer at first.

Then: "I think he's part of it. But I don't think he's the end of it."

Fi leaned back in the chair, the weight of memory still heavy in her limbs.

"What do we do?"

Cassie reached for the journal. "We read. We remember. And then we build something stronger than he's ever faced before."

And somewhere beyond the walls, the wind picked up, carrying something older than fear.

Chapter Fifty-Five: What Protection Requires

Baz held the copper thread steady as Morgan twisted it through the anchor stone.

The rite they were building wasn't flashy. It wouldn't throw sparks or ripple through the sky like some dramatic warding spell. It would move quietly - rooted, layered, patient.

Like the land it meant to protect.

Morgan sat cross-legged on the floor of the greenhouse; tools spread around them like a painter's palette. Basil, salt, moss scraped from the north side of the boundary stone. Iron shavings. A small bundle of larkspur from Bram.

And at the center, a smooth river stone etched with three spiraling lines - one for each of them.

Baz wrapped the final knot and exhaled. "That should hold the outer thread. It'll pull the rest into place when we set the anchor."

Morgan nodded. "We'll bury it at the grove just past the bend. Right under the old ash."

Baz didn't speak for a moment. Morgan didn't push.

But the silence had shape.

"You're thinking about her," Morgan said gently.

Baz nodded. "She's been through this before. Maybe not this exact shape, but... the fire underneath is familiar."

Morgan pressed a thumb to the river stone, then looked up. "She stood at the edge of town alone. Again. That's a kind of bravery that shouldn't have to repeat itself."

"She carries more than she lets on," Baz said. "Even with me."

Morgan offered a small, rueful smile. "That's how you know it matters. She holds it close when it's real."

Baz looked at the bundle of herbs beside the charm. "I just don't want her doing that until she breaks."

"She won't break," Morgan said.

"No," Baz agreed. "But she might disappear. Piece by piece. And I've only just gotten her back."

Morgan picked up the copper spool and began weaving a second thread—slimmer, meant to tie back to the inner ward. "Then we stay close. We hold where she's thinned. We don't ask her to speak before she's ready."

Baz knelt beside them, adding a pinch of salt to the thread's binding. "And we remind her that this time, she doesn't have to stand alone."

Morgan glanced sideways. "And maybe remind her how to rest."

Baz smiled softly. "We'll sneak it into the ritual. Make rest part of the structure."

Morgan laughed, but it was quiet. Reverent.

The rite was taking form now.

It would take more than the two of them to seal it. But for now, it was enough to begin.

They worked in silence, the kind that heals rather than hides.

And as the charm hummed beneath their hands, the land began to lean in.

Listening.

Waiting.

Ready.

Chapter Fifty-Six: Faith and Faultlines

Fox wasn't looking for anything.

He was just trying to reroute the drainage channel along the back edge of the yard. Another one of those small, manageable projects that made him feel useful in a world that no longer fit into clean logic.

But when he reached the corner where the mulberry bush had overgrown into a snarl of brambles, he felt it.

Wrongness.

Not the kind that announces itself with cracking branches or swirling mists.

But a quiet dissonance.

Like stepping into a room and forgetting what you came in for. Like the static before a power outage. Like the air holding its breath too long.

He crouched, fingers brushing along the base of the stones.

And there it was.

A ripple.

Just one. Subtle.

But real.

Fox stood up slowly, eyes narrowing.

He wasn't a believer—not in magic, not in fate, not in anything that couldn't be tested or rewired. He'd always found more comfort in circuit boards than circles of salt.

But this, this was not normal.

And it wasn't natural.

Fi was in the kitchen, flipping through another of Thea's journals, her expression pinched. She looked up when he came in.

"You're not going to believe this," he said.

She raised an eyebrow. "You literally just described half our life now."

He didn't even smirk. That's how she knew it was serious.

"I felt something," he said. "Out by the back fence. The air went thin. Like the world skipped a beat."

Fi's breath caught. "That's where I found the iron stake."

Fox blinked. "What stake?"

Fi stood, crossing to the table. "Come here. There's more."

She told him everything. The memory. The man. The questions. The journal entries that hinted at sealed things and buried warnings.

And when she described the stranger in the coat, Fox's whole posture shifted.

"This guy," he said slowly. "He's a preacher?"

Fi shook her head. "He never used the word. But… yeah. It's faith. Twisted faith."

Fox's jaw tensed. "Of course it is."

She looked at him, puzzled. "What do you mean?"

He hesitated.

Then: "We grew up around that kind of certainty. The kind that says the world is only safe if you keep it small. That anyone who doesn't play by the rules is either lost or dangerous."

Fi stayed silent.

Fox kept going. "They talked about salvation, but what they meant was control. Fear wrapped in scripture. Love measured by obedience."

"And you left," Fi said.

"I ran," he replied. "And I never looked back. But people like that don't let go. They linger. And they don't come to listen. They come to name. To declare what's clean and what's not."

Fi sat down again, softer now. "He's circling. Looking for a crack."

Fox ran a hand through his hair, the muscle in his jaw tight. "Then we close them. Every one."

He looked around the kitchen.

The windows.

The door.

The floorboards that had once hidden a child's voice in a dream Fi couldn't forget.

"I may not believe in magic," he said. "But I believe in us. And I'm not letting some sermon in a borrowed coat unmake this place."

Fi gave a short, wry smile. "Careful. That almost sounded like belief."

Fox shrugged. "Call it rage with boundaries."

Outside, the wind picked up.

And somewhere beyond the stake line, the stranger turned and smiled before fading back into the trees.

Chapter Fifty-Seven: The House That Would Not Be Taken

The kettle was already hissing when Cassie arrived.

Fi had cleared the table of old notebooks and unwashed mugs, replacing them with bundles of herbs, a bowl of iron nails, and the last of the beeswax Morgan had infused with ash and rue.

Cassie stepped inside and took one deep breath.

The house was still listening. But it was no longer waiting.

Morgan arrived next, holding a basket of dried vervain and rosemary and a pouch of salt thickened with crushed bone and thread that was leftover from a protection circle they'd built after a wildfire three summers ago. The air around them shimmered faintly, like something beneath their skin was glowing low and steady.

They exchanged no greetings.

There wasn't need.

Fi sat at the head of the table, hands pressed flat against the wood. Her eyes were shadowed but focused. She looked, Cassie thought, like someone finally willing to hear her own blood sing.

"We don't want to trap him," Cassie began.

"Or challenge him," Morgan added.

"We want to make this house a place he cannot enter," Fi finished. "Not just physically. But energetically. Intuitively."

Cassie nodded. "He walks like someone who doesn't hear 'no.' So we make this place speak louder than he's ever known."

Morgan handed Cassie the pouch. "Ash line at every threshold. Window frames too."

"Iron at each corner of the foundation," Fi added, reaching for the small square nails. "Rust is fine. Actually, it's better."

"We need a central sigil," Morgan said. "One the house will recognize as its own. We're not imposing magic on it, we're helping it remember what it already knows."

Cassie moved to the counter and pulled a worn cutting board from the shelf. "Then we use Thea's."

They all looked at her.

Cassie set the board on the table and turned it over.

On the underside, carved faintly but clearly: a spiral nested within a ring, bracketed by four small crescents.

Fi leaned forward. "That was there the whole time?"

Cassie nodded. "I never sanded it. Something told me not to. She marked it in the old way. A memory sigil. Tied to lineage and place."

Morgan touched the edge of the spiral. "It's perfect. We inscribe it under the floor. Between the beams."

Fi added, "And we weave it into thread. Hide it in the curtains, the blankets. Places he'll never think to look."

Cassie drew in a long, quiet breath. "We make the house speak in its own language."

They worked for hours.

Infusing the wax with rosemary and salt. Wrapping iron nails in thread and embedding them behind old hinges. Sketching sigils in flour on the pantry floor, brushing them into the cracks with purpose.

At dusk, they stood in the kitchen, each holding a small charm in their palm. Cassie spoke first.

"This house held her. It holds you. And now it will hold what's needed."

Fi repeated the words, voice firm.

Morgan followed.

The charms warmed in their hands.

And above them, the house groaned—softly, but not unhappily. Like a creature stretching, remembering how its limbs worked after too long curled tight in defense.

The ward wasn't a wall.

It was a heartbeat.

And it would not be stilled by the cold stare of a zealot who did not know how to listen.

Chapter Fifty-Eight: Strange Bedfellows

Cassie lay sideways across the couch, one leg draped over Baz's lap, a mug of lukewarm tea resting precariously on her chest.

"Do you think warding counts as cardio?" she asked.

Baz didn't look up from the book balanced on his knee. "Depends how fast you were running from your existential dread."

"I wasn't running," she said. "I was aggressively pacing."

"Then yes. Cardio."

She snorted, shifting the mug to the side table and squinting at the ceiling like it had recently betrayed her.

The room smelled like sage and sleep. The fireplace still held a faint glow, and somewhere near the back door, a protective charm clicked softly in rhythm with the wind.

Baz closed his book and set it aside. "How are you really?"

Cassie didn't answer right away.

She stared at the ceiling another moment, then said, "I keep thinking about how many people have tried to control what we don't understand. And how often they end up controlling each other instead."

Baz ran a hand lightly along her shin. "You mean the stranger."

"I mean zealotry in general." She rolled her head to look at him. "Do you know how many times in my life I've been told I was going to hell?"

"Do I want to know?"

"My personal favorite was a guy at a bus stop in Asheville who handed me a tract titled *Wicca and the Rise of the Jezebel Spirit.*"

Baz blinked. "That's… specific."

"He told me my tattoos were demonic. I told him his shoelaces were untied and walked away. Which they weren't, but he looked anyway. Still satisfying."

Baz chuckled, but the warmth faded quickly.

"I grew up in a church that taught obedience was the same as love," he said. "And that asking too many questions meant you had a rebellious spirit."

Cassie's expression softened. "Ah, so you were also raised by people who thought free will was a liability."

"They meant well. But everything had to be tidy. Explained. Anything mysterious was suspicious."

"Which," Cassie said, "makes you very suspicious of magic."

Baz didn't deny it.

"I don't mistrust you," he said. "Or Morgan. Or any of this, really. I just…" He sighed. "I have to feel it for myself. I can't accept it just because someone says it's true."

Cassie smiled. "That's exactly what makes you the safest person to have near power."

Baz looked at her, curious. "Why?"

"Because the people who scare me are the ones who want certainty. Not truth. Certainty. That's how you get crusades. Burnings. Forced purity in all its ridiculous, fragile forms."

She paused, then added, "Magic doesn't demand belief. It just keeps moving."

Baz looked down at her, admiration flickering in his tired eyes. "Sometimes I forget how sharp you are until you start casually dismantling centuries of theocracy during a cuddle."

Cassie grinned. "It's a gift. Like sarcasm. Or cinnamon rolls."

He leaned down and kissed her forehead. "Thank you. For holding the line."

Cassie snuggled in closer, her voice sleep-blurred now.

"We all hold it. Some of us just do it with salt and sass."

Baz pulled the blanket over them both and let the quiet settle.

Outside, the night stretched long and silent.

But in this room, between the two of them, the line held.

Chapter Fifty-Nine: The Stranger Steps In

Fox had never thought he'd come to appreciate how weirdly normal Emerdeen could be.

The way shopkeepers nodded with just enough curiosity to keep you honest. The handwritten signs that never matched but still told you where to go. The post office with its crooked bell and three shelves of communal books no one returned on time.

He was picking up coffee beans and a replacement part for the rain barrel spigot when the atmosphere shifted.

It wasn't loud.

Just... too still.

The kind of stillness that made animals stop moving. That made people check over their shoulder without knowing why.

Fox felt it as he stepped out of the general store, holding a paper bag under one arm. He spotted a few familiar faces on the street—Kara from the bakery, Old Reed muttering to himself by the benches—but they were quieter than usual.

And then he saw him.

Standing just beyond the flower cart outside the café.

Coat too clean. Posture too straight.

Fox didn't change direction.

He walked straight toward him.

The stranger watched him approach with an expression that might've passed for pleasant if you didn't know how people smiled when they meant it.

"You're Thea Carrow's nephew," the man said, voice even.

Fox stopped a few paces away. "That's one way to phrase it."

"Your sister remembers me," he said. "I could see it on her face."

Fox didn't answer.

The man smiled. "And you—you're not quite convinced any of this is real, are you?"

Fox raised an eyebrow. "I believe in wind when it knocks me over. Don't need a hymn about it."

The man chuckled. "Fair. But wind can be summoned. Magic can be twisted. And the wrong hands can leave a town like this in ruin."

"Funny," Fox said, "that's exactly what we think about you."

For the first time, something flickered behind the man's eyes. He stepped forward, not threatening, but not hesitant either.

"My name is Amos."

Fox nodded once. "Took you long enough."

"I've come to see if this place still knows what it is. Or if it's been bewitched into believing it can be something else."

Fox stared at him. "You're walking around judging a town you don't even know. That's not discernment. That's theater."

"I know places like this," Amos said, quietly now. "I've seen what they become when no one challenges the delusion."

"You mean when no one follows your rules."

Amos smiled again, but it was thin. "I mean when no one remembers what truth feels like."

Fox's jaw tensed.

"You think truth is a knife," he said. "We think it's a root."

Amos didn't respond.

Just looked past Fox, toward the direction of the Carrow house.

Then, almost gently, he said, "I don't want to hurt anyone."

Fox stepped into his line of sight. "But you're willing to."

A long silence followed.

Then Amos nodded once, almost like a blessing, and walked away without another word.

Fox didn't move until the man was halfway down the block.

And even then, he didn't breathe easily.

Because Amos hadn't come to test the town anymore.

He'd come to decide what needed to be broken.

Chapter Sixty: Names Carry Intent

"Amos? His name is Amos?" Cassie repeated, her voice edged with equal parts disbelief and grim amusement. "How biblical."

She stood in the Carrow kitchen, still wearing her coat though the fire had already warmed the room. The mug in her hand had gone cold, but she hadn't noticed. Her fingers tapped anxiously against the ceramic as she stared at the floor, like she was listening for something beneath it.

Fox leaned against the doorframe, arms crossed tightly across his chest. He hadn't even sat down since he walked in and relayed what happened in town. "That's what he said. He waited until the very end of our little sidewalk sermon and then just dropped it like punctuation. 'My name is Amos.'"

Fi sat at the kitchen table, one leg pulled up beneath her. Her eyes were shadowed from too little sleep and too many pages of old journals. She looked over at Cassie. "You've heard that name before, haven't you?"

Cassie finally moved, setting the mug down with a quiet clink. "It's not the name, exactly. It's the kind of person who chooses it. Amos isn't just a name. It's a signal. It's meant to carry authority. Righteousness. Judgment." She looked out the window into the grey edge of late afternoon. "He's telling us who he thinks he is."

Fox scoffed. "Yeah, he definitely carries himself like someone who thinks he's been given special permission by the universe."

"He has," Cassie said plainly. "In his own mind. People like him don't need facts or consent. They just need conviction. Everything else is decoration."

Fi shifted forward, resting her elbows on the table. "In the dream, he didn't have a name. But the way he spoke, the way he looked at me—like I was a passage he already knew by heart—it makes sense now. He didn't see me. He saw what he expected."

Cassie walked slowly around the table and sat beside her, brushing a few dried herb leaves off the table. "He doesn't see towns, or people, or even danger. He sees things to be purified. Anything complex is corruption in his eyes."

Fox pushed off the doorframe and started pacing slowly, his footsteps a steady rhythm against the creaking wood floor. "He told me he wasn't a threat. Said he was just trying to understand what this town had become. But the way he looked at me? He's not here to understand. He's here to dismantle."

Cassie nodded. "And now that he's named himself, we're no longer just a curiosity to him. We're a challenge."

Fi opened one of Thea's journals and flipped to a dog-eared page covered in looping, hurried script. "We have to assume he's going to act soon. The protective charms are in place, but if he's been here before; if he knows this land the way Thea hinted; then he may already be looking for its weak points."

"We warded the house," Fox said. "What else do we need to do?"

Cassie looked at him, her expression shifting to something softer, more worn. "Wards protect the walls. But protection isn't just about stone and charm lines. We need to understand what he's here to undo. He's not just threatening this house. He's threatening the memory it carries. And if Thea sealed something—something tied to him—then that's what he's come back for."

Fi nodded slowly. "You think he wants to unseal it."

Cassie's voice dropped. "I think he believes he's the only one who should be able to open it. And whatever's behind that seal, whatever truth or magic or memory, it doesn't want to be opened by force."

Fox stopped pacing and turned toward them. "So, we're not just protecting the house. We're protecting the story it holds."

"Exactly," Cassie said. "Magic lives in memory. In threads and stories and names. If Amos thinks he can rename this place in his own image, he's going to be met with a lot more than salt lines and old wood."

Fi closed the journal gently, her eyes fixed on the sigil carved into the table's edge. "Then let's give this house its name back, before he tries to rewrite it."

A long silence settled over the room, but it wasn't empty. It was full of resolve, quiet and deep as soil. The kind of silence that held room for what came next.

Cassie exhaled. "He's declared himself. So now we respond. Not in fear. Not in rage. But with the kind of strength he'll never understand."

Fox raised an eyebrow. "You mean rational boundaries and lovingly weaponized folklore?"

Cassie smirked. "Exactly."

Chapter Sixty-One: Uneasy Bloom

Bram was elbow-deep in goldenrod when he heard the crunch of footsteps on the gravel path.

The late morning sun hung low behind a veil of slow-moving clouds, and the scent of rosemary and wet earth clung to the hem of his tunic. He didn't look up immediately. Visitors were rare this early, and most of the town knew to wait at the gate.

But the man didn't stop.

He walked the narrow path without hesitation, his long coat brushing against the garden's border plants like he belonged there.

When Bram finally glanced up, the man was already close enough to greet.

"Good morning," the stranger said, voice warm but unhurried.

Bram straightened slowly. "Good morning."

The man offered a modest smile. "Quite a space you've cultivated here."

Bram nodded, brushing the dirt from his hands. "I try to listen to what the plants ask for."

"I imagine they speak often, in a place like this."

There was something oddly familiar in the man's tone. Not in its content, but in its cadence. Like a teacher who'd studied the local language just enough to sound polite.

Still, Bram found himself answering more easily than he expected. "They do. Most people just forget how to listen."

The man tilted his head as if in approval. "Not you."

A pause.

Then: "Do you mind if I walk a bit?"

Bram hesitated, and then surprisingly stepped aside. "Go ahead. Just don't touch the yarrow. It's in a temper this week."

The man chuckled softly, the sound more genuine than Bram was ready for. "Wouldn't dream of it."

He strolled slowly down the row, careful not to disturb the path. He didn't reach for any leaves or inspect the roots. He simply walked, hands folded behind his back.

"You're not from here," Bram said at last.

"No," the man replied. "But I've walked through places like this before."

"And what do you hope to find in them?"

The man looked back over his shoulder.

"Memory," he said. "Truth. What's hiding in plain sight."

Bram felt a strange warmth creep into his limbs; not pleasant, exactly. Just soft. Dulling.

He didn't move.

Didn't challenge the man.

And when he left, offering a parting nod and a quiet, "May your roots run deep," Bram returned it with something dangerously close to a smile.

It wasn't until dusk that the feeling wore off.

Morgan arrived just before the sky turned indigo, bringing a parcel of dried sage and an armful of runes they were working into the town's boundary charm.

They barely made it through the gate before Bram called out, "I need to talk to you."

Morgan paused. "Something wrong?"

"I don't know," Bram said honestly. "That man—the stranger—he came to the garden."

Morgan's expression darkened instantly. "Did he try anything?"

"No," Bram said. "That's the problem. He didn't do anything."

He sat on the low bench near the arnica patch, running his fingers through the thin clay bowl of soil he'd been mixing.

"I didn't ward him off. I didn't question him. I let him walk my garden like he belonged."

Morgan crouched beside him. "Did he say anything strange?"

"He said exactly the kind of things that would make someone feel seen," Bram admitted. "He knew how to sound like belonging. And I believed it, for a minute. I forgot what I knew."

Morgan watched him closely. "You think he charmed you."

"Not with magic. Not with spellwork." Bram's voice dropped. "With something older. Something colder. The kind that doesn't come through the weave, but through intention. Like he wore something I used to trust."

Morgan exhaled slowly. "You mean like an old mask."

Bram nodded. "Exactly."

They sat in silence as the sun dipped below the trees.

"I won't let him back in," Bram said. "But I needed you to know that I didn't stop him today. And I don't know why."

Morgan laid a hand on his shoulder.

"You remembered now. That's what matters."

But in Bram's chest, something still didn't feel like it had settled.

Chapter Sixty-Two: The Fire Beneath the Root

Amos moved through the undergrowth with a practiced stillness, the kind learned by men who believed the world owed them quiet. Branches bent away from his coat. Fallen leaves did not crunch beneath his boots. It was not grace that carried him forward, but expectation. He had learned long ago how to take up space without announcing himself, how to move as though the land were already in agreement.

He had found the place two days earlier.

An old clearing north of the boundary stones, just beyond the reach of Emerdeen's habitual paths. Forgotten by the town's daily rhythm. No footprints pressed into the soil. No charms nailed to bark. No lanterns hung as offerings or warnings. The trees here grew close together, their canopies knitted tight enough to thin the light.

It was quiet.

And beneath that quiet, there was magic.

Amos felt it humming underfoot as soon as he stepped into the clearing. Not the wild surge he had been trained to fear. Not the sharp sting of curses or the rot of corruption. This magic was woven deep into the rootlines, layered and old, pulsing faintly like a second heartbeat beneath the forest floor.

That was what disturbed him most.

This was where the sickness lived.

Not in chaos. Not in spectacle. Not in anything that announced itself as wrong.

But in peace.

In harmony that asked nothing of him. In a balance that did not demand repentance. In a stillness that existed without hierarchy or punishment.

Amos lowered himself to one knee and unlatched the worn satchel at his side. The leather creaked softly, familiar as a prayer spoken too many times to question. From within, he removed three objects, handling each with the careful reverence of a man who believed himself custodian of truth.

A strip of linen, once wrapped around a broken charm taken from a house he had helped cleanse years ago. A corked bottle of ash from a circle burned to the ground in another town, the smoke still clinging to it in memory. And a slim leather-bound text, its pages thin and brittle, marked with red thread at five places where doctrine sharpened into command.

He arranged them in a triangle on the moss-covered ground, adjusting their placement until the angles felt exact.

"This town lies to itself," Amos said quietly.

The words were not offered upward. They were not asked to be received. They were placed into the world like a verdict.

"They call it balance," he continued. "Healing. Intuition. But it is rebellion. It is pride dressed in calm. A refusal to submit to the order written into the bones of creation."

He drew a line in the soil between the linen and the bottle of ash, then another, and another, sealing the triangle with deliberate strokes. Inside it, he etched a spiral. Not the open, outward-reaching forms carved into Emerdeen's stones, but a reversed spiral, turned inward, drawing everything toward a single consuming center.

Control disguised as revelation.

"I ask not to destroy," he said, though no voice had accused him. "I ask to reveal. Let the truth come forward. Let what festers speak. Let the veil be torn."

The wind stirred through the branches overhead, leaves shifting restlessly, but it did not answer.

Amos reached into the satchel once more and withdrew the final object.

A sliver of black glass.

It caught no light. Reflected nothing. A surface that refused recognition, honed sharp enough to cut without gleaming. He placed it at the center of the spiral and pressed two fingers to its edge, ignoring the sting as it bit into his skin.

"Let them see themselves," he whispered.

A tremor moved through the soil.

Small. Barely perceptible. The kind that could be dismissed by anyone not looking for it.

But Amos felt it all the same.

He closed the satchel and rose, brushing moss from his knee. The clearing remained unchanged. No fire. No flash. No dramatic response to announce his righteousness.

That was fine.

This work was patient.

He would return in three days. By then, the ritual would have ripened, feeding on tension and doubt, amplifying the smallest fractures. By then, the land would begin to show what it truly held beneath its leaves and stones.

Not beauty. Not healing. Not truth.

But weakness.

And once exposed, Amos believed, weakness could be cut away.

He turned and left the clearing without looking back, convinced he was walking toward salvation rather than away from it.

Chapter Sixty-Three: Spirals and Signals

Cassie thumbed slowly through the brittle pages of Thea's weathered journal; her fingertips stained faintly with ash from the sigil work they'd done earlier that morning. Fi sat cross-legged beside her, poring over the corner margins where Thea often scribbled notes too quickly for neatness but too urgently for nonsense.

They had been looking for details about the old boundary wards.

What they found instead made both women go still at the same time.

Cassie read aloud, voice low.

"If the spiral turns backward, it doesn't call power in, it unthreads it. Slowly at first. Then faster. Until even memory begins to loosen. I saw it once, in a village farther west. It didn't destroy the people, not directly. But it hollowed them out. They forgot why they were kind. Why they trusted. By the time we reversed it, the only thing they believed in was doubt."

Cassie swallowed.

Fi looked up from the page. "She underlined it."

Cassie nodded. "Twice."

Under the entry, in a smaller, ink-blotted scrawl, was a single sentence:

Reversal is not noise; it is silence wearing your voice.

Fi's voice was quiet. "You think that's what Amos is doing?"

"I think he knows exactly how to dismantle a place without ever lifting a hand," Cassie said.

They sat in silence for a long moment, the sounds of late afternoon wind rattling the shutters lightly. The warmth from the hearth didn't quite chase off the weight that had settled in the room.

Then Cassie stood.

"Come on," she said.

Fi blinked. "Where?"

"To find Baz. If someone's trying to rewrite the weave from the inside out, we're going to need more than thread and salt. We're going to need something that can listen beneath the spiral. Something that can catch the silence before it spreads."

Baz was on the back porch of their home, coaxing signal out of an old radio rig he'd been experimenting with for months. When Cassie and Fi arrived, he looked up with a grin that faded almost instantly at the expressions on their faces.

"Please tell me we're here for tea and harmless weirdness."

"We found a journal entry from Thea," Cassie said, cutting right to it. "It talks about reversed spirals. And what they do to memory, to energy. We think Amos is working one now. Quietly. Somewhere near the edge of town."

Baz's brow furrowed. "And you think it's already taking effect?"

"We don't want to wait to find out," Fi said. "We want to build a way to detect it. Before it hits the rest of us."

Cassie added, "We think it starts with doubt. Not fear, not attack. Just that slow erosion of certainty. And Thea said the spiral doesn't shout. It whispers in your voice."

Baz nodded slowly, rubbing his thumb across the tuner dial. "I've been picking up weird interference in the last day or so. It's not radio chatter. It's background noise with… gaps. Like something's humming on a frequency that's not meant for speech."

Cassie stepped closer. "What if that's it? What if he's using intention through ritual to broadcast the reversal, and it's slipping into the threads that way?"

Baz was already standing. "Then we build a receiver that's part machine and part ward. We'll triangulate the silence. Find the center of the spiral."

Fi tilted her head. "Can you really do that?"

Baz grinned again, and this time it stayed. "You two bring the magic. I'll bring the copper wire and spite."

Cassie smiled back, though it didn't quite reach her eyes. "Let's make some noise before the silence spreads."

Chapter Sixty-Four: Where the Edges Blur

Morgan had learned to pay attention to the almosts.

The way someone almost remembered your name but didn't, pausing just a beat too long before settling on a polite substitute. The way a shopkeeper almost offered a joke, lips curving upward before the moment slipped past and the smile faded unfinished. The way a neighbor almost waved, hand lifting halfway before dropping again, as if the reason for the gesture had dissolved mid-motion.

Those were the tells.

Emerdeen had always hummed with layers. Emotion braided with memory. Presence woven into place. The town's rhythm wasn't loud or demanding, but it was unmistakable. You could feel it in the way bread rose too fast in the eastern kitchens, yeast responding eagerly to something in the air. In how the crows favored the same rooftops every dusk, punctual as prayer. In the way people lingered just long enough in doorways to matter.

But lately, something was thinning.

Morgan noticed it first in the café that morning. Two regulars sat at their usual table, mugs cooling between their hands, but they didn't speak. It wasn't companionable silence. It wasn't tension. It was vacancy. As if both were waiting for a memory to arrive and tell them why they had come.

Morgan watched Kara behind the counter, her movements still precise, still practiced. She slid a cinnamon roll across the case to a boy standing on tiptoe, his nose barely clearing the glass. Normally he would have lit up, eyes wide, fingers twitching with anticipation. Instead, he just stared at it.

Kara laughed softly and pushed the plate closer. "On the house today."

The boy blinked. Once. Twice. Then shook his head as if waking up. "I… I don't want anything."

Kara smiled, but it didn't quite reach her eyes. There was fog there. Not sadness. Not fear. Just the sense that she was reaching for the shape of kindness and couldn't quite find the outline.

When Morgan stepped back outside, the air felt wrong.

Not empty. Not hostile.

Muted.

Like the world had been wrapped in felt, edges softened, sound absorbed. The street noises dulled. Footsteps landed without echo. Even the wind seemed unsure of itself.

Morgan pressed their fingers to the seam of the thread tattoo winding up their arm, the familiar texture grounding them. The weave was still present. Still alive.

But it wasn't untouched.

Walking down Main Street toward the herb stand Bram usually manned, Morgan spotted Old Reed standing alone in front of the war memorial. He had one hand braced on the stone, head bowed slightly. His lips moved.

No sound came out.

Morgan approached slowly, careful not to startle him. "You okay, Reed?"

The old man blinked, eyes unfocused and then sharpening as if he were surfacing from deep water. "What?"

"Just checking in," Morgan said, voice low and steady.

Reed's gaze slid past them, then back again. His brow furrowed. "I was… I was supposed to…" He trailed off, frustration tightening his mouth. Then, almost pleading, "What day is it?"

Something dropped in Morgan's chest, heavy and cold.

They answered him gently and stayed until Bram arrived, already assessing, already reaching for the kettle without asking questions. He handed Reed a cup of tea like it was the most natural thing in the world.

Morgan didn't linger.

They turned toward the grove near the boundary. The one no one had touched in weeks. The one that marked the edge not of town, but of agreement.

They didn't need proof yet. They trusted what they felt.

What was moving through Emerdeen wasn't loud. It didn't tear or burn or curse.

It eroded.

It scraped feeling off the edges of days. Made memory just a little harder to hold. Made presence flicker like a candle caught in a draft that never quite went out.

Emerdeen's magic had always been built on attention. On showing up. On remembering together.

And now, presence itself was beginning to slip.

Morgan quickened their pace.

The almosts had become too many to ignore.

Chapter Sixty-Five: Tuning the Thread

Baz's workshop looked like a place where a hedge witch and a radio engineer had been trapped together for days and decided to compromise.

Spools of copper wire sat beside bundles of mugwort. Circuit boards rested on top of cloth dyed with elderberry and salt. A soldering iron blinked patiently next to a teacup that someone, probably Cassie, had scrawled a protective rune on with a gold paint pen.

Fi stepped carefully between the chaos and tried not to knock over a tangle of string lights that may or may not have been enchanted.

"So," she said, crossing her arms, "this is what magic-tech synergy looks like."

Baz didn't look up from his work. "It looks like a mess because it is a mess. But it works."

She crouched beside him as he wrapped fine copper wire around a piece of river quartz. "How exactly is this going to 'listen' to the weave?"

"It's not listening in the way people expect," Baz said. "It's tuned to frequencies where energy gets weird. Like static that pulses between emotional spikes and memory decay."

"Sounds made up," Fi muttered.

"Most things worth doing do, at first."

He passed her a small ceramic disk etched with spirals (Cassie's handiwork), energized earlier that morning with a sun spell and a very serious chant that ended with her muttering about needing coffee.

Fi turned the disk over in her hands. "You're building this to track the spiral?"

Baz paused. "To track its echo. It's subtle. Like a thread that's been slowly unspooling while no one watches."

He glanced up at her, expression sober. "Don't be hypnotized by the complexity."

Fi raised an eyebrow. "What's that supposed to mean?"

"It means the spiral wants you to focus on its form; how intricate it is, how clever. But that's a trap. The danger isn't in how it looks. It's in what it undoes. One thread at a time."

Fi was quiet for a long moment, then said, "That's pretty poetic for a guy who swears at wires."

Baz smirked, tapping the quartz with a tuning fork. "Cassie's rubbing off on me."

They continued working in a rhythm that felt strangely comfortable. Fi wound thread through a copper ring, her fingers steadier than she expected. Baz adjusted the tuner array, splicing it to a shortwave transmitter he'd repurposed from an old ham radio.

"It should be able to pick up deviations in the natural weave," Baz explained. "If Amos's ritual is broadcasting a reversed spiral, this should find the frequency and anchor us to the right one."

"And if it doesn't?"

"Then we recalibrate. And maybe throw salt at something."

Fi nodded once. "Reasonable."

When they finished the first prototype, Baz turned a dial slowly. The faintest hum filled the room. Not noise, exactly. A presence. Like something searching for its own reflection in the dark.

They didn't speak. They didn't need to.

Because in that moment, they both understood: the spiral was already speaking.

But now, Emerdeen was finally listening back.

Chapter Sixty-Six: Following the Hollow

Morgan entered the grove the way one enters a conversation already in progress.

Slowly. Respectfully. Listening before speaking.

The trees stood in a loose circle here, their trunks older than the town's oldest buildings. Moss clung thickly to their roots, and the ground dipped just enough at the center that rainwater always gathered, even after long dry spells. It was a place people avoided without knowing why. Not out of fear, exactly. More out of instinct.

Morgan paused at the threshold and closed their eyes.

The numbness was stronger here.

Not painful. Not sharp. It pressed instead, like wool packed into the ears. Like trying to remember a word that stayed stubbornly out of reach. The weave still existed, but it felt dulled, as though something had wrapped itself around the threads and smothered their vibration.

"This is where you're thinning," Morgan murmured.

They knelt and pressed a palm flat to the earth.

The ground answered. Not with warmth, but with resistance.

Something had been laid here recently. It hadn't been buried, but impressed. A pattern pushed down into the soil and left to settle. Morgan followed the sensation inward, tracing the shape with their awareness instead of their eyes.

A spiral.

Reversed.

Morgan drew back sharply and stood.

"So that's how you're doing it," they said quietly. "You're not tearing the weave. You're convincing it to forget itself."

The grove shifted, leaves whispering uneasily.

Morgan moved deeper, careful with each step. They noticed signs others would miss. A fern that should have unfurled had remained tight. A stone that normally hummed faintly underfoot felt inert. Even the birds had gone silent, leaving the air strangely vacant.

They reached the center and stopped.

Here, the numbness pooled.

Morgan reached into their satchel and withdrew a small bundle of thread Bram had dyed with elderberry and ash. They looped it around their fingers, letting it brush the surface of the soil.

The thread did not glow.

That confirmed it.

"Not a curse," Morgan said. "Not a binding. A withdrawal."

They felt a flicker of anger then, sharp and unwelcome. Whoever had done this had not challenged the land. They had undermined it. Whispered doubt into its roots and called it righteousness.

Morgan exhaled and steadied themselves.

They could not confront this directly. Not yet. Force would only deepen the hollow. What was needed was mapping. Understanding. Witness.

They placed three small stones in a loose triangle; each etched with a listening sigil. Not to amplify power, but to record absence. To note where the weave grew thin and where it still held.

As they worked, Morgan felt the faintest tug at their awareness. Not from the grove, but from elsewhere. A ripple moving outward, slow and deliberate.

"Cassie," they whispered.

Whatever Amos had begun, it was spreading.

Morgan gathered the stones and retreated carefully, marking the path with quiet gestures meant only for the land to see.

At the edge of the grove, they turned back once.

"This place remembers how to heal," Morgan said firmly. "So do we."

Then they headed back toward town, already planning who needed to know first.

Because numbness was not emptiness.

It was a warning.

And now they had a direction.

Chapter Sixty-Seven: What Still Holds

Cassie was re-shelving jars when Morgan came in.

She didn't look up at first. She felt them before she saw them, the way she always did when Morgan carried something heavy. The air in the shop tightened slightly, like a held breath.

"You found it," Cassie said.

Morgan nodded and closed the door behind them, sliding the latch into place with care. "I found where it's pooling."

Cassie set the jar down slowly and turned. "The grove."

"Yes."

Morgan crossed the room and placed three small stones on the counter. They were dull, unremarkable to the eye, but Cassie felt the absence clinging to them the moment they touched the wood.

"He's using a reversed spiral," Morgan said. "Not to break the weave. To quiet it. To convince it to forget how to respond."

Cassie's jaw tightened. "That explains the numbness. Why people feel off but can't name it."

"He's not attacking Emerdeen," Morgan continued. "He's hollowing it. Making it doubt itself. If the land forgets how to hold, the wards won't fail. They'll simply stop mattering."

Cassie leaned back against the counter, thinking. "Which means brute force won't stop him."

"No," Morgan agreed. "If we push too hard, we risk reinforcing the hollow. He wants opposition. He wants proof that he's right about corruption."

Cassie huffed a quiet, humorless laugh. "Of course he does. Men like that always confuse resistance with validation."

They stood in silence for a moment, the shop creaking softly around them.

Then Cassie straightened. "So, we don't confront the spiral directly."

Morgan looked up. "We reinforce what it's trying to erase."

"Yes," Cassie said. "Presence. Memory. Choice. We remind the town why it belongs to itself."

Morgan's eyes sharpened. "Distributed anchors."

Cassie smiled faintly. "Exactly. Not one big ritual. Lots of small ones. Everyday magic. Meals shared. Stories told out loud. Touchstones that don't look like spells."

"And we map the hollow," Morgan added. "Quietly. Using listening wards, not barriers. We track where the numbness spreads and strengthen those places gently."

Cassie nodded. "Baz and Fi are already working on the listening ward. That will give us a center point. From there, we stitch outward."

Morgan hesitated. "There's something else."

Cassie waited.

"The grove resisted me," Morgan said. "Not fully. But enough that I know this isn't the first time. Amos has done this before. Somewhere else."

Cassie's expression softened, then hardened with resolve. "Then Emerdeen will be the place where it stops."

Morgan met her gaze. "We'll need everyone. Bram. Baz. Fi and Fox. Not all at once. But intentionally."

Cassie reached for the iron key she kept beneath the counter and wrapped her fingers around it. "I won't let him turn this into a war. But I will let it become a reckoning."

Morgan nodded. "Then we begin tonight."

Cassie tilted her head. "Dinner?"

Morgan smiled. "Dinner. Stories. Light in the windows. No secrecy. No fear."

Cassie exhaled, some of the tension leaving her shoulders. "You know, for someone trying to erase us, Amos picked the worst possible town."

Morgan glanced around the shop, at the jars and threads and quiet hum of things that remembered.

"Yes," they said. "He did."

Outside, the late afternoon sun dipped lower, and Emerdeen leaned toward evening.

Chapter Sixty-Eight: The Shape of His Faith

Amos lit the candle with a steady hand. The flame caught quickly, climbing the wick like it had been waiting. He watched it for a long moment, his lips moving silently as he counted his breaths. This part mattered. Control mattered. Precision mattered.

People assumed zealotry was loud.

It rarely was.

The ritual space was spare. No circles of salt. No offerings laid out with reverence. Just the objects he required, placed with intention. Ash from a burned chapel beam. The black glass shard. The linen strip marked with inked scripture, folded so tightly it creased.

He knelt and pressed his palm to the earth.

The land recoiled slightly.

Good, he thought. It still knows shame.

His mind drifted, as it often did during this phase, to the first time magic had lied to him.

It had been his sister.

Ash had been gentle, once. Curious. The kind of person who believed the world could be coaxed into kindness if you asked the right way. She had learned the names of plants and spoken to them like companions. She had lit candles and whispered promises over water and believed she was protecting their home.

She told him it was harmless. She told him it was healing. She told him God would understand.

Then came the sickness. The kind that did not show up on skin or bone, but in attention. Ash stopped listening to anyone who questioned her. Stopped eating. Stopped sleeping. She said the magic would hold her.

It did not.

When Ash collapsed, the candle burned on long after she stopped breathing.

Amos had stood in the doorway and watched the flame flicker.

It did not go out on its own.

He had blown it out himself.

From that moment, magic ceased to be mystery. It became seduction. A false promise that offered control and delivered chaos.

People said grief made him rigid.

They were wrong.

Grief made him focused.

He opened the book and read the passage he always read, not aloud but inwardly. Words about false prophets. About fires that tested truth. About cleansing the house so it would not fall.

He believed them.

He always had.

What others called spellwork, he called discipline. What others called intention, he called obedience. He did not see the contradiction in using ritual to dismantle ritual. To him, the power was not in the act. It was in who claimed the right to wield it.

Magic that named itself was blasphemy.

Magic that submitted was tool.

He drew the reversed spiral again, slower this time, deeper into the soil. The numbness spread outward in response, like frost along glass.

"Be revealed," he whispered. "Be emptied."

The land resisted, faintly.

Amos smiled.

Resistance meant it was working.

They would feel it soon. The doubt. The quiet second guessing. The sudden hesitation before reaching for what once felt natural.

And when they faltered, even briefly, he would step in.

Not as a destroyer.

As a savior.

He rose, brushing the dirt from his knees, and gathered his tools. The ritual would continue for another night. Perhaps two. He was patient.

Faith always outlasted beauty.

As he left the clearing, the candle guttered but did not go out.

And far away, in a town that refused to forget itself, the land gathered its memory like breath before speech.

Chapter Sixty-Nine: The Day That Slipped

The bell above the bakery door rang at eleven forty-two in the morning. That alone was strange.

The bakery never closed before three, not on weekdays, not on holidays, not even during storms. People planned their days around it. Coffee after errands. Bread before meetings. Cinnamon twists wrapped in wax paper for the walk home.

Cassie noticed the silence first.

She had been shelving jars when the absence pressed against her ribs. Not a sound, not a sensation. Just the sudden awareness that something habitual had gone missing.

She stepped outside the shop. The bakery windows were dark.

The sign was flipped to CLOSED, the chalk lettering neat and deliberate, as if it had always belonged there.

Cassie frowned and crossed the street.

Kara stood behind the counter, coat on, hands folded tightly around her purse. The trays behind her were still half full. Bread cooling where it always cooled. Rolls untouched.

"Kara?" Cassie said gently. "Everything okay?"

Kara blinked at her, as if the name had to travel a long way to reach her. "I just felt like I should close."

Cassie did not miss the flatness in her voice.

"Did something happen?" Cassie asked.

Kara shook her head. "No. Nothing. I just couldn't remember why I was supposed to stay open."

Cassie's chest tightened.

"You've been opening this shop every morning for twelve years," Cassie said carefully. "You bless the ovens before the first loaf. You hum while the dough rises."

Kara's brow furrowed. "I do?"

"Yes," Cassie said. "You always say it helps the bread remember what it's meant to be."

Kara stared at the counter. Her fingers flexed once, sharply. "That sounds... silly."

The word landed wrong. Cassie felt it in her bones.

"Silly isn't the word you use," Cassie said.

Kara's jaw set. "Maybe I've just been indulging nonsense for too long."

There was no anger in her voice. No fear.

Only rigidity.

Cassie glanced around the shop. The air felt dull, like felt laid over sound. Even the yeast smelled muted.

"Kara," Cassie said, grounding her voice. "Go sit. Don't lock the door yet."

Kara hesitated, then obeyed, sinking into the chair behind the counter like someone relieved to stop pretending they knew what they were doing.

Cassie stepped outside and inhaled deeply.

Across the street, Old Reed argued with a lamppost.

Not loudly. Just firmly. As if it had personally disappointed him.

Down the block, a couple who had walked hand in hand for years stood facing opposite directions, neither speaking.

This was not chaos.

This was forgetting.

Cassie turned and nearly collided with Morgan.

They took one look at her face and said, "It's spreading."

Cassie nodded. "It's not erasing memory completely. It's hollowing meaning. Rituals without explanation feel unnecessary. Care becomes indulgence. Familiar becomes foolish."

Morgan's hands curled slowly into fists. "The reversed spiral is accelerating."

"And it's smart," Cassie added. "It's not attacking belief. It's attacking reason for belief."

Morgan glanced back at the bakery. "If people decide their rituals are pointless, they'll abandon them willingly."

"Yes," Cassie said. "And they'll call it clarity."

They stood together in the street as the town continued around them, slightly off rhythm, like a song played half a beat too slow.

"We need to counter this now," Morgan said. "Before it feels normal."

Cassie looked at the bakery door, still unlocked.

"Tonight," she said. "We gather people. Not for magic. For memory."

Morgan nodded. "Food. Stories. Shared work."

"And light," Cassie added. "Every window."

Across the street, Kara stood and slowly flipped the sign back to OPEN.

She looked confused. But she stayed.

For now.

And that was enough to know the line had not fully broken.

Yet.

Chapter Seventy: The Needle Jumps

Baz was halfway through convincing himself the listening ward was working exactly as intended when the needle slammed to the right.

Not drifted. Not wavered.

Jumped.

The meter on the repurposed radio rig let out a sharp click, followed by a low, sustained hum that vibrated through the worktable and straight into his bones.

Baz froze.

"Okay," he said aloud, because silence felt like a bad idea. "That's new."

He leaned closer, careful not to touch anything yet. The copper coils Cassie had threaded with rosemary fiber glowed faintly, not with light exactly, but with presence. The quartz core hummed like it was trying to remember a song it had never learned.

The needle trembled again.

Then steadied.

Dead center.

Baz swallowed.

The ward was not picking up noise. It was picking up absence.

He reached for the notebook he had been pretending was just for diagrams and started writing fast.

Time: 2:14 p.m.
Location bias: North-northeast
Signal type: Sustained null

A null meant something was actively canceling signal. Not overpowering it. Not scrambling it. Just flattening it. Like white noise, but deliberate.

"Don't be hypnotized by the complexity," he muttered, hearing his own words thrown back at him.

He adjusted the tuner slowly; fingers light on the dial. As he shifted frequencies, the hum deepened, resolving into a pattern that made the hair on his arms lift.

There it was.

A pulse.

Regular. Measured. Almost patient.

Baz leaned back in his chair and let out a breath. "You've got to be kidding me."

The pulse aligned perfectly with the reversed spiral Cassie had sketched earlier that morning.

Same rhythm. Same cadence. Same quiet insistence.

The ward wasn't just detecting it.

It was syncing.

"Nope," Baz said, and slapped the grounding switch hard.

The hum cut out instantly. The needle snapped back to zero.

Baz sat there for a long moment, heart racing, palms damp.

Then he laughed once, sharp and incredulous.

"Oh, you sneaky bastard," he said to no one in particular.

He stood and paced the room, running both hands through his hair.

This wasn't theoretical anymore.

The spiral wasn't just a ritual sitting in a clearing somewhere. It was broadcasting. Leaking into the town's rhythms, slipping into habits and hesitations and the quiet decisions people made when no one was watching.

And now they had proof.

Baz flipped the rig back on, this time with the grounding loop partially engaged. The needle twitched but did not spike.

Good.

He scribbled another note.

Containment possible with counter-frequency.
Requires anchor points. Multiple. Human-scale.

Human-scale.

That was the key.

You couldn't out-shout a thing like this. You had to out-belong it.

Baz grabbed his jacket and headed for the door, nearly colliding with Fi on the way in.

"You felt it too?" she asked.

"The ward spiked," he said. "Hard. We're not imagining this anymore."

Fi's face tightened. "Cassie needs to know."

"So does Morgan," Baz replied. "And we need to move fast."

Fi glanced back toward the house, then met his eyes. "How bad is it?"

Baz hesitated.

Then chose honesty.

"It's not destroying anything yet," he said. "It's just… convincing the town to let go."

Fi nodded slowly. "That tracks."

Baz grabbed the notebook and tapped it against his palm. "The good news is, we can hear it now. Which means we can answer it."

"And the bad news?"

Baz opened the door.

"It knows we're listening."

Behind them, the listening ward gave one soft click.

Not a spike.

A response.

Chapter Seventy-One: When the Doors Stay Open

Cassie did not ring a bell.

She did not light candles in the street or carve sigils into the pavement. She did not call it a gathering, a ritual, or anything that might make people hesitate.

She simply opened the doors.

The shop doors went first, propped wide despite the chill that had settled into the late afternoon. Then she crossed the street and knocked on the bakery window, gently, until Kara looked up.

"Stay open tonight," Cassie said through the glass. "You don't have to do anything special. Just be here."

Kara hesitated, then nodded.

Cassie moved down the block, stopping at the café, the post office, the bookstore. She didn't explain. She didn't warn. She didn't say something is wrong.

She said things like:

"Come sit for a while."
"Bring something warm."
"Don't rush home tonight."

Most people didn't question it.

A few almost did, then stopped, as if the question slid away before it could fully form.

By dusk, light had begun to gather in the windows along Main Street. Not coordinated. Not dramatic. Just present. Lamps turned on earlier than usual. Doors left ajar. The sound of voices drifting out instead of being sealed in.

Cassie stood in the middle of it; hands wrapped around a mug she hadn't realized she'd poured.

Morgan appeared at her side, quiet as breath. "The numbness is resisting."

Cassie nodded. "Good. That means it can still feel us pushing back."

"What if he interferes?" Morgan asked.

Cassie smiled faintly. "Then he'll have to explain why he's afraid of people sharing soup."

At the edge of the street, Bram set up a long wooden table and began laying out bread, herbs, jars of honey. No ceremony. Just food. Old Reed wandered over and sat down without being asked.

Fi and Fox arrived next, carrying bowls and mismatched utensils. Fox paused, scanning the street.

"This feels… intentional," he said.

"It is," Cassie replied. "But it's not magic in the way Amos understands it."

People began to drift closer, drawn not by announcement but by gravity. Someone started telling a story about a storm years ago. Someone else laughed too loudly, then laughed again when it didn't feel wrong.

Cassie cleared her throat once.

No one shushed her.

She didn't raise her voice.

"I don't have a speech," she said. "I just didn't want anyone eating alone tonight."

There was a murmur of agreement. A clink of mugs. The scrape of chairs being pulled closer.

Cassie felt it then.

Not the weave.

The weight.

The collective presence of people choosing to stay instead of retreat. Choosing familiarity over isolation. Choosing each other without knowing why it mattered.

She caught Morgan's eye across the street.

The hollow was thinning.

Somewhere beyond the lights, beyond the town's edge, something strained against its own certainty.

Cassie lifted her mug. "To Emerdeen," she said simply.

The reply came not as a cheer, but as a chorus of quiet affirmations. Nods. Smiles. The sound of a town remembering itself in real time.

And far away, in a clearing where silence had been carefully cultivated, the spiral faltered.

Not broken.

But challenged.

And that was enough to change everything.

Chapter Seventy-Two: The Silence Pushes Back

Amos felt it like grit between his teeth.

Not pain.
Not fear.

Resistance.

He had returned to the clearing before nightfall, earlier than planned, compelled by an unease he did not name. The reversed spiral lay etched into the soil exactly as he had left it, the lines sharp, obedient, drawing the land inward toward stillness.

But the air was no longer compliant.

He knelt and placed his palm to the earth.

The numbness was thinner.

Interrupted.

Something was interfering with the quiet he had so carefully cultivated. The hollow had not spread the way it should have. Instead of deepening, it felt… crowded. Pressed upon from the inside.

Amos drew back sharply.

"No," he said aloud.

He reached for the black glass shard and held it up, angling it toward the trees. The surface should have swallowed the light. Instead, it shimmered faintly, as if struggling to maintain its emptiness.

That was not possible.

The ritual had been precise. The cadence correct. The scripture aligned. He had followed every step exactly as he always had.

And yet—

Voices.

Not here, but nearby. Too many of them. Overlapping. The low, constant murmur of people gathered together without fear or permission.

Amos stood.

"They should be doubting," he muttered. "They should be hesitating."

Instead, the land vibrated faintly beneath his boots. Not with magic in the way he despised it, but with something far more dangerous.

Belonging.

He closed his eyes and focused, extending his awareness outward, searching for the familiar drift of detachment, the subtle surrender of meaning. He found pockets of it still clinging to the edges of town, but at the center, something had flared.

Light.

Windows. Voices. Shared breath.

Someone had answered the silence.

Amos's jaw tightened.

"So," he said softly, "you've noticed."

He paced the perimeter of the spiral, boots disturbing the soil for the first time. The ritual resisted him now, the lines less eager to obey. The land had begun to remember itself, and memory was stubborn.

He pressed his heel down hard at the spiral's center.

The pulse wavered.

But did not collapse.

"Clever," he admitted. "You didn't confront it. You drowned it."

Food. Stories. Togetherness. Small rituals hidden inside ordinary choices.

They were not fighting him with force.

They were starving him of isolation.

Amos laughed once, quietly. There was no humor in it.

"Fine," he said. "If you insist on staying awake, then I will give you something clearer to see."

He gathered his tools with sharp, efficient movements. The spiral would hold, for now. But he would adjust. Refine. Shift from erosion to revelation.

He would make the town choose.

Faith thrived on contrast.

And Emerdeen had not yet been tested by fire.

As he stepped away from the clearing, the land shuddered—not in fear, but in warning.

Amos smiled.

"Good," he said. "Now it matters."

Behind him, the spiral pulsed once more, no longer alone.

Detected.

Answered.

And no longer inevitable.

Chapter Seventy-Three: Resonance

Fi did not intend to touch the dial.

She had come into Baz's workspace only to check on the rig, to make sure it was still grounded the way he insisted it had to be. The room hummed faintly, a low sound you felt more than heard, like a refrigerator working too hard in the next room.

The needle was steady.

That alone made her uneasy. She leaned closer, reading the notes Baz had taped along the edge of the table. Handwritten labels. Frequencies. Warnings.

Anchor engaged.
Human scale only.
Do not amplify.

Her fingers hovered. The hum shifted.

It was not louder. It was clearer.

Fi inhaled sharply and froze.

The counter frequency did not feel like sound. It felt like recognition. Like a pressure behind her eyes and a sudden tightening in her chest that had nothing to do with fear.

She saw the house.

Not as it was now, but as it had been when Thea first sealed it. Windows open. Floors bare. The smell of lemon oil and wet earth. Her aunt standing in the center of the living room with her hands pressed flat to the wall, listening.

Then the image fractured.

The reversed spiral pressed in, trying to quiet the memory, trying to convince it that it had never mattered. That care was excess. That belief was indulgence.

Fi gasped. Her hand landed on the dial.

The needle jumped.

The hum snapped into alignment, not louder but deeper, threading itself through her like a tuning fork struck against bone.

"No," she whispered, not to the rig, but to the feeling that tried to flatten her thoughts. "You do not get to tell me what mattered."

The counter frequency surged.

Not outward.

Inward.

Fi staggered back against the table, heart racing, breath uneven. Images flashed through her mind in quick succession. Kara's bakery at dawn. Fox laughing on the porch despite himself. Cassie standing in the street with a mug in her hands, refusing to call it a ritual.

Presence. Meaning. Choice.

The numbness recoiled.

Not violently. Not angrily.

It thinned.

The rig gave a single sharp click and then steadied, the needle settling just left of center, vibrating softly.

Fi slid down onto the chair, hands trembling.

"What the hell was that" she breathed.

The door creaked open.

Baz froze in the doorway when he saw her face. "Fi. Did you touch it?"

She nodded, once.

"I didn't amplify," she said quickly. "I didn't push. I just listened back."

Baz crossed the room in three long strides and checked the grounding loop, then the tuner, then the notes. Everything was stable.

Too stable.

"That's not possible," he muttered. "It should not have synced to you."

Fi looked up at him, eyes bright and shaken. "It did not sync to me. It recognized me."

Baz went very still.

"You are part of the anchor," he said slowly.

Fi swallowed. "So is the house. So is the memory he is trying to erase."

Baz exhaled, something between awe and fear. "That means the counter frequency is not just a signal. It is a relationship."

"Yes," Fi said. "And he underestimated that."

The rig hummed again, softer this time.

Not a warning.

An answer.

Fi closed her eyes and pressed her palms to the tabletop, grounding herself in the solid wood, the very real room around her.

"We can hold this," she said. "But not alone. It needs witnesses. It needs people who remember on purpose."

Baz nodded. "Then we build anchors everywhere he tried to hollow."

Fi stood, steadier now.

"And we start with the house," she said. "Because it already knows how to refuse him."

Outside, the evening deepened.

And for the first time since Amos began his quiet unmaking, the numbness did not spread.

It retreated. Just a little.

Enough to prove it could.

Chapter Seventy-Four: The Missing Thread

Fi did not tell Fox everything at once. She told him enough to make him sit down.

They were in the back room of the house, the one that still smelled faintly of cedar no matter how many windows were opened. The listening ward hummed quietly from the other side of the wall, subdued now, like a cat that had finally settled.

"I touched the rig," Fi said. "Not on purpose."

Fox stared at her. "You touched the thing everyone told you not to touch."

"Yes," she said. "But not recklessly. It… responded."

He waited.

She explained what she could. The way the hum had aligned with her breath. The images of the house as it had been. The sensation of being recognized instead of overwhelmed.

Fox leaned back in his chair; hands folded behind his head.

"So, you tuned into a magical frequency, and it decided you were authorized," he said flatly.

"When you say it like that, it sounds irresponsible."

"It sounds impossible," he replied. "Which is somehow worse."

Fi smiled faintly, then sobered. "It wasn't about me. It was about memory. About refusing to let something else define what mattered."

Fox's gaze sharpened. "And Amos hates that."

"Yes."

They sat in silence for a moment, the house creaking softly around them.

Fox broke it. "This doesn't start with us, does it."

Fi shook her head. "No. It starts with Thea. And before that, I think, with him."

She reached for one of the journals and flipped it open, stopping at a page marked with a dried marigold.

"She wrote about a man who came through once," Fi said. "Not by name. But by behavior. She called him a corrector."

Fox snorted. "That tracks."

"She said he spoke in scripture and certainty. That he believed the land needed discipline. That he accused her of misleading people."

Fox's jaw tightened. "And she sealed something after that."

"Yes. Not to trap him. To protect what he was trying to erase."

Fox leaned forward. "Us."

Fi nodded slowly. "Or what we would become."

He exhaled through his nose. "So, this guy didn't just wander into Emerdeen. He has history here. With our aunt. With this house."

"And maybe with our parents," Fi added quietly.

Fox stilled. "What do you mean."

"I remembered him from when I was a kid. But I don't remember why we never talked about it. Why we stopped visiting for so long."

Fox frowned. "We left fast. I always thought it was about money."

Fi shook her head. "No. It was fear. But not of magic. Of him."

Fox stared at the floor, memory clicking into place. "I remember a fight. Mom and Thea yelling in the driveway. Something about safety. About not opening doors."

Fi closed the journal. "I think Amos tried to force something open here once. And Thea stopped him. Or slowed him. And now he's back to finish it."

Fox ran a hand through his hair. "Using faith as a weapon. Again."

Fi met his eyes. "Which means whatever he wants is still sealed. And whatever it is, it involves us whether we like it or not."

Fox nodded slowly. "Then we stop pretending we're just visitors."

Fi's voice was steady. "We never were."

They sat together, the house warm and listening.

And beneath the floorboards, something old and patient waited.

Not to be opened.

But to be understood.

Chapter Seventy-Five: The House That Refused Him

Amos did not approach the Carrow house directly.

He circled it first, walking the long way around the block, letting his steps fall into the rhythm he preferred. Measured. Observant. Patient. The house sat quietly at the end of the street, its windows dark but not empty, as if it were holding its breath.

It always had.

He stopped at the fence line and studied it, jaw tight.

Some places bent easily. Others resisted at first and then broke. This one had done neither. It had absorbed his presence once and then closed itself, not violently, not dramatically, but with resolve.

He remembered that.

He had not meant to come back to Emerdeen for this house. Not consciously. He told himself the town was the problem. The indulgence. The unchecked belief. The way magic had been allowed to nest and grow.

But the spiral had pointed him here repeatedly. As if the land itself knew where the fault line ran.

"You won't stay hidden forever," Amos murmured.

"Talking to buildings again?"

Amos turned sharply.

Morgan stood a few yards away, hands loose at their sides, posture open but not unguarded. They were dressed for the greenhouse, soil still clinging to their cuffs, the scent of crushed leaves faint in the air.

Amos recovered quickly. "I find it useful to understand what people choose to protect."

Morgan tilted their head. "That house has been protecting itself longer than you have been asking questions."

Amos's lips pressed thin. "That house is a problem."

"Because it holds memory," Morgan said calmly. "Or because it refused you?"

The words landed closer than Amos liked.

He straightened. "It was sealed improperly."

Morgan raised an eyebrow. "Improperly according to whom."

"According to order," Amos replied. "According to design. According to what is permitted."

Morgan stepped closer, not threatening, just present. "You have a habit of confusing permission with righteousness."

Amos's gaze flicked to the windows. "The woman who lived here interfered. She used magic to obstruct truth."

"Thea Carrow preserved something," Morgan corrected. "There is a difference."

"She chose what people were allowed to know," Amos snapped. "She decided which doors stayed closed."

"Yes," Morgan said. "Because some doors open into harm."

Amos laughed, sharp and humorless. "That is exactly what my sister said."

The words were out before he could stop them.

Morgan's eyes softened, just slightly. "And what happened to her."

Amos inhaled, then exhaled through his nose. "She trusted the wrong voice. She believed intention was enough. She died because no one told her no."

Morgan nodded slowly. "So, you made it your mission to become the no."

Amos bristled. "Someone had to."

"And the Carrow house," Morgan said gently, "stood in your way."

Amos did not answer immediately.

He looked at the fence again, at the way the ivy grew thickest near the foundation, at the subtle curve of the porch rail that suggested careful hands and long memory.

"She bound something here," he said finally. "Something that should not have been allowed to persist."

Morgan did not ask what.

They already knew the answer was not simple.

"And now," Morgan said, "you believe if you unravel the town, the house will open."

Amos's silence was confirmation enough.

Morgan crossed their arms. "You are wrong about Emerdeen. And you are wrong about that house."

Amos met their gaze, eyes bright with conviction. "We will see."

Morgan shook their head. "No. We will remember."

They turned and walked away, not rushing, not looking back.

Amos stood alone again at the fence line, the house unmoved by his scrutiny.

For the first time since his return, doubt flickered. Not about his cause, but about his certainty.

Because the house had not weakened.

It had waited.

And now, he suspected, it was no longer waiting alone.

Chapter Seventy-Six: What Was Interrupted

Morgan found Cassie and Fi in the back of the shop, surrounded by journals, loose pages, and one very judgmental teacup.

Cassie looked up first. "Please tell me you've come bearing clarity and not more ominous half sentences."

"I have context," Morgan said. "Which may or may not feel worse at first."

Fi straightened. "Start talking."

Morgan set their bag down and leaned against the table. "Amos knows the Carrow house. Not abstractly. Personally. He tried to open it once before."

Cassie's expression sharpened. "Tried and failed?"

"Yes."

Cassie smiled faintly. "Good. I like a man with a history of losing."

Fi folded her arms. "He told you this."

"Not intentionally," Morgan said. "But he talked about Thea. About interference. About something she sealed that he believed had no right to exist."

Cassie's fingers stilled on the edge of a journal. "Something or someone."

Fi inhaled slowly. "Ash."

Morgan nodded.

The name settled into the room like a held breath finally released.

Cassie reached for another journal and flipped quickly, practiced now at finding what mattered. "There are gaps," she said. "Years where Thea writes around a person without naming them. References to shared work. Shared grief. Shared laughter."

Fi's voice was quieter. "She stopped writing altogether for a while. Right after the incident with Amos."

Morgan watched Fi carefully. "You knew Ash."

Fi nodded. "Not well. But enough. They were around when I was little. I remember warmth. Music. Someone who listened without correcting."

Cassie glanced up. "That tracks. Amos strikes me as deeply allergic to joy."

Fi gave a weak smile.

Morgan continued. "Amos talked about his sister. About losing her. About deciding that magic was the enemy rather than grief."

Cassie snorted. "A classic misdiagnosis. Happens all the time."

Fi looked between them. "So, Thea and Ash were more than friends."

Cassie tilted her head. "I would say yes. And I would say it mattered."

Morgan nodded. "Enough that Amos tried to intervene. Enough that he decided Thea was dangerous."

"And enough," Cassie added, "that Thea chose the house over him."

Fi swallowed. "She sealed something to protect Ash."

"Or to protect the choice they made," Morgan said. "Which Amos could not tolerate."

Cassie leaned back in her chair and crossed her arms. "So let me summarize. We have a man who confuses control with virtue, shows up years later with a reversed spiral, and is deeply offended by a house that remembers love."

Fi huffed a quiet laugh. "When you put it like that."

"I always do," Cassie said. "It's a gift."

The humor faded, replaced by something steadier.

Fi looked down at the journal. "So, what is actually sealed."

Cassie met Morgan's eyes. "Not a weapon. Not a curse."

"A promise," Morgan said. "A truth that refuses to be disciplined into silence."

Fi nodded slowly. "And Amos believes if he hollows the town enough, the house will be forced to open."

Cassie stood. "Which means we stop playing defense."

Morgan raised an eyebrow. "You have a plan."

Cassie smiled. "I always do. It just improves with company."

Fi looked up. "What kind of plan."

"The kind," Cassie said, "where instead of hiding what was interrupted, we finish it."

Morgan exhaled. "You want to complete whatever Thea and Ash began."

"Yes," Cassie replied. "On our terms. In the open. With witnesses."

Fi straightened, resolve settling into her posture. "Then I'm in."

Morgan nodded. "So am I."

Cassie gathered the journals into a neat stack and tapped them once on the table. "Excellent. Because if Amos thinks he's the only one allowed to bring the past into the present, he's about to be very disappointed."

She paused, then added, "Also, if he tries to lecture me about morality, I will absolutely interrupt him."

Fi smiled for the first time in hours.

Outside, the town continued to glow with quiet light.

And somewhere beneath the Carrow house, something old and unfinished stirred.

Not in fear.

But in readiness.

Chapter Seventy-Seven: Where Sparks Gather

Baz smelled it before he saw it. Not smoke. Not exactly.

Heat.

The listening ward had settled into a steady rhythm after Fi's contact, a low hum that felt almost companionable. Baz had been monitoring the readings, jotting down notes, recalibrating small things that did not matter until they suddenly did.

The copper coil twitched.

Baz frowned.

"That's new," he muttered.

He leaned in, checking the grounding loop first. Still intact. The quartz core pulsed once, brighter than before, then dimmed. The meter needle wavered, not spiking this time, but dragging. Like something pulling current through a space not designed to hold it.

Baz's stomach tightened.

"No no no," he said quietly.

He followed the line of wire back toward the junction point where magic and circuitry met. Cassie's threading was still perfect. Fi's anchor loop still held. But the energy was not staying contained. The counter frequency was doing its job too well. It was amplifying presence faster than the system could disperse it.

Baz touched the table and yanked his hand back.

Hot.

"Damn it."

This was the problem with hybrid systems. Magic flowed where it was welcomed. Electricity flowed where it was forced. When they aligned too closely, the margin for error vanished.

Baz flipped the rig off and the hum cut out, but the heat did not dissipate.

Instead, it spread.

The rosemary fiber began to smolder.

Baz swore and grabbed the fire blanket from the wall, smothering the coil just as a thin ribbon of smoke curled upward. He stood there for a long second, heart pounding, staring at the scorched edge of the table.

Fire.

Not symbolic. Not ritual.

Real.

And if the ward overloaded again, it would not stop at the workbench. It would follow the threads.

To the shop. To the Carrow house. To the grove where the spiral strained against resistance.

Baz straightened, adrenaline sharp and clear.

This was not an accident.

The reversed spiral was pushing back. Meeting amplification with pressure. Turning connection into friction.

"Okay," Baz said aloud, steadying himself. "So, this is how you want to play it."

He grabbed his notebook and flipped to a fresh page.

Risk: thermal cascade across anchored nodes.
Trigger: sustained counter frequency without dispersal.

In plain terms, they were creating too much resonance in too small a space. Which meant the solution was not to shut it down.

It was to spread it out.

Baz grabbed his jacket and headed for the door, already running the map through his head. The house. The shop. The grove. People gathering. Lights on. Stories told.

Every thread was already live.

If the energy had nowhere to go, it would burn.

But if it moved through the town, through shared presence instead of concentrated machinery, it could ground itself safely.

Baz paused at the threshold, glancing back at the singed table.

"This is going to get dramatic," he said.

He stepped into the night, moving fast now. Because fire did not wait for permission.

And if they did not act soon, Amos would not be the only one who learned what happened when belief met heat.

Everything was coming together.

Whether they were ready or not.

Chapter Seventy-Eight: Fire, Contained

Baz did not knock. He hit the door with his shoulder hard enough to make the bell above it jingle in protest, then caught himself before he took the whole frame with him. Cassie looked up from the back table where she and Morgan had been sorting journals into neat, angry stacks.

"Either you are dying," Cassie said, "or you found something that wants to kill us."

Baz held up his notebook like evidence in a trial. His face was pale in the lamplight. "Both, potentially."

Morgan was already moving, crossing the room with that quiet urgency they got when the weave was shifting beneath their feet. "Talk."

Baz took one breath, then another, like he was trying to keep his lungs from making this dramatic. "The listening ward almost ignited. It is not just a machine problem. The counter frequency is building heat. If we keep amplifying presence through a concentrated node, it can cascade across any anchored points."

Cassie blinked once. "Translate."

Baz met her eyes. "If we keep doing what we are doing, we could accidentally burn down half the town."

Cassie stared at him for a long, flat second.

Then she said, "I was hoping for a normal Tuesday where our biggest problem was someone mislabeling lavender as lilac."

Baz did not laugh. He wished he could have.

Morgan's voice stayed calm. "Why now."

"Pressure," Baz said. "The reversed spiral is pushing back. It is meeting resonance with friction. It is turning connection into heat."

Cassie exhaled slowly through her nose, the way she did when she was deciding whether to panic or plan. She chose plan.

"Okay," she said. "So, we stop amplifying."

Baz shook his head. "If we shut down completely, the spiral wins. We lose the signal and the town keeps slipping into numbness."

Cassie nodded. "Then we do something that feels insane but is actually practical."

Morgan's eyebrows rose. "Go on."

"We disperse it," Cassie said. "We stop trying to hold presence in one box of copper and quartz and instead spread it through the town like a network. Human scale. Multiple anchors. A lot of small, grounded points."

Baz stared at her. "That is literally what my notes say."

Cassie gave him a look. "Yes. Because I also have notes. They are just in my head and occasionally on napkins."

Morgan leaned in slightly. "If we disperse it, where does the energy go."

Cassie lifted her mug. "Into the places already awake. Into the windows that are lit. Into the people who are choosing to be together."

Baz frowned. "That still risks ignition if any one point overheats."

Cassie nodded. "Which is why we do not hide in our houses tonight. We do not isolate. We keep doors open, air moving, people moving."

Morgan caught the shape of it and their posture shifted. "You are talking about building a living circuit."

"Yes," Cassie said. "A closed loop of presence. A pattern that cannot be hollowed because it is constantly witnessed."

Baz swallowed. "Cassie, this is going to feel like a ritual."

Cassie lifted an eyebrow. "Everything is a ritual if you do it on purpose. Tonight, we just do it with soup and stubbornness."

She was already moving, grabbing a basket from under the counter. She started filling it with small objects. Candles. Matches. A pouch of salt. A jar of honey. Not for show, but for touchstones.

Morgan reached for their coat. "We should warn Fi and Fox."

Cassie pointed at Baz's notebook. "You are going to take that to Kara and Bram. Tell them not to close. Tell them to keep water nearby. Not because we are expecting flames, but because we are refusing surprises."

Baz nodded, then hesitated. "If this goes wrong—"

Cassie stepped closer, her voice dropping. "It will not. Because we are not going to do it alone. And because we are not going to do it scared."

Morgan's gaze flicked to the door. "We need to include the Carrow house."

Cassie stilled for half a beat. "Yes."

Baz's mouth tightened. "That is the most anchored point we have. It is also the most targeted."

Cassie nodded. "Which means it is the safest place to ground the excess, if the house is willing."

Morgan's eyes sharpened. "The house is already willing. It has been waiting."

Cassie's expression softened, then hardened into resolve. "Then we go there first."

They left the shop with purpose, not haste. Cassie did not run, because running made fear contagious. She walked like she owned the night.

When they reached the Carrow house, the porch light was already on. Fi opened the door before Cassie could lift her hand.

"I felt it," Fi said, voice tight. "The frequency rose and then snapped."

Baz nodded. "It almost burned."

Fox appeared behind her, eyes narrowed. "You mean the zealot is turning the town into a toaster."

Cassie pointed at him. "Yes. And I appreciate the clarity."

Fi stepped aside. "Come in."

The house felt different than the shop. The shop held warmth like a hearth. The Carrow house held it like a promise.

Cassie stood in the entryway and closed her eyes. She did not reach for the weave the way she usually did. She listened for the house itself.

The walls creaked softly, settling.

The air moved, subtle but present.

Morgan murmured, "It knows we are here."

Baz swallowed. "We need it to help us disperse the load. If the house can act as a grounding anchor, it can pull the excess into the structure and release it safely."

Fox frowned. "You are proposing we use the house like a lightning rod."

Baz nodded. "Yes. But for memory."

Fi placed her palm on the doorframe. "It already does that."

Cassie opened her eyes and spoke to the room in the simplest language she had.

"We are not here to force you," she said quietly. "We are here to ask. Will you help us hold."

The house answered.

Not with words.

With a breath.

A gentle shift of air that moved through the hallway and out the back door that had been cracked open, as if the house were creating its own draft, its own path for heat to travel.

Baz let out the breath he had been holding. "It is opening a flow."

Morgan's face softened. "It is choosing."

Cassie's smile was small and fierce. "Good. Because I have been in enough buildings with opinions to know when one is cooperating."

Fi's eyes shone, unsettled and awed. "So, what now."

Cassie turned to them all. "Now we do what Amos cannot comprehend."

She lifted the basket slightly. "We gather the town, keep the doors open, and we tell stories that cannot be edited by silence."

Fox snorted. "I hate that I am living inside a metaphor."

Cassie smiled at him. "You are not. You are living inside a plan. Try to keep up."

Outside, the wind picked up. The porch light flickered once, then steadied.

And somewhere beyond the boundary stones, a reversed spiral pressed outward and met something it had not planned for.

A town refusing to close its doors.

Chapter Seventy-Nine: The Living Circuit

By the time twilight settled over Emerdeen, the town had already begun to rearrange itself.

Not because anyone announced an emergency. Not because sirens sounded or bells rang. It happened the way Emerdeen always did things. Through suggestion. Through habit. Through someone saying, "You might want to leave that open," and another person deciding it felt right to listen.

Cassie stood at the center of Main Street with a notebook tucked under her arm and a mug in her hand that had gone cold an hour ago.

"Open doors," she called, not loudly, just enough to carry. "Open windows if you can. Water on every table. If you have candles, great. If you don't, lamps work just fine. This is not a performance."

A few people laughed, the tension easing.

"It's more of a vibe," Cassie added. "Please hydrate accordingly."

That got a real laugh.

She moved from group to group, steady and visible, assigning nothing that felt mystical. Just practical adjustments. Chairs pulled closer together. Walkways cleared. Porch lights turned on earlier than usual.

People complied because it made sense, even if they could not explain why.

Morgan moved along the edges, quieter, eyes half unfocused as they tracked something deeper than foot traffic. They paused at corners where the air felt heavier, where conversations stalled or tempers flared for no reason. With a small stone placed here, a hand to a shoulder there, they marked the places where the numbness still clung.

"Hotspot by the post office," Morgan murmured into the small receiver Baz had given them. "It's thinning but not gone."

Baz's voice crackled back, controlled and focused. "Copy. Keep it gentle. We are dispersing, not correcting."

Baz stood near the bakery, his repurposed rig now broken into smaller units, each one barely humming. No spikes. No amplification. Just a low, steady pulse spread across the street like a heartbeat you had to lean in to feel.

He watched the meters carefully.

The needle stayed calm.

That was everything.

At the Carrow house, Fi stood in the doorway with her palms resting lightly against the frame. The front and back doors were both open, creating a slow, deliberate current through the hall. Curtains stirred. The air moved.

Fox hovered nearby, pretending he was not paying attention while paying attention to everything.

"You are sure this is safe," he said, for the third time.

Fi smiled faintly. "No. But I am sure the house knows what it is doing."

The floor beneath their feet warmed slightly, not hot, just alive. The house responded to the flow of people, to the sound of voices drifting in from the street, to the quiet laughter that carried through the open windows.

Fi closed her eyes and breathed.

The counter frequency threaded through her, not overwhelming, not demanding. It recognized her again, the way it had earlier, like a familiar hand at her back.

She did not push. She held.

Fox watched her shoulders settle, the tension easing. "You are acting like a conduit."

"I am," Fi said. "So are you."

He scoffed. "I am aggressively unqualified."

"And yet," she replied, opening her eyes, "here you are."

Outside, tables filled. Someone passed around a basket of bread. Children darted between adults, carrying cups of water like it was a game with very serious rules.

Cassie paused at the edge of the crowd and took it in.

This was the circuit.

Not wires. Not sigils.

People choosing to remain present. Choosing not to retreat inward when discomfort brushed against them. Choosing to stay connected.

She caught Morgan's eye across the street. They nodded once.

The hollow was not spreading.

It was thinning.

Baz's rig clicked softly, not in alarm but acknowledgment. The readings evened out, the excess energy bleeding harmlessly into warmth, into light, into the simple fact of people being together.

Cassie let out a breath she had been holding since before dusk.

"Okay," she muttered to herself. "We are doing this."

No one in Emerdeen would later say they had participated in a ritual that night.

They would say things like, "I don't know. It just felt wrong to go home."

Or "I stayed because someone asked me to."

Or "The bread was good."

But the weave knew better.

And somewhere beyond the glow of the town, a spiral strained against a pattern it could not hollow.

Because it had underestimated one thing.

Emerdeen did not protect itself with secrecy.

It protected itself by staying open.

Chapter Eighty: The Sermon in the Street

Amos stepped into the light as though it had been waiting for him.

He did not arrive with spectacle. No raised voice. No dramatic gesture to announce himself. He simply moved into the space where people had gathered, hands folded loosely at his sides, his posture calm enough to be mistaken for kindness.

The street quieted without instruction.

Cassie felt it before she saw him, the way attention shifted toward certainty like iron filings toward a magnet. The numbness had not vanished completely. It lingered in people's bones, making clarity feel like relief rather than danger.

Amos let the silence stretch.

"My friends," he said finally, voice smooth and measured. "I can see you are uncomfortable."

A few heads nodded.

He smiled gently. "That is not your fault."

Cassie exhaled through her nose and took a deliberate sip from her mug. She did not move. She did not speak. Rage would give him what he wanted.

Amos continued, walking slowly between the tables as though he belonged there. "When confusion settles in, when familiar things begin to feel unnecessary or indulgent, it is often because something has been allowed to grow without guidance."

Someone near the bakery murmured agreement.

"The world has a way of telling us when it has been misled," Amos said. "Heat rises. Restlessness spreads. You feel it, do you not?"

People shifted in their seats. A woman near the café pressed her hands together tightly.

"I am not here to accuse," Amos said, lifting his hands slightly. "I am here to offer clarity."

Cassie's jaw tightened.

He stopped near a table where two men sat with half-finished bowls of soup. "You feel tired," he said kindly. "You feel unmoored. That is what happens when false comfort replaces truth."

The word false landed like a hook.

"This gathering," Amos said, gesturing to the open doors and glowing windows, "this attempt to drown discomfort in noise and light, is proof of how deeply the corruption runs."

A ripple moved through the crowd.

Cassie set her mug down.

She stepped forward, slow and unhurried, as though she had all the time in the world.

"Corruption," she said pleasantly, "is a strong word to use when people are sharing bread."

Amos turned toward her, expression composed. "Sometimes poison tastes sweet."

Cassie smiled, sharp and bright. "And sometimes certainty is just fear wearing a nicer coat."

A few people laughed, unsure if they were allowed to.

Amos did not rise to the bait. He never did. "I understand why you would resist this message," he said, eyes fixed on Cassie. "You have invested much in these practices."

Cassie nodded. "Yes. Like caring about my neighbors."

"That is not what I mean," Amos replied. "I mean the rituals you refuse to name."

Morgan stepped closer, standing at Cassie's shoulder. They did not speak. Their presence was enough.

Amos addressed the crowd again. "You feel the heat building. The strain. That is not community. That is consequence."

Baz felt the readings twitch and adjusted the distributed ward slightly, keeping the frequency low and steady.

Cassie folded her arms. "You are very good at pointing to symptoms and calling them sins."

Amos inclined his head. "And you are very good at turning indulgence into virtue."

Cassie shrugged. "It is a talent."

A few more people laughed. The tension wavered.

Amos pressed on. "I can help you. I can show you what must be removed so peace can return."

That did it.

Cassie stepped fully into the circle now, her voice still calm, still dry. "You keep saying 'removed' like it is a kindness."

She gestured to the street. "Look around. No one is trapped. No one is being compelled. They stayed because they wanted to."

Amos's eyes narrowed slightly. "Choice is not always freedom."

"No," Cassie agreed. "But coercion is never faith."

The words hung in the air.

Somewhere behind them, a child laughed. The sound cut clean through the tension, startling in its normalcy.

Amos felt the shift. He masked it quickly, but it was there. A subtle resistance. Not rage. Not defiance.

Connection.

"You feel uncertain because you have been misled," he said, voice firmer now. "Because meaning has been replaced with sensation."

Cassie shook her head. "No. They feel uncertain because you hollowed something out and then offered yourself as the cure."

A murmur rippled through the crowd.

Amos straightened. "I am offering truth."

Cassie met his gaze evenly. "You are offering control and calling it salvation."

Silence followed.

Not empty.

Listening.

Amos realized, too late, that the gathering had not thinned. No one had backed away. The doors remained open. The windows glowed steadily.

The circuit held.

He had expected confrontation.

What he had not expected was refusal.

And that, more than any spell or ward, unsettled him.

Chapter Eighty-One: The House Remembers Out Loud

The house chose the moment.

Fi was standing alone in the hallway when it happened, her back against the familiar wallpaper, her fingers tracing the small crack near the baseboard she had memorized as a child. The sounds of the gathering drifted in through the open windows. Laughter. Cutlery against bowls. Someone calling another name twice, just to be sure it landed.

The house exhaled.

It was not dramatic. There was no sudden cold, no rush of wind. Just a subtle loosening, like a clenched jaw finally relaxing.

Fi felt it before she saw it.

A pressure behind her eyes. A warmth in her chest that did not belong to the present. The hallway stretched, not physically, but in memory. The walls brightened, colors sharpening into something older and cleaner.

She turned slowly.

The door at the end of the hall was no longer flush with the frame.

It stood open by the width of two fingers.

Her breath caught.

That door had never opened. Not in her lifetime. Not once. It had always been sealed, painted over, folded into the architecture like it was never meant to exist.

"Okay," Fi whispered. "Okay."

She stepped closer. The house did not rush her.

The door opened another inch.

Inside was not a room in the usual sense. It was small, barely larger than a walk-in closet, its walls lined with shelves that held objects carefully spaced, as though each had been given permission to exist only where it was.

The air smelled faintly of beeswax and dried lavender.

And memory.

Fi crossed the threshold and the door closed behind her, not locking, just settling.

The room breathed.

Images pressed gently at the edges of her mind, not forcing themselves forward but waiting to be acknowledged. She reached out instinctively and touched the nearest shelf.

The memory unfolded around her.

Thea stood in the center of the room, younger than Fi had ever known her, hair loose and hands stained with ink and soil. She was laughing, unguarded, her voice warm and low.

Ash stood opposite her, sleeves rolled up, holding a pressed flower between careful fingers. A small sigil had been inked along the stem, subtle and precise.

"You're sure this will hold," Ash said.

"It doesn't have to hold forever," Thea replied. "It just has to hold long enough."

They leaned into one another, foreheads touching. The affection between them was quiet but unmistakable. Not secret. Chosen.

Fi's throat tightened.

Another memory layered over the first.

Amos stood in the doorway, rigid with certainty, his presence sharpening the air. He spoke in absolutes, in warnings, in words like order and correction. He told Thea she was misleading people. He told Ash they were indulging something dangerous. He told them love did not sanctify disobedience.

"You do not get to decide what survives," he said.

Thea's voice did not rise. "I am deciding what is worth protecting."

Amos's gaze flicked to the shelves. To the objects. To the pressed flower now resting in Fi's hand.

"You are sealing corruption," he said.

"I am sealing truth," Thea replied.

The memory shifted again.

The sealing itself.

Thea and Ash stood together, hands linked, breath synchronized. There was no urgency, only resolve. They did not hide what they were doing. They named it. They spoke aloud what they were protecting.

Not power.

Not magic.

Love. Choice. The right to remember oneself without fear.

Ash pressed the flower into a small cloth and tied it closed with thread dyed the deep red of elderberry. Thea added letters, folded carefully, each page marked with a simple symbol of continuation.

"This is not an ending," Ash said.

"It is a pause," Thea agreed.

They sealed the space not to imprison it, but to keep it safe until it could be witnessed without being destroyed.

The memory softened and released Fi gently back into the present.

She stood in the room, hands shaking.

On the shelf in front of her lay the physical truth of it all.

A bundle of letters, edges worn but intact.

A small cloth pouch tied with red thread.

Inside it, the pressed flower, still bearing the faint trace of its sigil.

Fi sank to the floor, breath hitching as the weight of it settled.

"This is what you were protecting," she whispered. "This is what he tried to erase."

The house creaked softly, a sound that felt like affirmation.

Fi gathered the items carefully and stood.

The door opened again, just enough to let her pass.

As she stepped back into the hallway, the space behind her closed, seamless once more. Not gone. Not lost.

Held.

She walked toward the front room where the voices from outside drifted in stronger now. Cassie's laughter carried through the air, dry and defiant. Morgan's calm tone followed.

Fi clutched the letters to her chest.

The house had not revealed a weapon.

It had revealed a witness.

And that was far more dangerous to a man like Amos than any spell could ever be.

Chapter Eighty-Two: The Fire Line

The first sign was not flame.

It was smell.

They were all still outside. Baz caught it near the bakery, just as the crowd shifted and someone laughed too loudly at a joke that did not quite land. It threaded through the warm evening air, sharp and wrong. Not smoke exactly. More like scorched metal and dry herbs heated past their welcome.

His head snapped up.

"No," he said under his breath.

He checked the handheld meter clipped to his belt. The needle trembled, then crept higher, not spiking but straining, like a held breath that had gone on too long.

Across the street, a wisp of smoke curled up from the edge of a table where a candle had burned down faster than it should have.

Cassie saw it at the same moment.

She did not shout. She did not run. She lifted her hand.

"Water," she said clearly. "If you have it, pour a little now. Not all of it. Just enough."

People hesitated for half a second, then obeyed. Cups tipped. Pitchers tilted. Someone dumped a whole bowl of water onto the pavement and winced.

"That is fine," Cassie called. "Overachievers are welcome."

A few nervous laughs rippled outward, tension easing just enough to keep panic from catching.

Morgan moved swiftly, redirecting foot traffic away from the hotspot with gentle pressure. A hand to an elbow. A murmured suggestion. They placed a stone at the edge of the warming air, grounding it, letting the excess bleed into the earth.

At the Carrow house, Fi felt the heat roll through the walls like a pulse.

She pressed her palm flat against the doorframe, breathing steadily. The counter frequency surged, not violently, but insistently, as if the house were saying, This is too much. Share it.

"I need airflow," Fi said.

Fox was already moving, throwing open another window, then another. The house responded immediately, the warmth shifting, thinning as the current carried it through and out.

Outside, the reversed spiral pushed hard.

Amos stood at the edge of the gathering, eyes bright, chest lifted, mistaking the rising heat for confirmation.

"Do you feel it now," he called out. "This is what happens when you invite disorder. Fire always follows false worship."

Baz's hands curled into fists.

False worship. The phrase hit him harder than the heat.

He looked down at his notes, at the equations and flow charts, at the careful balance they had been maintaining, and something clicked into place with brutal clarity.

"He is using ritual mechanics," Baz muttered. "Cadence. Focus. Collective attention."

Morgan glanced at him sharply. "While denying they are ritual."

"Yes," Baz said. "He calls it faith, but he is doing the same thing we are doing. He just pretends his intent exempts him from responsibility."

Cassie heard them and turned, smoke curling faintly behind her now as another candle guttered dangerously close to a stack of napkins.

"Of course he is," she said. "That is always how it works."

She stepped into the center of the street, voice calm but carrying.

"Everyone," Cassie said, "look at me."

They did.

She waited until the heat eased just a fraction.

"This is not punishment," she said. "This is friction. When too much care is forced into too small a space, it gets hot. That is true of wires, and it is true of people."

Amos scoffed. "You reduce sacred truth to metaphor."

Cassie turned her head slightly toward him, not fully giving him her attention. "No. I am expanding the metaphor to include you."

A ripple of laughter moved through the crowd, shaky but real.

Cassie continued, "Some of us were taught that faith means obedience. That love requires discipline. That fire proves purity."

She gestured to the glowing windows, the open doors, the hands passing water.

"But love that cannot breathe burns things down," she said. "And magic that is forced instead of shared does the same."

The heat surged again, sharper this time. A curl of smoke rose from the edge of the bakery awning.

Baz's voice cut in, urgent but steady. "Cassie, we need to widen the circuit now."

Cassie nodded once. "Do it."

She turned back to the crowd. "If you are standing still, move. Slowly. Walk. Talk. Keep the air moving."

People began to circulate, not chaotically, but like a tide adjusting itself. Conversations picked up. Laughter returned in uneven bursts. The circuit widened.

At the Carrow house, the heat drained away like water finding its level. The house creaked, releasing it, distributing it into the night.

Amos watched, confusion cracking his certainty for the first time.

This was not collapse. This was containment.

"This should not be possible," he said.

Cassie met his gaze fully now. "It is, when you stop trying to control what love looks like."

She stepped closer, smoke dissipating behind her.

"You talk about tenants," she said, voice sharp with wit and steel. "Rules. Order. Submission."

She gestured around them. "We talk about care. Consent. Memory. Turns out those hold better under pressure."

The fire risk eased, then receded. The smoke thinned and vanished. Candles steadied. The night exhaled.

Baz checked the meters and let out a shaky laugh. "We are stable."

Morgan closed their eyes briefly. "The spiral lost momentum."

Fi leaned against the doorframe, breath finally steady. The house settled, warm and intact.

Amos stood alone at the edge of the street, watching a town refuse to burn for his certainty.

For the first time, he looked afraid.

Not of magic.

But of love that would not be corrected.

Chapter Eighty-Four: The Final Ritual

The ritual did not begin with words. It began with stillness.

After the heat receded and the smoke thinned, no one rushed to fill the quiet. People stood where they were, cups of water still in their hands, shoulders brushing shoulders. The night air moved gently through open doors and windows, carrying the smell of bread and wax and damp pavement. The town did not retreat indoors. It stayed present.

Cassie felt the moment settle. Not as triumph, not as relief, but as readiness.

"This is the part," she said softly, more to herself than to anyone else.

Morgan stood beside her, eyes half closed, listening not for danger but for alignment. The weave no longer strained. It waited.

Cassie stepped forward and spoke clearly, without ceremony.

"We are not here to undo anything," she said. "We are here to remember it correctly."

No one argued. No one asked what that meant.

Baz moved quietly through the crowd, adjusting the small, distributed nodes. He kept the power low, barely more than a suggestion. The instruments no longer hummed with warning. They glowed faintly, as if relieved to be allowed to rest.

At the Carrow house, Fi stood at the threshold with Fox beside her. The doors were open wide now, front and back, creating a clean line of air through the center of the house. The walls felt warm but steady, like a body returning to its natural temperature.

Fi held the bundle she had brought out from the sealed space. The letters. The cloth pouch. The pressed flower marked with its careful sigil. She did not lift them high. She simply held them where they could be seen.

"This belonged to my aunt," she said. Her voice shook once, then steadied. "And to someone she loved."

The word love landed gently, without demand.

"This house was sealed to protect a promise," Fi continued. "Not power. Not secrecy. A choice. The right to be known without being corrected."

A murmur moved through the gathering. Recognition, not surprise.

Cassie nodded. "That is the heart of it. The weave holds when people consent to be part of it. Not because they are commanded. Because they choose."

Morgan stepped forward and placed three stones at the center of the street, forming a loose arc rather than a circle. Not closed. Open. The stones bore simple listening marks, nothing ornate.

"This is not a boundary," Morgan said. "It is an orientation."

Cassie took a length of herb dyed twine from Bram and held it loosely. "We are not reversing anything tonight," she said. "We are turning toward each other."

She handed the twine to the nearest person, who tied a simple knot and spoke one word aloud. Home.

The twine passed from hand to hand. Each knot was different. Some words were spoken with confidence. Others came out tentative, then stronger once heard. Kindness. Memory. Laughter. Rest. Courage. Forgiveness.

As the words accumulated, the air brightened. Not with glare, but with warmth. The heat that had threatened to burn now softened into light, reflecting in windows and on faces.

The spiral responded.

Amos felt it before he saw it.

He stood at the far edge of the gathering, rigid, hands clenched at his sides. The reversed spiral he had laid into the land faltered, its pull weakening as the pattern around it shifted. Not against it. Around it.

The spiral could not draw inward when the town was moving outward.

He stepped forward once, as if to speak, then stopped.

His ritual required isolation. Focused certainty. A narrowing of attention until doubt felt like relief.

But here, doubt had no foothold. People were remembering together. Witnessing without shame. Choosing without permission.

The mechanics failed him.

The spiral collapsed quietly, not shattering, not exploding, simply losing coherence. The lines blurred, then vanished into the soil like something exhaled and released.

Baz watched the meters flatten to calm. "It is done," he said quietly. "The load is gone."

Amos stared at the scene in front of him. At the open doors. The linked twine. The way the Carrow house stood illuminated but unexposed.

This was not repentance.

This was not submission.

"This is disorder," he said, though his voice no longer carried.

Cassie looked at him, not unkindly. "No," she replied. "This is consent."

He shook his head once, sharp and final. "Love does not absolve corruption."

Cassie shrugged. "No one asked it to."

For a moment, it seemed as though he might argue. Might escalate. Might demand acknowledgment.

Instead, he turned.

He did not curse them. He did not recant. He did not bless or threaten.

He simply walked away, boots striking the pavement in measured steps, his certainty intact but unshared. The night swallowed him without ceremony.

No one followed. No one cheered.

The ritual completed itself in the absence he left behind.

The twine was tied off and laid gently at the base of the stones. The light settled into something sustainable. The weave eased into place, not tightened, not locked, but aligned.

Cassie exhaled slowly and smiled, small and tired and satisfied.

"Well," she said. "That could have gone worse."

Fox snorted. "I feel like that should be engraved somewhere."

Fi laughed, the sound breaking open something that had been held too tightly for too long.

Morgan closed their eyes and felt the land answer, steady and whole.

The ritual ended not with an ending, but with people lingering. Talking. Eating. Carrying chairs back inside only when they felt ready.

The town did not return to normal.

It returned to itself.

And that was enough.

Chapter Eighty-Five: Afterglow

Morning arrived gently, as if it had learned something from the night before.

The light came in low and gold through the windows of the Carrow house, touching the edges of furniture and catching on dust motes that drifted lazily through the air. The house felt different now. Not louder. Not brighter. Simply settled, like a body after a long-held breath finally released.

Cassie stood at the kitchen sink with a mug of coffee she had reheated twice and still forgotten to drink. Outside, someone laughed. Somewhere down the street, a door opened and closed with the easy familiarity of routine restored.

Emerdeen felt like itself again. Not unchanged, but intact.

Baz came up behind her without announcing himself and leaned one hip against the counter. He did not speak right away. He did not need to. The quiet between them was not empty. It was earned.

"You stayed," Cassie said eventually, eyes still on the window.

Baz smiled. "I had some concerns about leaving you unsupervised with a town and a half-dismantled ideology."

Cassie snorted. "That is fair. I am notoriously reckless with communal healing."

He shifted closer, their shoulders brushing. "I meant it, though. About staying. About choosing this."

Cassie turned then, really turned, and studied his face. The exhaustion there. The relief. The unmistakable resolve.

"I know," she said. "I am choosing it too. You. Us. Not as a reaction. Not because everything almost burned down."

Baz lifted an eyebrow. "Though that does add romance."

Cassie smiled softly. "I am choosing you because when things got hard, you did not try to control the outcome. You built something that could listen. And then you trusted people with it."

Baz swallowed. "I choose you because you refuse to disappear when things get dangerous. And because you never confuse fear with wisdom."

She reached for his hand. He laced his fingers through hers without hesitation.

Outside, Morgan stood near the long table that had been left out overnight, now covered in empty bowls and folded cloths. People moved around them naturally, asking quiet questions, offering help without being asked.

Someone approached Morgan hesitantly. Then another. By midmorning, it was no longer hesitation. It was recognition.

"You knew what to do," Bram said, handing Morgan a mug of tea. "You listened when the rest of us felt lost."

Morgan accepted the mug, expression thoughtful. "I did not know everything. I just paid attention."

"That is leadership," Bram replied simply.

Later, Kara from the bakery stopped by with a loaf still warm. "You should teach something," she said. "Not magic. Or maybe magic. I do not know. But the way you help people remember what they already know."

Morgan blinked, caught off guard.

"I already do," they said slowly. "I just did not call it that."

Across the yard, Fi sat on the front steps with the bundle from the sealed room resting beside her. The letters were wrapped carefully now, the pressed flower returned to its pouch. She had read enough to understand the shape of Thea and Ash's love. Quiet. Fierce. Deliberate.

Not tragic.

Fox dropped down beside her, stretching his legs out into the sun. "So," he said, "we accidentally inherited a house with opinions and a legacy of inconvenient truth."

Fi laughed. "We could sell it."

He looked at her sideways. "You are not serious."

"No," she admitted. "I am not."

They sat quietly for a moment, the decision settling between them without drama.

"I think," Fi said, "we stay because this place lets us choose who we are. Not who we are supposed to be."

Fox nodded. "I stay because it pisses off the kind of people who think certainty is a virtue."

Fi smiled. "That too."

In the afternoon, Cassie gathered everyone briefly, not for a ritual, not for instruction.

She held up the cloth pouch and the letters. "These belonged to Thea and Ash. They were part of why this house held when it needed to. Their story does not belong to secrecy anymore."

She placed the bundle on a shelf near the window, visible but not exposed.

"No monument," Cassie said. "No moral. Just acknowledgment."

The house creaked softly, approving.

As evening crept back in, Emerdeen resumed its familiar rhythms. Shops closed at their proper times. People went home because they wanted to, not because something pressed them there.

The afterglow lingered. Not as triumph.

As tenderness.

Cassie stood on the porch with Baz, watching the light fade. Morgan walked past, deep in conversation with Bram. Fi and Fox argued cheerfully about dinner plans.

The town breathed.

Cassie leaned into Baz and murmured, "We are not done, are we."

He kissed the top of her head. "No. But we are not starting from fear anymore."

She smiled, content. The story had not ended.

It had rooted.

And whatever came next would rise from something whole.

Chapter Eighty-Six: Open Hands

The sign went up quietly.

Cassie taped it to the front window of Stirred & Spellbound one morning while the kettle warmed and the shop still smelled faintly of lemon oil and old paper. She stood back, tilted her head, then straightened it by half an inch because crooked signs made her irrationally cranky.

WORKSHOPS.
NO EXPERIENCE REQUIRED.
CURIOSITY WELCOME.

She considered adding something wry, then decided the invitation was enough.

By midmorning, people were already drifting in.

Not the usual crowd. Not only the ones who already knew how to name herbs or trace a spiral without thinking. These were neighbors who had stood in the street during the gathering and felt something shift without knowing how to talk about it. People who had stayed because staying mattered. People who wanted to understand what had happened without being handed doctrine in exchange.

Cassie greeted everyone with a mug or a chair or a simple question. "What brought you in today."

No one answered the same way.

"I just want to feel less… foggy," one woman said.

"I want to know how to pay attention without feeling stupid," another offered.

"I liked that no one told me what to believe," a man near the back said. "I liked that I got to decide."

Cassie smiled. "Excellent. That means you are in the right place."

Morgan arrived carrying a stack of notebooks and a bundle of twine, their posture relaxed but focused. They took in the room with a teacher's eye, already mapping how energy settled and where it snagged.

Baz followed with a box of small lamps and extension cords. He set them up without explanation, spacing them out so no one section of the room felt spotlighted or ignored.

Fi hovered near the shelves, listening. Fox leaned against the counter, arms crossed, wearing the expression of someone who had agreed to be present but not impressed.

Cassie clapped her hands once, gently. "Okay. Ground rules. There are very few."

She held up one finger. "No one here is an authority over your experience."

Another finger. "Nothing you learn today requires belief."

A third. "If something does not work for you, that is not a failure. That is information."

A pause. "Also, there will be snacks. Because learning is harder when you are hungry."

That earned a laugh.

Morgan stepped forward next, setting a notebook on each table. "We are starting with noticing," they said. "Noticing is not mystical. It is a skill. You already do it when you walk into a room and know whether to stay."

They guided the group through simple exercises. Paying attention to breath without changing it. Noticing temperature shifts. Tracking when attention wandered and gently bringing it back.

No symbols. No incantations.

Just awareness.

Baz followed with a short explanation of how systems behaved under pressure. He talked about circuits and flow and why bottlenecks caused heat. He talked about how people were not so different.

"You do not need to control everything," he said. "You just need to give energy somewhere safe to go."

A few people nodded slowly.

Fi spoke last, unexpectedly. She did not plan to. It just happened.

"I did not believe in any of this," she said plainly. "I still do not believe in parts of it. But I believe in paying attention. And I believe in consent. Those two things changed everything."

Fox snorted softly, then added, "And if you are allergic to spiritual language, you can think of this as learning how not to let someone hijack your nervous system."

That got real laughter.

The workshops unfolded over the afternoon, overlapping and organic. Knot tying that focused on intention without symbolism. Journaling that asked better questions instead of offering answers. Walking the block together and noticing which spaces felt lighter or heavier.

People left with tools, not commandments.

By evening, Cassie leaned against the counter, watching the last group trickle out. Her feet hurt. Her voice was tired. Her heart felt full in a way that did not demand anything from her in return.

"This worked," Baz said quietly beside her.

"Yes," she agreed. "Because we did not try to teach magic."

Morgan closed a notebook and smiled. "We taught literacy."

Fi glanced around the shop, then at the people still talking outside, reluctant to leave. "I think," she said slowly, "this is how the town stays awake."

Cassie nodded. "Not by guarding the door. By opening it."

She reached up and flipped the sign in the window to read *SEE YOU NEXT WEEK.*

And for the first time since the spiral began, the future did not feel like something to brace against.

It felt like something they could build together.

Chapter Eighty-Seven: The Quiet After Teaching

The shop was quieter than Cassie expected it to be.

Not empty. Not hollow. Just settled, like a room that had finally exhaled after holding too many voices for too long. The kind of quiet that did not feel like absence, but completion.

Cassie moved slowly through the space, wiping down the long worktable even though it was already clean. It was out of habit more than necessity, a way of letting her hands stay busy while her thoughts loosened their grip. The smell of tea and citrus cleaner hung in the air, layered over the deeper, familiar scent of old paper, wood polish, and whatever faint trace of magic had long ago seeped into the bones of the place.

Stirred & Spellbound had been full lately. Not just of people, but of questions. Of hesitation and cautious hope. Of that particular relief that comes when someone realizes they are not broken for feeling the way they do.

Now it held only her.

Cassie paused near the shelves where the workshop notebooks were stacked. Their corners were already softened, pages bent and marked by use. Some had smudges where hands had lingered too long. Others held uneven handwriting, starts and stops where people had wrestled with words before letting them land.

She smiled faintly.

For so much of her life, she had believed magic required defense. She had tried to convince people it was real when disbelief felt like dismissal, and she had hidden it when belief felt dangerous. Magic had been proof, shield, and justification all at once.

Today, it had been none of those things.

She had not performed. She had not dazzled. She had not wrapped insight in mystery to make it more palatable.

She had listened.

The realization settled into her with a surprising weight. Early on, magic had felt like the thing she needed to earn her place. Proof that she belonged here. Proof that walking away from her old life had been more than fear dressed up as courage.

But now, magic felt like language.

Optional. Useful. Something to reach for when it helped and set aside when it did not.

Not a demand.

Cassie leaned against the counter and took in the shop as a whole. The mismatched chairs. The shelves arranged with care and imperfection. The small scuff near the baseboard that she had never quite managed to fix. This place had been her anchor. Her refuge. Her excuse when she needed one.

It was still all of those things.

But it was also something else now.

It was shared.

The thought brought an unexpected tightness to her chest, quickly followed by relief. She was no longer the sole keeper of what happened here. She did not have to hold it alone.

She spotted a small charm left behind near the edge of the table. Nothing elaborate. Just twine and a single bead, unevenly knotted. An attempt, earnest and imperfect.

Cassie picked it up and turned it over in her palm, smiling to herself. She set it gently in the lost and found jar with the others.

"You did good," she murmured.

The words were not for the charm.

They were for her.

When she flipped the sign in the window to *CLOSED*, the bell above the door chimed softly, the sound familiar and grounding. Cassie left one lamp on, low and warm, its glow pooling gently across the front of the shop.

She paused for a moment at the bottom of the stairs, listening.

The quiet did not press in. It did not ask her to fill it or fix it or prove anything within it.

For the first time since the beginning, the quiet simply was.

And that was enough.

Chapter Eighty-Eight: Baz, Before and After

Baz sat on the floor with parts spread out around him like the remains of an old map, each piece marking a place he had once stood.

Copper wire coiled loosely beside him. A cracked casing rested near his knee. The faint smell of ozone still clung to the components, though the device had not been powered in days. This was the first prototype he had built after arriving in Emerdeen, back when every unknown felt like a threat and every system felt safer if it was monitored closely. Back when vigilance had masqueraded as care.

He turned the device over in his hands and traced the familiar seams with his thumb. He remembered the night he had assembled it, sitting at the same spot on the floor with a mug of burnt coffee and too many open notebooks. He had believed then that if he could just anticipate every failure point, nothing would slip through.

And it had worked.

That was the complicated part. The device had done exactly what he had designed it to do. It had listened. It had warned. It had held a boundary long enough for him to feel competent and useful and necessary.

It was just no longer necessary.

Baz set the casing down gently and began dismantling the device piece by piece. He did not rush. He did not hesitate. Each screw came loose with a soft, familiar resistance. Each wire released without protest.

He did not feel frustration. He did not feel loss.

What he felt was appreciation.

Each component carried a story. The early clumsiness of his designs, when he compensated for uncertainty with redundancy. The refinement that came after, when he learned how to trust materials to behave as they were meant to. The quiet panic beneath it all, the part of him that believed unseen forces would always do harm if left unchecked.

He smiled to himself, a little ruefully.

He had been solving emotional problems with engineering for most of his adult life. It had worked often enough to feel justified. But it had never made him peaceful.

When Cassie leaned against the doorway, he sensed her presence before he heard her. He did not look up right away. She did not press. She had learned, like he had, that some moments needed space to finish unfolding.

"You taking it apart," she asked eventually, her voice light but careful, "or laying it to rest?"

Baz considered the question honestly. "Yes," he said.

She smiled and crossed the room, lowering herself to the floor beside him without ceremony. She tucked one leg beneath her and rested her elbow on her knee, watching his hands move.

"You okay," she asked.

He nodded. "I am better than okay."

He set a small coil of wire aside and leaned back slightly, letting himself sit with the feeling that had been building quietly all morning. "I do not want to build things to contain you anymore," he said. "Or the town. Or myself."

Cassie did not interrupt him. She studied his face, the tension that was no longer there, the resolve that had replaced it.

"I never asked you to," she said gently.

"I know," Baz replied. "That is the point."

He picked up the last remaining piece, a small stabilizer he had once been proud of, and placed it carefully with the others. Then he turned fully toward her.

"I am not here because something needs fixing," he said. "I am here because I want to be. Because this place matters to me. Because you matter to me."

Cassie reached for his hand and held it without hesitation. "Good," she said. "Because I am done surviving my way into love."

Baz let out a quiet laugh, the sound carrying relief more than humor. "That sounds like something we should put on a sign."

She raised an eyebrow. "Do not tempt me. I own a shop."

They sat together on the floor, surrounded by parts that had once felt essential. The pieces no longer formed a system. They were simply materials now, waiting to be repurposed or released.

There was no urgency between them. No problem left to solve.

Only choice.

And that, Baz realized, felt like the safest design he had ever trusted.

Chapter Eighty-Nine: The Grove at Rest

Morgan returned to the grove alone.

They did not announce themselves with words or intention. They did not carry tools, charms, or offerings tucked into their pockets. There was no need. The path was familiar beneath their feet, worn smooth by years of quiet passage. As they walked, the canopy slowly closed overhead, branches knitting together until the light softened and the air shifted into that particular hush that existed nowhere else.

The grove greeted them without urgency.

The land was calm.

Not dormant. Not asleep. Simply balanced, like a body at rest that no longer braced for pain.

Morgan slowed near the center, letting their steps fall where they always had, trusting memory rather than sight. The tree stood as it always had, broad and steady, bark textured with age and weather and patience. Morgan placed a hand against it and felt warmth there, not heat, but recognition.

They closed their eyes.

The echo of strain still lingered faintly in the weave, the way a muscle remembers effort after healing. But there was no pull now. No resistance. No sense of being tested or watched. The land no longer asked Morgan to intervene.

It simply existed.

Morgan breathed, letting the air fill their lungs without shaping it into anything else. For so long, they had come to this place seeking answers, seeking confirmation that what they felt was real, that they were not alone in it. They had come fractured, uncertain, searching for language to name themselves.

"I am not asking," Morgan said softly, voice barely more than a vibration against the bark. "I am listening."

The grove answered the way it always had, not with signs or visions, but with the absence of urgency. With stillness that felt earned rather than imposed. With the quiet assurance that balance did not require constant correction.

Morgan smiled.

Once, this place had reflected their fragmentation back at them, amplifying the pieces they had not yet learned how to hold together. Now, it reflected something whole. Not perfected. Not finished. Simply aligned.

They knelt at the base of the tree and pressed a small marker into the soil. It was unremarkable. A smooth stone etched with a simple line, easily overlooked by anyone not paying attention.

Not a ward. Not a boundary.

Just a sign that someone had stood here and listened well.

"For those who come after," Morgan murmured.

They lingered for a moment longer, palm resting against the earth, feeling the steady rhythm beneath it. The grove did not cling. It did not close around them as they rose.

Morgan left the way they had arrived, without ceremony, without backward glances.

They trusted now that balance did not require constant supervision.

Some things, once restored, knew how to remain at rest.

Chapter Ninety: The Carrow House, Unsealed

The Carrow house felt lighter.

Not because something had been taken away, but because nothing was being forced to stay hidden anymore. The tension that had once threaded through the walls, subtle but persistent, had eased. The air moved differently now, no longer catching in corners or settling too heavily in rooms that once felt reluctant to be entered.

Fi stood in the doorway of the hall where the sealed space had been, its presence now acknowledged rather than denied. The door itself was closed again, plain and unremarkable, blending seamlessly back into the architecture. It no longer carried the weight of secrecy. It simply existed.

In the front room, the letters and token rested on a small shelf near the window. They were not framed. They were not elevated or hidden away. They were visible without being displayed like relics. Part of the house, not an attraction.

Fox leaned against the wall nearby, arms crossed loosely, watching Fi more than the room. "So, we are not turning it into a museum," he said.

"No," Fi replied without hesitation. "Or a shrine."

"Good," he said, relief clear in his voice. "I draw the line at guided tours."

Fi smiled. "The house does not want that anyway."

They moved through the rooms together, not inspecting so much as noticing. Small changes revealed themselves easily now. A draft that had always snagged at the corner of the hall no longer caught. A floorboard near the kitchen that used to complain underfoot stayed quiet. Even the light felt different, spreading evenly instead of pooling in careful, defensive patches.

It felt as though the house had stopped bracing itself.

Fi paused near the front window and looked out toward the street. Emerdeen moved through an ordinary afternoon, people passing with bags and conversations, nothing remarkable and everything restored. The normalcy caught her off guard.

"They loved each other," Fi said quietly.

Fox followed her gaze. "And they were stopped."

"Yes," Fi said. "But not erased."

She swallowed, surprised by the weight of the words. That distinction mattered more than she had expected. Thea and Ash had not been preserved as a warning or a tragedy. Their story had endured as proof that love had existed here without apology.

They began making decisions together then, practical and unceremonious. Which rooms would remain private. Which spaces could be opened for workshops or gatherings. Where boundaries belonged and where they were no longer needed.

Fi spoke. Fox listened. Fox questioned. Fi adjusted. The house responded with quiet acceptance, creaking softly at the right moments, as if acknowledging consent.

When they finished, Fi placed her palm against the wall and waited for the familiar resistance she had grown up sensing without understanding. There was none.

Nothing pushed back. Nothing held tight.

The house was not guarding anymore. It was not holding its breath or preparing for intrusion.

It was home.

Chapter Ninety-One: What Emerdeen Keeps

Emerdeen did not celebrate its survival.

There were no banners strung across Main Street, no announcements, no collective sigh of relief that demanded to be shared. The town simply resumed its rhythms, altered just enough to notice if you were paying attention.

Cassie was paying attention.

She noticed it first in the way people lingered.

Outside the bakery, a conversation continued well past the point where both participants had already said what they came to say. No one checked a watch. No one apologized for taking up space. A laugh rose and fell without hurry, as if time itself had loosened its grip.

At the café, chairs were pulled closer together instead of pushed back. Someone refilled another person's cup without asking. The barista paused mid-motion to listen fully, hands still, eyes focused.

These were not grand gestures.

They were choices.

Cassie walked the length of the street slowly, her steps unhurried, her hands tucked into the pockets of her coat. She greeted people by name, and they returned the greeting with warmth that lingered just a moment longer than politeness required.

The town felt awake in a different way.

Morgan noticed it too, though they named it differently. To them, it showed up in the weave. Not brighter, not louder, but steadier. Places that once felt thin now held weight. Attention settled into the land like dew rather than rain.

At the greenhouse, Morgan watched two people pause mid-argument and start again, softer this time. They did not resolve the disagreement, but they did not escalate it either. The moment passed without leaving a bruise.

Bram felt it in his garden. Plants he expected to struggle took root without fuss. The soil held moisture better. Not because it had changed, but because it was being tended with presence rather than habit.

Fi noticed it at the Carrow house when a neighbor stopped by with no reason at all and stayed to talk on the porch. The conversation wandered. It did not need direction. The house seemed to approve, the air inside staying warm and receptive.

Fox noticed it when he realized he had been listening to someone's story without planning his rebuttal. The thought surprised him enough that he almost laughed.

Cassie reached Stirred & Spellbound just as the afternoon light slanted through the front windows. She paused before unlocking the door, taking in the quiet hum of the street behind her. It did not feel victorious.

It felt intact.

Inside the shop, she moved through familiar motions. She straightened a stack of books. She adjusted a display that did not need adjusting. She noticed how often people had touched certain items, the way fingers left small signs of hesitation and return.

Emerdeen had not won anything.

That was the realization that settled into her bones as she stood behind the counter and watched the street through the glass.

Winning implied opposition. A defeat. A thing overcome.

What Emerdeen had done was remember.

It had remembered how to stay with discomfort without needing to crush it. It had remembered that attention could be an act of care rather than control. It had remembered itself.

Cassie leaned her elbows on the counter and exhaled slowly.

She thought about the workshops she had begun to plan. About the quiet expectation people carried when they stepped into her shop. About the old impulse to teach magic as a thing that could be mastered, a skill that could be learned if one just tried hard enough.

That was not what was needed now.

Magic had never been the point. Discernment was.

The ability to notice what tightened the body and what softened it. To recognize when certainty was being used as a weapon. To tell the difference between guidance and coercion, between ritual that opened and ritual that closed.

Cassie picked up a notebook and wrote a single line across the first page.

Attention is care.

She underlined it once, then set the pen down.

When the bell chimed later and the first person stepped inside with a hesitant smile and no clear question, Cassie met them with steady presence rather than answers.

"Take your time," she said.

And Emerdeen did.

Chapter Ninety-Two: Intention Is Not a Wish

The chairs were arranged in a loose circle, not because circles were sacred, but because no one liked sitting with their back to the door.

Cassie noticed that immediately and adjusted without comment. She had learned to read rooms the way some people read weather. Where tension gathered. Where attention slipped. Where people needed an exit even if they never used it.

The workshop filled slowly. A few familiar faces. Several new ones. Some people held notebooks. Others came empty handed, wary but curious. No one looked certain, and Cassie took that as a good sign.

She waited until everyone had settled, until the small sounds of discomfort faded into a shared quiet.

"Today is not about getting what you want," she said calmly. "So, if that is what you were hoping for, I recommend the bakery instead."

A ripple of laughter loosened the room.

Cassie reached into the basket at her feet and lifted a small bowl filled with clear quartz. The stones caught the light without effort, plain and unadorned.

"This," she said, passing the bowl slowly around the circle, "is clear quartz. People like to call it an amplifier."

She paused until the bowl completed its slow circuit and returned to her hands.

"Which sounds impressive," she continued, "but it is also deeply misleading. This does nothing on its own. No agenda. No opinion. It reflects and magnifies what is already present. That is all."

Baz, sitting quietly near the back, nodded once.

Cassie set the bowl on the floor between them. "That is why we are starting here. Intention works the same way. It is not a lever. It is a direction."

Morgan watched the group carefully. They saw shoulders ease at the absence of promise. Relief flickered across more than one face.

Cassie handed out paper and pens. "Write an intention," she said. "But do not use verbs that imply control."

A few brows furrowed.

"No manifest," Cassie added. "No force. No make. No ensure. If your sentence sounds like you are filing a request with the universe, try again."

Someone near the window laughed quietly and scratched out a line.

Fi leaned over her page, thoughtful. She crossed out want and replaced it with remain.

Fox stared at his paper for a long moment before writing anything at all.

As the pens moved, Cassie spoke again, softer now. "An intention is not a wish. A wish hands responsibility outward. An intention names who you are willing to be, regardless of outcome."

She let that land.

"In many traditions," Cassie continued, "prayer is taught as a request. Ask. Hope. Wait. That works for some people, and I am not here to take that away."

She glanced around the circle, meeting eyes rather than avoiding them.

"But intention asks something different. Intention asks who you will be if no one intervenes on your behalf."

Baz watched someone straighten in their chair at that.

Cassie gestured toward the quartz. "This does not give you power. It gives you clarity. Which is sometimes harder."

Morgan spoke then, briefly. "Clarity changes what you notice. Not what exists."

Cassie smiled in agreement.

After a few minutes, she invited anyone who wanted to share. No pressure. No obligation.

A woman near the front spoke first. "I wrote - I intend to respond instead of react."

Another voice followed. "I intend to stay present when things get uncomfortable."

Fi hesitated, then read quietly, "I intend to trust my own timing."

Fox cleared his throat. "I wrote, I intend to stop arguing with ghosts."

That earned a laugh, including his own.

Cassie nodded at each offering, treating them as complete, not improvable.

"Notice something," she said. "None of those sentences demand an outcome. They do not promise success. They name orientation."

She held the quartz up once more, letting the light pass through it. "This will amplify what you practice. Not what you want. That distinction matters."

The room was quiet again, but it was a different quiet now. Focused. Attentive.

Cassie set the stone down gently. "Intention asks who you are willing to be," she said. "Prayer often asks who will save you."

She did not say it as an accusation. She said it as an offering.

As the workshop ended, people lingered, rereading what they had written. Some folded their papers carefully. Others tucked them into pockets without ceremony.

Emerdeen held the moment the way it had learned to do.

Without rush.

Without demand.

With care.

Chapter Ninety-Three: The Weight of Words

The attendance at workshops continued to grow. Not by leaps and bounds, but by interest.

Morgan began the newest workshop session without asking anyone to sit.

They moved quietly through the room instead, setting small bowls along the tables and windowsills. Dried lavender rested beside fresh lemon balm, their scents gentle but unmistakable. As people entered, the air softened around them, not enough to distract, just enough to slow the breath.

"Before we talk," Morgan said calmly, "I want you to notice how you arrived in your body."

A few people shifted. Someone laughed nervously. Someone else closed their eyes without realizing they had done it.

Morgan waited.

"This is not about belief," they continued. "It is about response."

They invited everyone to sit only after the room had settled. The chairs formed no particular shape. Morgan stood where they could be seen easily, but they did not command the space. They shared it.

"Language shapes nervous systems," Morgan said. "Not metaphorically. Literally."

They gestured toward the herbs. "Lavender and lemon balm are not magic. They signal safety. Your body responds before your mind does. Words work the same way."

They asked the group to place a hand on their chest or stomach. Somewhere that felt neutral.

"Now," Morgan said gently, "I am going to say some phrases. You do not need to analyze them. Just notice what happens."

They spoke slowly.

"Submit your will."

A few shoulders tightened. Someone inhaled sharply.

"Trust without question."

A hand curled into a fist.

"Be worthy."

A woman near the back swallowed hard.

Morgan nodded, as though this confirmed something they already knew.

"Now," they said, "notice your body."

They gave the room time. Long enough for discomfort to be felt without being pushed away.

"These phrases are not wrong," Morgan said. "They are powerful. That is the point. Power without examination leaves marks."

They picked up a small bundle of lavender and crushed it lightly between their fingers. The scent lifted, immediate and grounding.

"Many of us learned faith through language that tightened us," Morgan continued. "That does not mean faith itself is harm. It means the words were carrying more than they admitted."

They paused, eyes moving across the room, attentive.

"I want you to think of a prayer you know by heart," Morgan said. "One that feels familiar. You do not have to share it."

Pens were passed out. Paper followed.

"Write it down," Morgan instructed. "Exactly as you remember it."

The room filled with the quiet scratch of ink.

Fi wrote quickly, then stopped, staring at the page. Fox hesitated longer, then wrote only a single line.

Morgan let the silence hold.

"Now," they said, "rewrite it. Not as a request. As a statement of presence."

Confusion flickered across faces.

"If your prayer asks for guidance," Morgan explained, "rewrite it as attention. If it asks for forgiveness, rewrite it as accountability. If it asks for protection, rewrite it as awareness."

Cassie watched as someone near the window crossed out nearly everything they had written and began again, slower this time.

Morgan gave an example, not from scripture, but from experience.

"I once prayed to be made whole," they said quietly. "I rewrote it as, I am here with what is broken, and I will not abandon myself."

The room stilled.

A woman near the front lifted her head, eyes bright with something like shock. Her hand trembled slightly as she looked down at her page.

"I always prayed to be strong," she said softly. "I rewrote it as - I am allowed to rest."

The words seemed to surprise her as they left her mouth.

Her breath caught.

"Oh," she whispered.

Morgan watched the realization move through her, the way her shoulders lowered, the way her spine softened.

"That," Morgan said gently, "is an epiphany your body has been waiting for."

Around the room, others were feeling it too. Not fireworks. Not revelation. Just the quiet recognition of how much effort it had taken to carry certain words for so long.

Morgan concluded the session without ceremony.

"You do not need to abandon your language," they said. "You need to listen to what it does to you. Faith that cannot be felt safely in the body will always demand silence."

As people left, one by one, the scent of lavender lingered. The woman who had spoken earlier paused at the door and turned back.

"Thank you," she said. "I did not realize I had been bracing my whole life."

Morgan nodded. "Most of us do not. Until we stop."

The room emptied slowly.

And something unseen loosened its grip.

Chapter Ninety-Four: Manifestation Without Control

The room felt lighter when people arrived, as if something from the previous session had followed them in and decided to stay.

Cassie noticed it immediately. The way shoulders dropped more quickly. The way people chose seats without hovering. The way no one asked, right away, whether this was going to work.

She took that as progress.

"Today," Cassie said, leaning casually against the counter, "we are going to talk about manifestation. Which means I am about to disappoint at least half of you."

A few people laughed. One person groaned theatrically.

Cassie grinned. "If the universe worked like customer service, we'd all be angrier. And on hold."

That earned a fuller laugh, the kind that carried relief with it.

She reached into a small bowl and lifted a smooth piece of moonstone, pale and softly luminous. She did not hold it up like a prize. She simply let it rest in her palm.

"Moonstone is often associated with manifestation," she said. "Which is unfortunate, because it is really about timing."

She passed the stone to the person nearest her and waited as it moved slowly around the room, hand to hand.

"This stone does not make things happen," Cassie continued. "It reminds us that things happen in cycles. That not everything responds to urgency. That some things unfold only when the conditions are right."

Baz, sitting near the back, watched a man turn the stone over in his fingers, brow furrowed as if this contradicted something he had been taught.

Cassie noticed.

"The myth," she said, "is that manifestation is about control. That if you think the right thoughts hard enough, or say the right words often enough, the universe will comply."

She made a vague twisting motion with her hand. "Like a vending machine. Insert affirmation, receive outcome."

A few people chuckled. A few shifted uncomfortably.

"The reality," Cassie said, more gently now, "is that manifestation is about orientation. It is about how you face the world, not how you demand from it."

Morgan nodded slightly, tracking the shift in tone. This was where people often resisted. Control was comforting. Orientation required trust without guarantee.

Cassie handed out paper. "Write down something you are committed to," she instructed. "Not something you want to get. Something you are willing to show up for."

The pens moved slowly this time.

"No timelines," Cassie added. "No ultimatums. And no bargaining."

Someone laughed softly and crossed out an entire sentence.

Cassie continued, "Now, underneath that commitment, write what you are afraid will happen if it does not work out the way you imagine."

The room grew quieter. Heavier, but not tense.

Fi stared at her page for a long moment before writing a single line. Fox scribbled, paused, then sighed and kept going.

Cassie gave them time.

"Here is the hard part," she said eventually. "Read both sentences and notice which one tightens your body."

Several people exhaled sharply.

"That tightness," Cassie said, "is attachment. Attachment is not bad. It just becomes dangerous when it pretends to be faith."

She reached for the moonstone again as it completed its circuit and held it up briefly.

"This stone does not rush the moon," she said. "It does not scold the dark. It reflects what is already in motion."

She set it down between them.

"The exercise," Cassie said, "is to release attachment to outcome while keeping commitment. You do the work. You stay present. You adjust when necessary. And you stop treating the future like it owes you something."

A woman near the front raised her hand hesitantly. "So, if I let go of the outcome, how do I not give up."

Cassie smiled. "You do not give up. You give in. To the process. To learning. To becoming someone who can respond instead of react."

The woman nodded slowly, eyes distant as something rearranged itself.

Afterward, as people gathered their things, Cassie watched one man carefully fold his paper and tuck it into his pocket instead of tearing it up. She saw the way he touched the moonstone once more before leaving, not like a talisman, but like a reminder.

As the room emptied, Cassie leaned against the counter beside Morgan.

"You think that landed," Morgan said.

Cassie shrugged lightly. "If it did not, they will try to manifest understanding later."

Morgan laughed quietly.

Outside, the light shifted as clouds moved across the sun, altering the day without asking permission.

Cassie watched it happen and smiled.

Orientation, she thought, was everything.

Chapter Ninety-Five: Obedience Is Not Love

The variety of the class had grown as much as the attendance.

Cassie noticed it before she noticed the numbers. The mix of ages. The way some people came alone while others arrived in pairs that sat carefully apart. The clothing that suggested different lives, different histories, different reasons for being here. Some faces carried openness. Others carried caution so practiced it looked like calm.

This was the session she had both anticipated and delayed.

Consent and agency were not abstract ideas. They were lived ones. Scarred ones.

Cassie had arranged the room differently this time. The chairs were spaced with more intention, not close enough to feel confining, not so far apart that people could disappear. Small bundles of dried rose and hawthorn rested at the center of each table. Rose for tenderness. Hawthorn for boundaries that protected rather than closed.

Morgan moved quietly through the space, making tea. The scent softened the air without overwhelming it. Cassie waited until everyone had settled, until the room found its own stillness.

"This is not a light topic," she said plainly. "You are not required to speak. You are allowed to leave. You are allowed to change your mind at any point."

A few people nodded, visibly relieved by the permission.

Cassie continued, her voice steady. "Obedience is often taught as virtue. Especially in systems that promise safety or belonging. For many people, obedience is not a moral failing. It is a survival strategy."

That landed hard.

She let it.

"When you grow up needing approval to stay safe," Cassie said, "compliance becomes a skill. You learn when to be quiet. When to agree. When to disappear just enough."

She did not dramatize it. She did not soften it either.

"And sometimes," she added, "that skill saves your life."

A man near the window exhaled sharply and stared at the floor.

Cassie rested her hands on the table. "The problem comes later. When survival habits get mislabeled as love."

She picked up a sprig of hawthorn and turned it between her fingers, careful of the thorns. "Love that requires you to abandon yourself is not devotion. It is erosion."

The room grew very quiet.

"I want you to think," Cassie said gently, "about where you learned that love meant compliance. Not intellectually. In your body. In the way you learned to stay."

Pens were set aside. This was not a writing exercise.

A woman near the front spoke first, her voice barely above a whisper. "Church."

Another voice followed. "My family."

"My first marriage," someone said from the back.

Each answer added weight, but also clarity. Threads that had been tangled began to separate.

Cassie nodded. "None of those people set out to teach you harm. But harm can still be taught."

She gestured toward the rose. "Rose reminds us that softness does not require surrender."

Then to the hawthorn. "And hawthorn reminds us that boundaries are an act of care."

She met the eyes of the group, one by one. "Love that demands silence is not love. It is management."

The words hung in the air, unmistakable.

Someone's breath hitched. Someone else wiped their eyes without apology.

Cassie did not rush to comfort. She trusted the room to hold what had been named.

"We are not here to shame obedience," she said. "We are here to notice when it is still running the show. Agency does not mean rebellion. It means consent."

Morgan spoke then, quietly. "Consent can be withdrawn."

A woman in the second row nodded slowly, her expression changing as something clicked into place. "I thought love was something I had to earn by being agreeable," she said. "I did not realize I was allowed to say no and stay."

That was the moment.

Not loud. Not dramatic. Just a soft rearranging of truth.

Cassie smiled, gentle and fierce at once. "You are."

The session ended without applause. People left slowly, many lingering near the herbs, touching them as if testing the idea of gentleness paired with strength.

Cassie stayed behind, collecting cups and folding chairs, her chest heavy but steady.

This work was not comfortable.

But it was honest.

And honesty, she had learned, was the beginning of love that did not require obedience to survive.

Chapter Ninety-Six: What She Takes With Her

Her name was Hazel, though most people in Emerdeen knew her only as the woman who ran the small alterations shop two doors down from the bakery.

She left Stirred & Spellbound later than most that afternoon, lingering just long enough to make sure Cassie had not called her back for anything. She had not spoken much during the workshop. She had not needed to. The words had settled into her body like a stone dropped into water, sending quiet ripples outward.

Love that demands silence is not love. It is management.

The sentence followed her down the street.

Hazel stopped once, halfway to her shop, because she realized her jaw hurt. She had been clenching it. Out of habit. Out of training so old she no longer remembered learning it.

She forced herself to unclench, rolling her shoulders back, letting her breath drop lower into her chest. It felt unfamiliar. Like walking with a different gait.

That was when she saw Bram.

He was crouched near the edge of his garden plot behind the greenhouse, hands sunk into the soil as he teased apart a cluster of roots. He looked up when he sensed her standing there, dirt smudged across his knuckles, expression open in a way that made conversation feel possible without commitment.

"Afternoon," he said easily. "You look like someone who just rearranged something important."

Hazel laughed despite herself. "Is it that obvious?"

Bram stood and brushed his hands together. "Sometimes people leave that shop like they have finally stopped holding their breath."

She considered that, then nodded. "That sounds right."

She hesitated, then gestured toward the rows of plants. "Those were in the workshop today. Rose and hawthorn."

Bram smiled softly. "Ah. That explains the energy in the air."

She stepped closer, curiosity overtaking caution. "Cassie said rose was for softness and hawthorn for boundaries. I have always thought of boundaries as hard."

"They can be," Bram said. He knelt again and beckoned her closer. "But in plants, boundaries are how life continues."

He gently lifted a branch of hawthorn, careful to avoid the thorns. "These look aggressive if you do not know them. But they protect without choking the plant. They define where it ends so it can keep growing."

Hazel reached out, then stopped herself. "So, boundaries are not punishment?"

Bram glanced up at her. "No. They are maintenance."

Something in her chest loosened at that.

"And rose," she prompted.

Bram plucked a fallen petal from the soil and placed it in her palm. "Rose teaches resilience through softness. It heals without pretending the wound did not exist."

Hazel stared at the petal resting against her skin. "I was taught that love meant being agreeable. That if I pushed back, I was being difficult."

Bram considered her carefully before answering. "Plants that never push back get trampled."

She laughed, surprised by the sound of it. "That is not very poetic," she said.

"It is very botanical," Bram replied, deadpan.

They stood together in companionable silence for a moment. Hazel felt the urge to explain herself, to justify why the workshop had affected her so deeply. She resisted it. She did not owe a defense.

"I think," she said slowly, "I am going to stop apologizing at work for things that are not mistakes."

Bram nodded as if she had announced a perfectly reasonable plan. "Good place to start."

She hesitated again, then asked, "Do you think it is okay to change like this. Quietly. Without asking permission."

Bram smiled, warm and certain. "That is how most real changes survive."

Hazel left the garden with a small bundle of rose and hawthorn Bram pressed into her hands. Not as instruction. As reminder.

Later that evening, when a familiar voice in her life expected her silence out of habit, Hazel felt the weight of the herbs in her pocket and chose differently.

Not loudly. Not cruelly.

But clearly. And for the first time, the choice felt less like defiance and more like care.

Chapter Ninety-Seven: Faith as Relationship, Not Rule

The room filled more slowly than it had for the previous workshops.

Cassie noticed the difference immediately. The careful steps. The way people hovered at the doorway, scanning faces before choosing a seat. These were not newcomers to belief. They were people shaped by it. People who carried faith in their bodies the way others carried old injuries, sometimes protective, sometimes tender to the touch.

Cassie had prepared for this session with particular care.

The chairs were arranged with extra space between them, as if acknowledging that closeness could feel threatening when belief had once been used to crowd the soul. On the central table rested two small bowls. One held amethyst, deep purple and quiet. The other held sodalite, veined with white like truth trying to move through stone.

Morgan moved through the room with a kettle, pouring tea slowly. No incense. No ritual gestures. Just warmth.

When everyone had settled, Cassie did not begin with a lesson.

She began with acknowledgment.

"Faith has been part of our lives since before we had language for choice," she said. "For many of us, belief arrived before we knew how to question it. Before we knew how to consent."

A murmur of recognition passed through the room.

Cassie continued, her voice steady and unhurried. "Religion has shaped how we learned right and wrong. How we learned obedience. How we learned comfort. Even those who left it carry its imprint. We do not shed it just because we walk away."

She let the truth of that breathe.

"This session is not about rejecting belief," Cassie said. "It is about remembering that faith is a relationship, not a rulebook."

She lifted a piece of amethyst and held it loosely. "This stone is often associated with faith and spiritual insight. Not because it answers questions, but because it slows the need for certainty."

She passed it around, watching hands receive it with reverence that surprised some of them.

"Sodalite," she said, indicating the second bowl, "is linked to truth. Not truth as correctness. Truth as alignment. The kind that can change."

Cassie paused, choosing her next words with care.

"Many of us were taught that faith meant knowing," she said. "Knowing who is right. Knowing who is wrong. Knowing what happens if we step out of line."

Someone in the back nodded, eyes fixed on the floor.

"But relationship requires something else," Cassie continued. "It requires curiosity. Listening. The willingness to sit with mystery without demanding resolution."

She did not say the word danger, but everyone understood what she meant. They remembered what certainty had done when it hardened into weaponry. When belief had stopped listening.

"There are people who believe faith must be enforced to survive," Cassie said gently. "Who believe that if doubt is allowed, everything collapses."

She did not name him.

"They are wrong," she said simply.

A woman near the window lifted her head, eyes shining. "I always thought questioning meant I was failing."

Cassie met her gaze. "Questioning is often how relationships deepen."

Morgan spoke then, voice calm and grounded. "Rules close conversations. Relationships keep them open."

Cassie nodded. "Faith that cannot tolerate questions is not faith. It is fear wearing sacred language."

She invited the group to write one sentence. Not a creed. Not a confession.

"Write something you believe," she said. "And then write one question you are still willing to ask."

The pens moved slowly.

Fi wrote carefully, crossing out and starting again. Fox stared at his page for a long time before writing a single line, then another beneath it.

Cassie gave them time.

As people shared, the room softened. Beliefs were spoken without defense. Questions were voiced without apology.

One man said quietly, "I believe something larger than me exists. I do not believe it needs me to be afraid."

A woman added, "I believe love is sacred. I am still asking why I was taught to fear it."

Cassie felt something shift, subtle but profound.

This was not deconversion.

It was release.

When the session ended, people lingered longer than usual, touching the stones as if thanking them for their patience. Some left with tears. Others with relief.

Cassie stayed behind, collecting cups and listening to the quiet return.

Faith, she thought, did not disappear when rules loosened.

It breathed.

And in that breath, there was freedom.

Chapter Ninety-Eight: The Cost of Belief

His name was Thomas, though in Emerdeen he was mostly known as the man who fixed old radios and refused to throw anything away if it could be coaxed back to life.

He left the workshop later than most, not because he wanted to linger, but because his legs did not move when he told them to. The sentence he had spoken aloud kept replaying in his mind, louder now that the room was quiet.

I believe something larger than me exists. I do not believe it needs me to be afraid.

It had sounded reasonable when he said it. Even calm.

Now it felt dangerous.

Thomas walked home slowly, hands shoved deep into his pockets, shoulders tight against an evening that had not earned his distrust. The words followed him past the bakery, past the closed library, past the place where he used to kneel every Sunday without fail.

Fear had been the first thing he learned about God.

Not awe. Not mystery. Fear.

He had learned it before he learned to read, before he understood metaphor, before he could question who decided which stories were sacred and which were warnings. He had learned it in the rhythm of sermons that circled endlessly around obedience. In rules explained as love. In silence framed as virtue.

Do not ask. Do not doubt. Do not trust yourself.

Thomas stopped walking and leaned against a lamppost, breath shallow.

He had tried to obey. For decades. He had followed rules written by long dead figures whose voices came to him only through translations and interpretations layered thick with power and agenda. Characters elevated to authority by repetition rather than proof. Stories written by men who were trying, very successfully, to manage their own fear by controlling others.

The realization came with heat.

Anger flared in his chest, sharp and unwelcome. Anger at the manipulation. At the way society not only accepted it but endorsed it. At how easily fear had been called holiness. At how guilt had been installed so early that it felt like conscience.

He had been told his anger was sin.

But standing there, jaw clenched and hands shaking slightly, Thomas knew that was another lie.

This anger was not destructive. It was clarifying.

"You are allowed to be angry," a voice said gently.

He turned, startled.

Cassie stood a few steps away, coat pulled close, expression open and unguarded. She had not followed him deliberately. She had simply noticed.

"I did not mean to interrupt," she added. "But you looked like someone carrying something heavy without handles."

Thomas laughed once, the sound rough. "That is an accurate assessment."

They stood together beneath the lamppost, the quiet between them holding rather than pressing.

"I grew up believing fear was proof of devotion," Thomas said finally. "If you were not afraid, you were doing it wrong."

Cassie nodded. "Fear is a very efficient teacher. Especially if what you want is obedience."

He looked at her sharply, relief and disbelief crossing his face at once. "That is exactly it. And the worst part is how normal it all is. How much of it is treated like moral good."

Cassie leaned back against the lamppost beside him. "Power does not like to admit it is power. It prefers to call itself truth."

Thomas swallowed. "I feel angry. And then I feel guilty for feeling angry. Like I am betraying something sacred."

Cassie considered him carefully. "You are not betraying the sacred," she said. "You are noticing where it was misused."

He exhaled slowly. "No one ever told me that was allowed."

"They would not," Cassie replied softly. "Because once you notice, control gets harder."

They stood in silence for a moment, the street quiet around them.

"I do believe in something," Thomas said. "I just do not believe it needs my fear to exist."

Cassie smiled gently. "That sounds like a relationship finally allowed to breathe."

He laughed, a little broken but sincere. "It also sounds like rebellion."

"It is," Cassie agreed. "But not against mystery. Against manipulation."

Thomas felt something loosen in his chest, not resolve, not certainty, but space.

"How do you live with the guilt," he asked. "The kind that shows up even when you know better."

Cassie tilted her head. "You do not argue with it. You acknowledge where it came from. Then you choose differently anyway."

She met his gaze, steady and kind. "Guilt is just an echo. It gets quieter when you stop obeying it."

Thomas nodded slowly, the words settling into him with unexpected gentleness.

When they parted, he walked home lighter than he had in years. Not because the questions were gone, but because he no longer believed fear was the price of faith.

And that, he realized, changed everything.

Chapter Ninety-Nine: The Body Is the First Altar

Morgan prepared for this workshop more slowly than the others.

They moved through the greenhouse with deliberate care, touching leaves as they passed, inhaling deeply where vetiver roots dried on a low shelf and rosemary hung in loose bundles from the rafters. The scents grounded without demanding attention. Earth and memory. Sharpness and warmth.

Morgan paused, one hand resting against the worktable, and let their breath settle.

Their body had never been neutral territory.

For years, it had been a site of negotiation. Of contradiction. Of pain that arrived uninvited and stayed too long. Of dysphoria that spoke louder than any doctrine ever had. Their spirit had not floated above that experience. It had been shaped by it. Pressed into it. Sometimes bruised by it.

There had been seasons when their body felt like an obstacle to transcend. A thing to endure rather than inhabit.

Spiritual spaces had not helped. Too many teachings suggested that enlightenment meant rising above the flesh. Too many prayers framed the body as temptation, weakness, distraction.

Morgan had learned early how dangerous that idea could be. Ignoring the body did not make pain holy. It made it invisible.

They exhaled slowly and continued setting up the room.

When participants arrived, Morgan greeted them quietly, inviting them to choose a place where they felt comfortable. No assigned seats. No hierarchy. Small bowls of dried vetiver and rosemary rested nearby, offered without instruction.

Morgan waited until the room settled, then spoke.

"The body is the first altar," they said. "Not because it is sacred in some abstract way, but because it is where everything is felt first."

They did not smile. They did not soften the truth.

"Many spiritual systems bypass the body entirely," Morgan continued. "They treat it as something to overcome. Something to discipline into silence."

Cassie, seated near the wall, nodded. "Anything that tells you to ignore your body is afraid of your agency."

A murmur of agreement moved through the room.

Morgan invited everyone to stand or sit however felt natural. "We are not fixing anything today," they said. "We are noticing."

They guided the group through simple grounding practices. Feet against the floor. Breath moving without instruction. Hands resting where they felt most at ease.

"Notice what yes feels like," Morgan said. "Not intellectually. In your body."

They paused. "And now notice no."

People shifted. Some frowned. Some inhaled sharply as recognition sparked.

A woman near the window pressed her hand to her stomach. "My no is tight," she said quietly. "Like a knot."

A man across the room shook his head slowly. "Mine feels heavy. Like gravity."

Morgan nodded. "Both are correct."

They passed the rosemary around next, inviting people to smell it, to notice whether it sharpened or softened their awareness. Vetiver followed, its scent deeper, anchoring.

"These are not cures," Morgan said. "They are companions. They help you listen."

As the workshop continued, something subtle changed. People stopped performing stillness and began inhabiting it. Shoulders dropped. Spines adjusted. Breath deepened without instruction.

One participant began to cry quietly, not from pain but from relief.

"I thought my body was betraying me," they said. "I did not realize it was trying to protect me."

Morgan felt the words land in their own chest.

"Yes," they said softly. "The body speaks before the mind has permission."

When the workshop ended, no one rushed to leave. People lingered, touching the herbs, standing quietly with one another.

Morgan remained seated after the room emptied, palms resting on their thighs, feeling the steady presence of their own body beneath them.

It still caused pain sometimes. It still carried angst. It still asked difficult questions of their spirit.

But it was not an enemy.

It was the place where truth arrived first.

And honoring it felt like the most sacred practice of all.

Chapter One Hundred: Tools, Not Talismans

The tables were covered before anyone arrived. Not arranged for reverence. Not displayed for awe. Just laid out plainly, like a set of instruments waiting to be used. Clear quartz. Amethyst. Citrine. Smoky quartz. Jasper. Stones both polished and rough, their differences visible without explanation.

Cassie watched people enter and pause, the way they always did when faced with objects that had been assigned power by rumor rather than understanding. Some leaned in, curious. Some kept their hands firmly at their sides, wary of being asked to believe something they did not.

Baz stood beside her, arms folded loosely, observing with the same quiet attentiveness he brought to any system under examination.

"Okay," Cassie said once everyone had settled. "Let us start by lowering the stakes."

A few people laughed.

"These are not talismans," she continued. "They will not save you, curse you, protect you, or ruin your life. If they could do all that, I would not be allowed to keep them on open shelves."

Baz added dryly, "Insurance would be a nightmare."

That earned real laughter, the tension easing.

Cassie gestured to the stones. "Crystals are tools. That is it. Tools that hold structure well. Tools that respond predictably to pressure, heat, and repetition."

Baz stepped forward then, picking up a piece of quartz. "From a materials standpoint," he said, "this is remarkable because of how stable it is. It holds pattern. It does not invent one."

He tapped it lightly against the table. "It does not generate energy. It responds to it."

Cassie nodded. "Which is where the myths get it wrong. People want inherent power. They want something external to do the work for them."

She looked around the room. "Meaning does not come from the stone. It comes from how you use it."

Morgan, seated near the window, watched a woman relax visibly at that.

Baz continued, "Energy is not mystical," he said. "It is attention plus repetition. What you focus on consistently changes how you respond over time. The stone just gives that focus somewhere to land."

Cassie smiled at him. "See. Romance."

Baz rolled his eyes fondly.

Cassie turned back to the group. "Here is the exercise. You are not going to look up meanings. You are not going to ask what a stone is for. You are going to notice how your body responds."

She gestured toward the tables. "Walk around. Pick one up. Hold it. If nothing happens, put it back. That is useful information."

People moved hesitantly at first, then more freely. Hands hovered. Some stones were picked up and set down quickly. Others lingered in palms, brows furrowing as attention turned inward.

Fi picked up a smoky quartz and felt its weight settle her breath. Fox watched, skeptical, then picked up a stone himself and frowned.

"This one makes me want to argue," he said.

Cassie grinned. "Congratulations. You found your stone."

A man near the back shook his head slowly. "I always thought this was nonsense," he admitted. "But holding this one feels… steady."

Baz nodded. "Steady is a response. That is data."

Cassie watched a woman who had been tense since entering the room pick up a piece of amethyst and exhale without realizing it. The moment was small. It mattered anyway.

When everyone returned to their seats, Cassie spoke again. "If you decide to keep using a stone, you are not honoring the stone. You are honoring your own attention."

She paused. "And if someday it stops working, that does not mean you failed. It means you changed."

Baz added, "Tools evolve as users do. That is normal."

Cassie gathered the stones back into their bowls without ceremony. "There is no loyalty test here. No hierarchy of objects. Just curiosity."

As the workshop ended, people lingered longer than usual, not to ask for meanings, but to talk about sensation. Weight. Temperature. Memory.

Cassie leaned against the counter beside Baz once the room cleared.

"That went better than expected," she said.

Baz nodded. "Turns out people appreciate not being lied to."

She smiled. "Who knew."

Outside, the late afternoon light caught the stones briefly through the window, illuminating them without sanctifying them.

Tools, Cassie thought, were most powerful when they stayed honest. And honesty, like attention, was something you practiced.

Chapter One Hundred One: When Prayer Hurts

The session was optional. Clearly they all were, but she wanted these people – her friends, her neighbors – to understand how triggering this session could be.

Cassie made sure that was clear on the sign in the window and again when people stepped inside. No explanation offered. No reassurance layered on top of the truth. Optional meant optional, not a test of courage or commitment.

The room was arranged with only chairs. No tables. No stones. No herbs. Nothing to hold or hide behind. Just space and the quiet that settled into it when people chose to stay.

Not many did.

Those who remained took their seats slowly, leaving gaps between chairs, as if each person needed proof that they could leave without consequence. Cassie waited until the door was closed, until the last shuffling stopped.

She did not begin with instruction.

She began with honesty.

"There are prayers that heal," Cassie said. "And there are prayers that harm."

She did not raise her voice. She did not soften the words.

"Some prayers are used to erase parts of a person in the name of saving them," she continued. "Some are spoken over children who do not yet have the language to resist. Some are framed as love while demanding silence, obedience, and disappearance."

The room remained very still.

Cassie rested her hands on her knees. "I am not here to argue theology. I am here to name impact."

She told a brief story. Not the worst one. Just enough.

"There was a time when people prayed over me to make me smaller," she said. "To make me quieter. To make me easier to manage. Those prayers were called mercy. They felt like erasure."

A man in the second row closed his eyes. A woman near the wall pressed her palms together tightly.

Cassie let the silence stretch.

"If prayer has ever hurt you," she said gently, "you are allowed to say that. You are allowed to name it without fixing it or forgiving it."

One person spoke, voice shaking. "They prayed for my anger to leave. It was the only thing keeping me alive."

Another added, "They said my doubt was a demon."

Someone else whispered, "They prayed until I stopped talking about myself."

Each story was offered without commentary. Cassie did not correct or reframe. She simply witnessed.

"That was harm," she said quietly after a pause. "Holiness does not excuse it."

The session ended without a closing ritual. Cassie did not ask for resolution. She did not suggest hope. She simply opened the kettle and began pouring tea.

Chamomile and skullcap. Gentle. Nervine. Grounding.

People accepted the cups gratefully, wrapping their hands around the warmth. Some stayed seated. Some stood near the windows. Conversations remained low and careful, like walking on a healing limb.

One by one, people left.

Petra stayed.

She waited until Cassie had stacked the last chair and wiped the counter, until the shop felt small again.

"I did not plan to talk," Petra said finally.

Cassie turned and leaned against the counter. "You do not have to."

"I know," Petra said. "But if I do not say it now, I will keep swallowing it."

Cassie nodded once. "Okay."

Petra's hands trembled slightly as she held her empty cup. "They prayed for me every time I spoke up. For my stubbornness. For my questions. They said God would fix me if I was patient."

Her breath hitched. "I learned to disappear so well that I forgot how to come back."

Cassie felt the words land heavily, familiar and sharp.

"That hurts," Cassie said simply. "And it should not have happened to you."

Petra's eyes filled. "I still feel guilty for being angry."

Cassie met her gaze steadily. "Anger is often the part of you that knew something was wrong long before you had permission to name it."

Petra exhaled, something loosening.

They stood in silence for a moment, not awkward, not heavy.

"You are not broken," Cassie added. "And you do not owe anyone gratitude for surviving harm."

Petra nodded, tears slipping free without apology.

When she left, the shop felt quieter than before.

Cassie rinsed the last cup and turned off the lights, carrying Petra's words with care.

Some prayers, she knew, had to be unlearned before anything new could grow.

And naming that truth was its own kind of healing.

Chapter One Hundred and Two: Reclaiming Ritual

There had been a break. Not announced as such but felt all the same.

Stirred & Spellbound had gone quiet for a few days after the last workshop. The lights were still on in the evenings. The door still opened. Tea was still brewed. But the chairs stayed stacked. The long table remained bare.

Cassie needed the pause.

So did the town.

The workshops had been helpful, yes. Clarifying. Unsettling in the way truth often was. But they were also a lot. Each one pulled something loose. Each one asked people to notice what they had been holding in their bodies, their beliefs, their relationships. That kind of work could not be rushed without doing harm of its own.

Cassie had learned that the hard way.

When she finally announced the next session, she chose the word reclaim carefully.

Ritual as choice.

The room felt different when people returned. Softer. Less urgent. Some familiar faces were missing, choosing rest over participation. Cassie approved silently. The ones who came arrived without expectation of transformation.

Good, she thought. That was the point.

The tables held only two bowls this time. One with coarse salt. One with clear water.

Cassie stood at the front; hands relaxed at her sides. "Ritual has a reputation," she began. "Mostly earned."

A ripple of knowing laughter moved through the room.

"For a lot of us," she continued, "ritual was something inherited. Something imposed. Something you were told mattered whether it made sense to you or not."

She paused, letting people nod, shift, breathe.

"But ritual is not a relic," Cassie said. "It is a technology. A way humans mark meaning. And like any tool, it should serve the person using it."

She gestured to the bowls. "Salt and water show up everywhere. Cultures that never spoke to each other figured them out independently. Not because they are magical in themselves, but because they are accessible. Familiar. Useful."

She dipped her fingers briefly into the water. "Ritual starts with presence."

Then touched the salt. "And intention."

Cassie looked around the room. "Rituals are created, not inherited. And the most important thing about them is consent."

Morgan, seated near the wall, nodded.

"You get to choose when a ritual begins," Cassie said. "You get to choose when it ends. And you get to stop halfway through if something feels wrong."

She let that settle.

"Any ritual that cannot be interrupted is not sacred," Cassie added. "It is coercive."

That line landed hard, but clean.

She invited participants to design something small. Not dramatic. Not symbolic beyond what felt honest.

"A ritual for ending the workday," she suggested. "Or for beginning the morning. Or for letting something go without making it a performance."

People leaned in. Fingers traced lines in salt. Water was poured and repoured. Some closed their eyes. Others kept them open, anchoring themselves in the room.

Fi created something quiet and brief. Fox watched, then surprised himself by doing the same.

A woman near the window whispered, "I like knowing I can change it later."

Cassie smiled. "You should. Rituals that cannot adapt tend to fossilize."

When people shared what they had created, there was no ranking. No correction. Cassie listened with the same care she asked of them.

One ritual was only a breath and a hand over the heart. Another involved washing hands slowly at night. Another was simply saying no without explanation.

All of it counted.

As the workshop wound down, Cassie felt the familiar ache behind her ribs. Not exhaustion exactly. More like the soreness after using muscles you had neglected for too long.

She did not hide it.

"These workshops matter," she said honestly. "But so does rest. We will not meet every week. We will not keep digging if there is nothing ready to be unearthed."

No one argued.

People cleaned up together, rinsing bowls, stacking chairs. The room returned to its ordinary shape.

When Cassie finally locked the door, she did not feel depleted.

She felt grounded.

Ritual reclaimed, she thought, was not about doing more.

It was about choosing when to begin.

And when to stop.

Chapter One Hundred Three: Fox Asks the Hard Questions

Fox had not planned to attend.

He told himself that as he stood near the back of the room, arms crossed, weight settled into his heels like an anchor. He was not here for belief. He was not here for reassurance. He was here because something in him refused to leave questions unasked when language started getting slippery.

He had learned the cost of that too early.

Cassie noticed him immediately. She always did. Not with suspicion, but with the particular attention reserved for people who were listening hard enough to interrupt.

"Glad you're here," she said simply, as if his presence was expected rather than tolerated.

Fox nodded once. No promises implied.

The discussion began easily enough. People talking about what had shifted for them. What felt truer. What still snagged. Fox listened, cataloging words the way he always did. Meaning. Faith. Energy. Intention.

Eventually, he raised his hand.

"When we say belief," he asked, voice steady, "do we mean what people think is true, or how they actually behave."

The room quieted.

Cassie did not flinch. She smiled, the kind that said thank you rather than brace yourself. "Excellent question."

Fox continued before anyone could soften it for him. "Because I've met a lot of people who believe the right things and act terribly. And a lot of people who don't believe any of this and still show up with integrity."

A few people nodded. Someone exhaled in relief.

Cassie leaned against the counter. "I agree," she said. "Belief without behavior is decoration."

Fox snorted despite himself.

"What I'm trying to understand," he said, "is why belief keeps getting treated like the entry requirement."

Cassie tilted her head. "It isn't."

That stopped him.

"Say more," he said.

"We care about orientation," Cassie replied. "How you move through the world. What you do when no one is watching. Belief can inform that, but it doesn't guarantee it."

Fox considered that. "So, skepticism isn't a problem."

"Not if it's honest," Cassie said. "Skepticism is often just integrity refusing to be rushed."

Something loosened in his chest at that. He hadn't realized how tightly he'd been holding the line between curiosity and capitulation.

"I don't believe in magic," Fox said plainly. "Not the way people mean it."

Cassie nodded. "You've been clear."

"I'm staying," he added, surprising himself with the admission, "not because I believe. Because I trust the process. I trust that no one here is trying to manage me."

The word landed with weight.

Cassie's expression softened. "That was true for me once too," she said. "Long before I had language for what I was doing."

Fox looked at her, really looked. He could see it now. The early skepticism. The refusal to swallow certainty just to belong.

"So, belief isn't the point," he said slowly.

"No," Cassie replied. "Agency is."

The room breathed again.

As the discussion moved on, Fox stayed quiet, but it was a different quiet than before. Not defensive. Not withdrawn. Observant.

When the session ended, he didn't rush for the door. He lingered, listening to the scrape of chairs, the murmur of conversation.

Cassie caught his eye as he passed. "You're welcome to keep asking the hard questions," she said. "They help us stay honest."

Fox nodded. "Good. Because I'm not done."

He stepped outside into the cool evening air, the town settling around him in familiar ways. He still didn't believe.

But he trusted what was happening here.

And for the first time, that felt like enough.

Chapter One Hundred Four: Fi Chooses Meaning

Fi came to the session intending to sit near the window, to listen the way she had learned to do in Emerdeen. Attentive but unclaimed. Skeptical without being sharp. Present without volunteering herself as evidence of anything.

But as the discussion unfolded, something in her shifted.

People were talking about belief again. About what they had inherited without consent. About the quiet pressure of tradition that arrived bundled with love and expectation, handed down like a family heirloom no one remembered choosing.

Fi felt the familiar tightening in her chest, not resistance this time, but recognition.

When the pause came, the kind Cassie always left open on purpose, Fi heard her own voice before she had decided to use it.

"Can I add something," she asked.

Cassie looked at her, surprised but welcoming. "Please."

Fi stood, more out of instinct than confidence. She rested her hands lightly on the back of the chair in front of her, grounding herself in the ordinary weight of it.

"I don't believe in faith the way I was taught," Fi said. "But I don't think that means it's empty."

The room quieted in the way it did when people sensed something honest finding its shape.

"I think faith is an inherited story," Fi continued. "Not an obligation. A story someone told to explain how they survived, or what they loved, or what scared them."

She paused, choosing her words carefully. "Stories can be carried without being obeyed."

Morgan watched her with quiet attentiveness. Cassie did not interrupt.

Fi reached for the small bowl on the table and lifted a piece of smoky quartz, its surface dark and steady, light moving through it only at certain angles.

"This stone is heavy," Fi said. "Not dramatic. Not flashy. It doesn't promise clarity. It helps you feel what's already there."

She turned it in her palm. "That's what inherited belief feels like to me. Weight. Not something to throw away, but something to understand before you decide how to carry it."

She looked around the room. "I don't think we owe our ancestors obedience. But I think we owe them honesty."

A murmur of agreement moved through the group.

"My aunt," Fi said, voice steady now, "left us a house. And with it, a story she never got to finish telling."

She swallowed, then continued. "The Carrow house held what she couldn't say out loud. Not because it was sacred. Because it mattered."

Fox shifted in his seat; eyes fixed on her.

"When we unsealed it," Fi said, "we didn't inherit her choices. We inherited the chance to make our own."

She set the smoky quartz back in the bowl. "That's stewardship. Not belief. Choosing what to keep. Choosing what to tend. Choosing what ends with you."

The room was very still.

Cassie spoke softly. "Thank you."

Fi nodded, pulse racing, surprised by the steadiness she felt rather than the fear.

Later, as people filtered out, Cassie walked with her toward the door. "You didn't soften," Cassie said. "You integrated."

Fi smiled faintly. "I still don't believe the way people want me to."

Cassie returned the smile. "Neither did I. At first."

Outside, the afternoon light caught the street just right, and Fi thought of the Carrow house waiting quietly for her. No longer sealed. No longer burdened with guarding the past.

A living example.

Meaning chosen, not imposed.

And for the first time, Fi realized she wasn't standing apart from Emerdeen anymore.

She was tending something.

And that felt like its own kind of faith.

Chapter One Hundred Five: The Difference Between Hope and Escape

The room smelled warmer than usual.

Ginger and cinnamon steeped together on the side table, sharp and sweet at once, the kind of scent that traveled straight to the body before the mind had a chance to interpret it. Cassie had chosen them deliberately. Not soothing. Not sedating. Grounding. Waking.

Baz stood near the window, mug in hand, watching people arrive. He had agreed to be present for this one without being asked. Cassie noticed. She did not comment on it, but she felt the quiet steadiness of his choice.

This workshop always sat on a fault line.

Hope was not a gentle word for everyone.

Cassie waited until the chairs filled and the room settled into a listening posture that felt more guarded than curious. She understood why. Hope had been used as an exit ramp from pain far too often.

"We talk about hope like it's always virtuous," Cassie began. "Like it's something you should reach for automatically."

She rested her hands on the back of a chair, not pacing, not performing. "But hope can be misused. Especially when it's offered as a replacement for presence."

Baz nodded slightly.

"Sometimes hope is handed to people who are hurting as a way to make their pain inconvenient," Cassie continued. "Be hopeful. Stay positive. Look on the bright side."

A few people shifted uncomfortably.

"That version of hope doesn't help," she said. "It bypasses."

Baz spoke then, voice calm and precise. "In engineering, bypassing a system doesn't remove the problem. It just reroutes pressure until something fails somewhere else."

A low murmur of recognition moved through the room.

Cassie smiled at him briefly, then turned back to the group. "Exactly. Hope can be a way of staying. Or it can be a way of escaping."

She gestured toward the tea. "Drink if you want. Notice what warmth does in your body. Notice what happens when you stay with sensation instead of floating above it."

People wrapped their hands around mugs. Breath slowed. Color returned to cheeks.

"I want you to think about a time when hope helped you," Cassie said. "And a time when it hurt."

She did not rush them.

A woman near the front spoke first. "Hope helped me leave," she said. "It let me imagine a life that didn't hurt all the time."

A man across from her added quietly, "Hope hurt me when it was used to keep me where I was. When I was told things would get better if I just waited."

Baz watched the exchange, something thoughtful passing across his face.

"I was taught that hope meant ignoring data," he said after a moment. "If something wasn't working, you were supposed to believe harder instead of changing the system."

A few people laughed softly, not because it was funny, but because it was familiar.

Cassie nodded. "Hope that asks you to disappear isn't hope."

The sentence landed cleanly.

"It's a delay tactic," she continued. "Real hope stays with what's real. It doesn't demand you abandon yourself to earn relief."

Morgan, seated near the wall, added, "Hope that's grounded makes room for grief."

Cassie picked up a mug and inhaled the steam. "Ginger and cinnamon don't numb," she said. "They bring circulation. They remind the body it's still here."

She looked around the room. "Hope should do the same."

The exercise was simple. No writing. No sharing unless someone wanted to.

"Notice where you've used hope to stay," Cassie said. "And where you've used it to leave yourself behind."

The room grew quiet in a way that felt honest rather than heavy.

Baz caught Cassie's eye and spoke again. "Staying doesn't mean accepting harm," he said. "It means staying present enough to respond."

Cassie nodded, grateful.

As the workshop wound down, people lingered, not to seek reassurance, but to sit with what had surfaced. One person stared into their mug as if seeing something new. Another stretched their hands, testing sensation.

When the room finally emptied, Cassie leaned against the counter and exhaled.

"That one always costs," she said.

Baz smiled gently. "But it pays forward."

She reached for his hand briefly, grounding herself in the warmth that remained.

Hope, she thought, wasn't a promise.

It was a practice.

And like everything else worth keeping, it asked you to stay.

Chapter One Hundred Six: The Workshop That Was Just Tea

Cassie did not put a title on the chalkboard. She did not arrange chairs in a circle or line up objects on the tables. There were no handouts. No themes written neatly in advance. When people arrived, they hesitated in the doorway, scanning the room for cues that were not there.

The intensity had been growing with each workshop. Cassie could feel it in her bones. The way people arrived carrying more than curiosity. The way silence landed heavier. The way insight came with grief attached.

They needed a pause that was not framed as rest, but as presence. So, she made tea.

Kettles steamed gently on the counter. A few mismatched mugs waited nearby. Someone had brought honey. Someone else added lemon slices without asking. Cassie moved through the room easily, greeting people as they came, inviting them to sit wherever felt right.

"No lesson tonight," she said simply. "We're just here."

A few people blinked at her, uncertain.

"That's it?" someone asked.

Cassie smiled. "That's it."

The room settled slowly, like water finding its level. Conversations began hesitantly, then warmed. People talked about ordinary things at first. Weather. Work. The odd comfort of routines returning. Laughter broke out in one corner, unselfconscious and brief, then again, a little louder.

Crystals sat quietly on their shelves, untouched. No one reached for them. No one asked what they meant.

Morgan noticed and caught Cassie's eye, something like wonder passing between them.

Baz leaned against the wall, listening more than speaking, watching how people moved toward and away from one another naturally when nothing was being guided. Fi sat with Fox near the window, sharing a story that ended in a snort of laughter neither tried to suppress.

Bram arrived late with a basket of bread and set it down without announcement.

The room filled with the low hum of human presence.

Cassie stood behind the counter for a while, hands wrapped around her mug, observing. She noticed who gravitated toward silence and who needed words. Who sat alone comfortably and who drifted closer to others. No one was being led. No one was being corrected.

This, she realized, was the work integrating.

She thought back to her earliest days in Emerdeen. How she had believed she needed to explain magic to justify it. How she had felt responsible for people's understanding, their growth, their outcomes.

Now she watched people practice discernment without her prompting. She saw boundaries honored organically. She saw curiosity without hunger.

Teaching, she understood then, had worked because it had taught independence.

She had not given them answers. She had given them permission.

At one point, a woman who had barely spoken in previous workshops leaned over to someone beside her and said, "I think I'm okay not knowing what comes next."

The words were not announced. They were not claimed as revelation.

They were simply true.

Cassie felt something settle inside her chest, not relief exactly, but alignment.

This was the most powerful session they had held.

No curriculum. No objectives.

Just people choosing to be present with one another without instruction.

As the evening wound down, no one rushed to leave. Chairs were pushed back slowly. Mugs were rinsed without being asked. Someone turned off a lamp near the window, leaving the room in softer light.

Cassie locked the door later than usual and stood alone for a moment, listening to the quiet that followed genuine connection.

She smiled to herself.

Magic, she had learned, did not always arrive dressed as insight.

Sometimes it came as tea.

And laughter.

And the simple, radical act of being together without being managed.

Chapter One Hundred Seven: The Thread Holds

Cassie stood alone in the shop after closing, the quiet familiar enough now that it did not ache.

There had been a time when silence pressed against her ribs, when the absence of voices felt like failure or abandonment. Now it felt companionable. A pause rather than an ending. She moved slowly through the space, almost reverently, straightening things that did not need straightening. A stack of notebooks aligned just so. A chair nudged back beneath the table. A jar turned so its handwritten label faced forward.

None of it was necessary.

That was the point.

The ritual was not about order. It was about noticing where she was, and who she had become inside these walls.

This was how it had begun.

The first vignette had been an accident of attention. A moment of making something small and careful with no expectation beyond the act itself. She had not known she was opening anything. She had not been searching for a doorway. She had simply followed the quiet pull of curiosity, believing that wonder was something you encountered alone.

Back then, she had stepped forward without witnesses, convinced that crossing into magic was a solitary act. A private leap. A personal risk.

Cassie smiled faintly at the memory.

She was not alone now.

The shop held that truth without announcement. The shelves bore the marks of many hands, fingerprints smudged into glass and wood. The floor remembered footsteps that came and went without fear or ceremony. Stirred and Spellbound was no longer just her threshold. It was a place people entered knowing they could leave again. A place where no one was asked to stay smaller than themselves.

Cassie turned off the main lights and let the smaller lamps glow, warm and low. She did not rush upstairs. Instead, she stepped outside and followed the familiar path toward the Carrow house, the night cool and steady around her. The town breathed easily, as if it trusted the dark to pass.

The house greeted her the way it always did now.

Open. Unbraced. Alive without performing.

Fi and Fox had done something remarkable without ever naming it as magic. They had listened. They had chosen stewardship over certainty. They had resisted the urge to master what they had inherited, opting instead to tend it. The house no longer guarded a wound. It held a story that could breathe without being retold repeatedly.

Cassie rested her hand against the porch rail and felt nothing push back.

Emerdeen held steady.

That, more than anything else, felt like the miracle.

The town no longer felt like a place that required constant vigilance to survive. The weave did not hum with urgency or warning. It existed as it was meant to, present and responsive. Morgan's work had taken root in bodies and breath. Bram's gardens thrived without needing explanation or defense. Baz's systems rested lightly now, attentive rather than controlling, responsive rather than anticipatory.

Cassie exhaled and let herself feel the fullness of it.

The thread had not snapped.

It had stretched. It had been tested. It had frayed and been rewoven with care and consent. And now it held, not because it was unbreakable, but because everyone involved knew how to tend it.

She returned to the shop as the hour deepened, moving through spaces that had once felt like thresholds and now simply felt like home. Upstairs, the lantern waited by the window, its glass catching the low light of the street below.

Cassie lifted it gently.

Once, the lantern had been a promise. A symbol of passage. Of crossing. Of illumination earned through risk and uncertainty.

Now it was something else entirely.

Continuity.

She set it back in its place, not extinguished, not blazing, simply lit enough to be found by anyone who needed it.

Cassie leaned against the window frame and watched Emerdeen settle into itself for the night. Doors closed. Lights dimmed. Conversations softened and drifted into quiet. The town did not withdraw. It rested.

She did not feel the pull to step away.

She did not feel the need to prove anything.

The story did not end because nothing was broken.

It ended because the thread held.

And for the first time, Cassie understood that this, too, was an ending worth trusting.

Chapter One Hundred Eight: Baz and the Unreasonable Idea

Baz had always believed that relationships, like systems, revealed themselves under sustained use.

You did not really know how something worked in the testing phase. You knew it when it had been stressed, interrupted, adapted, and still chosen. When it had failed in small ways and been repaired without panic. When it no longer required constant monitoring to feel safe.

He sat at the worktable in the back room, hands idle for once, watching Cassie move through the shop upstairs. She was not doing anything remarkable. That was the point. She watered a plant. She paused to read a note someone had left on the counter. She laughed quietly at something only she knew.

The calm still surprised him. There had been a version of himself, not that long ago, who would have assumed this was temporary. A lull before the next complication. A system waiting to be destabilized.

He did not think that anymore. What he and Cassie had built was not elegant in the way his early designs had been. It was not optimized. It was not sealed against error. It was resilient because it was allowed to change.

He loved her for that.

Not just the wit, though that mattered. Not just the way she could name things without shrinking them. He loved her because she did not confuse intensity with intimacy. Because she did not ask him to contain her or himself. Because when something went wrong, the first question was not whose fault is this, but what do we do next.

That had rewired him more thoroughly than any circuit ever had.

Baz smiled to himself, a quiet, private thing.

He stood and joined her at the counter, leaning beside her without interrupting whatever thought she was finishing.

"You look settled," she said, not looking up.

"I am," he replied. "Which is new enough that I keep checking for hidden variables."

She glanced at him then, amused. "Find any."

"Only one," he said.

Her eyebrow arched. "I should be worried."

"Possibly," Baz said. "I am having an idea."

Cassie set the watering can down slowly. "That tone has preceded both excellent outcomes and at least one minor disaster."

"This one," Baz said carefully, "does not solve a problem."

She blinked. "Well now I'm intrigued."

He took a breath. This was the part that still felt strange. Offering something without justification.

"What if," he said, "we left Emerdeen for a while."

Cassie stared at him.

"Not running," he added quickly. "Not escaping. Just… going somewhere that has nothing to do with magic, or memory, or repair."

She folded her arms, studying him. "Continue."

"What if we took a train," Baz said, warming to it now. "Or a ferry. Somewhere inconvenient. Somewhere slow. We do nothing useful.

We eat food that does not carry symbolism. We argue about museums. We get lost on purpose."

Cassie laughed. "You are describing a vacation."

"Yes," Baz said. "But badly. On purpose."

She leaned against the counter, eyes bright. "That is… wildly out of character for you."

He nodded. "That's how I know it's not a control strategy."

Cassie considered him for a long moment. "You're serious."

"I am," he said. "I don't want our relationship to only exist in response to things needing us. I want to choose us in a context where nothing is at stake."

Something in her expression softened.

"You know," she said slowly, "I stepped into the first vignette because I thought wonder had to be earned through risk."

Baz reached for her hand. "And now."

"And now," Cassie said, squeezing his fingers, "I think wonder might just like good company."

They stood there together, the shop quiet around them, the town steady beyond the windows.

Baz did not know where they would go. He only knew this: whatever came next did not need fixing.

And that felt like the most radical idea of all.

Chapter One Hundred Nine: Leaving the Loom Lit

Cassie had always thought leaving would feel dramatic.

A last look. A weighted pause at the threshold. Some internal reckoning about whether she had done enough or missed something vital. The old version of her believed departures needed gravity to be legitimate.

This one did not.

The morning they chose to go, the shop opened as usual. Light filtered through the front windows. The bell chimed when Morgan arrived first, carrying a crate of herbs and a folded schedule tucked under one arm. Bram followed soon after, dirt already on his hands, smelling faintly of rosemary and earth. Fi and Fox arrived together, arguing about nothing important and smiling like people who trusted where they were.

Cassie watched them from the stairs, a mug warming her palms.

Baz leaned against the banister beside her. "They've got this," he said quietly.

"I know," Cassie replied. And she meant it.

Downstairs, the loom rested in its familiar place, thread drawn through not as a command but as a conversation. It no longer hummed with urgency. It existed, ready to be used when needed, left alone when not.

Cassie descended the stairs and joined them, not to instruct, but to witness.

Morgan stood at the counter, calmly assigning the day's rhythms. Not orders. Invitations. "If anyone feels the weave tighten near the back garden, let me know. I'll check in." Their voice held certainty without rigidity.

Bram nodded. "I'll keep an eye on the rosemary. It's teaching patience again."

Fi adjusted a stack of notebooks, thoughtful. "If anyone comes asking about meaning," she said, glancing at Fox, "we'll start with listening."

Fox smirked. "And if they ask for certainty, I'll ask what they're willing to do with it."

Cassie smiled so hard her chest ached.

This was leadership.

Not control. Not containment. Presence. Discernment. Trust.

She walked to the loom and rested her fingers briefly against the wood. No pull. No warning. Just steadiness.

"We're going," Cassie said simply.

Four faces turned toward her, not startled, not anxious.

Morgan met her gaze first. "Go," they said. "We'll tend."

Bram chuckled softly. "The garden grows whether or not you're watching."

Fi nodded. "The house knows how to hold."

Fox added, "And if something breaks, we'll fix it. Or decide it doesn't need fixing."

Cassie laughed, emotion rising unexpectedly. "That sounds familiar."

Baz stepped forward then, setting the keys on the counter. Not relinquishing. Sharing. "Call if you need us," he said. "Not because we're in charge. Because we're still connected."

Morgan slid the keys into the drawer without ceremony. "Of course."

Cassie took one last look around the shop. Not memorizing. Not bracing. Just noticing.

The lantern stayed lit.

Not as a beacon for return, but as a sign that the light did not depend on her presence anymore.

Outside, the town breathed easily. Doors opened. Conversations started. Emerdeen held.

As Cassie and Baz walked away, hand in hand, Cassie felt no tug back. No guilt. No fear that she was abandoning something fragile.

She was leaving something resilient.

The thread did not fray.

The loom did not go silent.

It continued, tended by many hands, exactly as it should.

And for the first time, Cassie understood that stepping away was not an ending.

It was proof that what they had built could stand.

On its own.

Join the Magic Beyond the Pages

I love connecting with readers and would be thrilled to visit your book club, whether that's in person (if you're local or semi-local!) or through a cozy Zoom chat across the miles. We can dive into the world of Emerdeen, swap favorite moments, talk creative sparks, and maybe share a few secrets about what's next.

If your club would like to schedule a visit, reach out to me at www.melodyksmith.com.

Let's make some bookish magic together!

Book Club Discussion Questions:

1. Cassie's role evolves from guide to witness over the course of the book. At what point did you notice that shift most clearly, and how did it change your understanding of leadership?

2. The workshops emphasize discernment over belief. Which workshop or concept felt most challenging or surprising to you, and why?

3. The book repeatedly contrasts control and consent in spiritual, relational, and communal spaces. Where did you see this tension play out most clearly?

4. Hope is framed as something that can either ground or bypass pain. Have you encountered forms of hope in your own life that felt more like escape than support?

5. The Carrow house becomes a living metaphor for inherited stories and unspoken truths. What do you think the house represents beyond its literal role in the story?

6. Fi's skepticism softens into stewardship rather than belief. How does this challenge the idea that faith requires certainty?

7. Morgan's workshops center the body as a source of truth. How did the book's treatment of somatic awareness reshape your understanding of spirituality or intuition?

8. Religion is not rejected in the book but examined. How did the story hold space for both harm and meaning within faith traditions?

9. Amos never "loses" in a traditional sense. He simply leaves. What does this suggest about how conflict, ideology, and power are resolved in Emerdeen?

10. The decision for Cassie and Baz to leave Emerdeen is quiet and intentional. Did this feel like an ending, a beginning, or something else entirely? Why?

11. Throughout the book, rituals are reframed as choices rather than obligations. What personal rituals in your own life might you want to reclaim, revise, or release?

12. The final chapters emphasize that teaching succeeded because it fostered independence. What does this book suggest about the difference between community and dependency?

About the Author

Melody K. Smith is an author, dreamer, tequila lover, wife, dog mom, and bestie material.

She has spent the past three decades bringing clarity and connection to the nonprofit world through organizational strategy, social media management, employee engagement and digital communications.

A lifelong creative, Melody channels her passion for storytelling into fiction that stirs the soul and sparks the imagination. When she isn't writing, she's elbows-deep in crafts, mixed media, and curated chaos—always drawn to the magic of making something from nothing. Her home is part art studio, part sanctuary, and part tasting room, where tequila is appreciated like fine poetry and poured with purpose.

Whether on the road, at her crafting table, or beneath the stars with a good drink in hand, she's always collecting stories and living a few worth telling.